PENGUIN BOOKS

KINGDOM'S END AND OTHER STORIES

Saadat Hasan Manto was born in Sambrala in Punjab in 1912. In a literary and journalistic career spanning more than two decades, he wrote over 200 short stories and scores of plays and essays. He died in Lahore, Pakistan, in 1955.

✢

Khalid Hasan is a Pakistani writer and journalist, who lives at present in Vienna where he works for a news agency. His own books include *A Mug's Game, The Crocodiles are here to Swim, Scorecard* and *Give us Back our Onions*. He has translated Fakhar Zaman's Punjabi novels, *The Prisoner, Dead Man's Tale, The Lost Seven* and *Versions of Truth*. He is the editor of *The Caravan of Pain*, the poetry of Faiz Ahmed Faiz.

SAADAT HASAN MANTO
KINGDOM'S END AND OTHER STORIES

Translated from the Urdu by Khalid Hasan

PENGUIN BOOKS

Penguin Books (India) Ltd, 72-B, Himalaya House
23 Kasturba Gandhi Marg, New Delhi-110 001. India
Penguin Books Ltd, Harmondsworth, Middlesex, England
Viking Penguin Inc, 40 West 23rd Street, New York, New York 10010, U.S.A.
Penguin Books Australia Ltd, Ringwood, Victoria, Australia
Penguin Books Canada Ltd, 2801 John Street, Markham, Ontario, Canada L3R 1B4
Penguin Books (N.Z.) Ltd, 182-190 Wairau Road, Auckland 10, New Zealand

First published by Verso Books 1987
Published in Penguin Books 1989
Copyright © Verso Books 1987

*Dedicated to the memory of Saadat Hasan
Manto, who was never to see any of his work
translated during his lifetime*
and
*the late Hamid Jalal, his nephew and literary
executor, who passionately believed in Manto's
greatness and his eventual recognition beyond
India and Pakistan.*

Contents

Introduction

Saadat Hasan Manto, little of whose work is known outside India and Pakistan, remains by any reckoning one of the world's major short story writers.

Born in Sambrala, now in the Indian state of Punjab, in 1912, he died in Lahore, Pakistan, in 1955 at the age of 43. In a literary and journalistic career spanning more than two decades, he wrote over 200 stories and scores of plays and essays; it is above all on his stories that his reputation rests.

Coming from a middle-class Kashmiri family of Amritsar, Manto showed little enthusiasm for formal education. He failed his school-leaving examination twice in a row; ironically, one of the subjects he was unable to pass was Urdu, in which he was to produce such a powerful and original body of work in the years to come. He was also to bloom into one of the language's great stylists.

Manto entered college in Amritsar in 1931, failed his first year examination twice, and dropped out. These were turbulent years in the history of India. The terrible Jallianwala Bagh massacre in Amritsar had taken place when Manto was a boy of seven, and it had left a deep and bloody imprint on the Raj. Indeed, it was something from which the British colonialists never recovered; 28 years after Jallianwala Bagh, the sun finally set on the Empire in India.

Punjab, and Amritsar in particular, were in constant turmoil throughout the 1920s. Political life was increasingly characterized by civil disobedience, often turning into open and militant defiance of British authority. Manto, restless and rebellious by nature, found the situation and the atmosphere intensely exciting. It was during these impressionable years that he fell under the influence of a man who was to push him towards literature and politics. That man, Bari Alig, now mainly remembered as the author of a history of the East India Company, was then a footloose writer and journalist, devoted to 'Revolution', but mortally afraid of the police. He was a man who had read extensively. He was the first to sense Manto's talent, and transformed Manto's vague fascination with revolution into strong literary commitment. It was Bari who introduced him to Russian and French literature, ultimately persuading him to undertake an Urdu translation of Victor Hugo's drama, *The Last Days of a Condemned Man*, something he accomplished in two weeks flat. It was accepted by a small publishing house in Lahore and printed.

Thrilled by his first success, Manto did a translation of Oscar Wilde's *Vera*, published in 1934. Manto was greatly inspired by the florid style of the original. As he later wrote, he and his friends, walking the streets of Amritsar, used to pretend that they were in Moscow making revolution. Manto was also much taken with the firebrand Punjabi revolutionary Bhagat Singh, who was hanged in Lahore for the murder of a British police officer. Those were heady times. There was a smell of revolt in the air and, for the first time, it looked possible to force the British to leave India.

Bari now began to urge Manto to write original stories in Urdu. Manto turned out to be a quick writer, who rarely revised his stories after the first draft. One of his longest stories, *Mummy* (included in this collection), was written in one marathon sitting. One of the first of Manto's Urdu stories, published in a small literary magazine, concerned the Jallianwala Bagh massacre. He was to return to the subject in his last years with the powerfully evocative

It Happened in 1919, also included here.

In 1934, under the influence of a schoolfriend from Amritsar, Manto decided to enter the famous Aligrah Muslim University. Predictably, he did not do well as a student, but he used the time to write and publish more original stories for magazines. Unfortunately, his stay at the University was to last only nine months. He was diagnosed as having tuberculosis — a false alarm as it turned out — and sent to recover at a small hill station in Kashmir for three months. He returned to Amritsar, then moved to Lahore to take up his first regular job with a magazine called *Paras*. But he soon tired of what he described as 'yellow journalism' and in 1936 arrived in Bombay to edit a film weekly, *Mussawar*. By this time, Bari had moved to Rangoon in search of employment. The two were never to be close associates again, though Manto, who was generally too vain to acknowledge a debt, always considered Bari the most important literary and political influence of his life. He wrote once that had he not met Bari in Amritsar, he might have become a criminal instead of a writer.

Manto loved Bombay, which was not only India's film capital, but its most stylish city. His love-affair with the city was to last throughout his life, though he left Bombay twice, once only briefly but for good the second time, after Partition in 1947. His last years in Lahore were years of intense creativity, extreme poverty and ill health caused by heavy drinking; he felt inconsolably nostalgic for Bombay and regretted ever having left it.

Manto was engaged as a staff writer by the Imperial Film Company in Bombay. He moved to Film City after one of the films he had written flopped at the box office, but at the urging of friends, returned to Imperial some time later. He was both fascinated and disgusted by the world of films. As he wrote to a friend in Lahore: 'The people who have the most influence in film companies are those whose ideas are old and useless, who are completely ignorant.'

At one time, he was not only writing for films, but also editing two magazines. In between, he was contributing to the All India Radio. His first collection of original stories was published in 1940, followed by a volume of essays in 1942, a year after he moved to Delhi to join the All India Radio as a staff writer. He was very unhappy at the time, because of the death of his mother and his first-born son.

He lived in Delhi for less than two years before returning to Bombay, the city which he once said had accepted him, a good-for-nothing family reject, without asking any questions. He went back to his old job at *Mussawar* and also began to freelance as a screenwriter. In 1943 he joined Filmistan, a company set up by a group of his friends from the famous Bombay Talkies. Manto wrote a number of successful films for the company, including *Eight Days*, the story of a shell-shocked soldier in the Second World War.

Soon after Manto had moved to Bombay Talkies itself, India was partitioned, on 14 August 1947. Communal tension was high in Bombay at the time. Hundreds of thousands of refugees had begun to move from one country to the other. Manto's own wife and children and some other members of his family had already migrated to what was now Pakistan, and he was in two minds himself about going. A new era had begun; few people felt sure what the future held in store. Perhaps what decided the issue for him was a string of threats to Bombay Talkies management that unless it sacked all its Muslim employees, its studios would be burnt down. One day in January 1948, Manto, who abhorred communalism, packed his bags and took a ship to Karachi, the capital of the Islamic state of Pakistan.

Manto wrote about his last days in Bombay in a powerful memoir devoted to his lifelong friend, the debonnaire screen actor Shyam who died in a tragic accident during the shooting of a film a couple of years before Manto's own death:

It seems such a long time ago. The Muslims and Hindus were engaged in a bloody fratricidal war. Thousands died every day from both sides. One day, Shyam and I were with a newly-arrived Sikh refugee family from Rawalpindi [Shyam came from Rawalpindi which was now a part of Pakistan] and listening in shocked silence to their horrifying account of what had happened. I could see that Shyam was deeply moved. I could well understand what was passing through his mind. When we left, I said to him: 'I am a Muslim. Don't you want to kill me?' 'Not now,' he replied gravely, 'but while I was listening to them and learning of the atrocities committed by the Muslims, I could have killed you.'

His remark shocked me deeply. Perhaps I could have killed him too when he made it. When I thought about it later, I suddenly understood the psychological background of India's communal bloodbath. Shyam had said that he could have killed me 'then' but not 'now'. Therein lay the key to the communal holocaust of Partition.

In Bombay communal tension was rising every day. Since Ashok Kumar [the famous Indian actor] and Wacha had taken over the Bombay Talkies, most senior positions had gone to Muslims by pure coincidence. However, this had caused much resentment among the Hindu staff of the company. Wacha had begun to receive a steady stream of hate mail containing threats of arson and bloodshed, not that he or Ashok worried much about that sort of thing. However, being sensitive by temperament, I felt greatly troubled in this atmosphere. A number of times, I expressed my unease to Ashok and Wacha and even suggested that they should sack me because some Hindu employees perhaps believed that the Muslim influx in Bombay Talkies was entirely my fault. They said I was out of my mind.

Indeed I was. My wife and children were in Pakistan, but they had gone there when it was still the India that I knew. I was also familiar with the occasional riots which broke out between Hindus and Muslims. But now that piece of land which I had once known as India had a new name. Had this changed anything? I didn't know. What self-government was going to be like, I had no idea, not that I hadn't tried to think it out.

The day of independence, 14 August, was celebrated in Bombay with tremendous fanfare. Pakistan and India had been declared two separate countries. There was great public joy, but murder and arson continued unabated. Along with cries of '*India Zindabad*', one also heard '*Pakistan Zindabad*'. The green Islamic flag fluttered next to the tricolour of the Indian National Congress. Pandit Jawaharlal Nehru and Quaid-e-Azam Mohamed Ali Jinnah's names were shouted by the people on the streets of the city.

I found it impossible to decide which of the two countries was now my homeland — India or Pakistan? Who was responsible for the blood which was being so mercilessly shed every day? Where were they going to inter the bones which had been stripped of the flesh of religion by vultures and birds of prey? Now that we were free, had subjection ceased to exist? Who would be our slaves? When we were colonial subjects, we could dream of freedom, but now that we were free, what would our dreams be? Were we even free? Thousands of Hindus and Muslims were dying all around us. Why were they dying?

All these questions had different answers: the Indian answer, the Pakistani answer, the British answer. Every question had an answer, but when you tried to look for truth they were no help. Some said if you were looking for the truth, you would have to go back to the ruins of the 1857 Mutiny. Others said, no, it all lay in the history of the East India Company. Some went back even further and advised you to analyse the Mughal Empire. Everybody wanted to drag you back into the past, while murderers and terrorists marched on unchallenged, writing in the process a story of blood and fire which had no parallel in history.

India was free. Pakistan was free from the moment of its birth. But man was a slave in both countries, of prejudice, of religious fanaticism, of bestiality, of cruelty.

I stopped going to the Bombay Talkies. Whenever Ashok and Wacha dropped in, I would pretend I wasn't feeling well. Shyam would look at me and smile. He knew what I was going through. I began to drink heavily, but got bored and gave it up. All day long I would lie on my sofa in a sort of daze. One day, Shyam came to the flat straight from the studio. I was lying listlessly on my sofa. 'Are you chewing the cud?' he asked.

I was peeved. Why did he not think like me? Why did he appear so calm? Why did he not feel that terrible sense of upheaval that was raging through my heart and mind? How could he keep on laughing and cracking jokes? Or had he perhaps come to the conclusion that the world around us had gone so completely insane that it was futile even to try to make sense of it?

It happened suddenly. One day I said to myself: 'The hell with it. I am going to leave.' Shyam was filming that night. I stayed up and packed my things. He came quite early in the morning, looked at my cases and said, 'Going?' 'Yes,' I replied.

We never mentioned the subject again. He helped me move odds and ends around while keeping up a steady stream of amusing stories about the night's shooting. He laughed a lot. When it was time for me to leave, he produced a bottle of brandy, poured out two large measures, handed me my glass and said, '*Hiptulla!*' [This was an all-purpose nonsense word coined by Manto to deal with all situations.] '*Hiptulla!*' I answered. Then he threw his arms around me and said 'Swine!' I tried to control my tears. 'Pakistani swine,' I said. '*Zindabad Pakistan*,' he shouted, sincerely. '*Zindabad Bharat*,' I replied. Then we walked down the stairs to a truck waiting to take me to the ship bound for Karachi.

Shyam came with me. There was still time to board. He kept telling funny stories. When the boarding bell was sounded, he shouted '*Hiptulla*' one last time and walked down the gangway, taking long, resolute strides. Never even once did he look back.

Manto detested bourgeois values and the pretentiousness of the respectable. He felt at ease with people who lived on the fringes of society. He found prostitutes more interesting than housewives, crooks more human than civil servants. The Progressive Writers' Movement denounced him as a 'reactionary' who was obsessed with sex and the seamy side of life, abuse he wore like a campaign medal on his chest.

He alone of the writers of his time was able to turn the bloody events of 1947 into great literature. He took no sides and wrote with detachment and passion about the brutalities committed by Hindus, Muslims and Sikhs in the name of religion and nationalism. It is the deep irony and humanism of stories like *Toba Tek Singh* that lives on, while most of the literature produced at the time is now either forgotten or unreadable.

Manto was an iconoclast, a man who defied social tradition and rejected the hypocrisy of the day. He was denounced for his 1947 stories and accused of cynicism and sensationalizing a tragedy. One critic even said Manto had desecrated the dead and robbed them of their personal possessions.

On at least two occasions, once in the early 1940s and the second time in 1948, Manto was prosecuted for 'obscenity'. The guardians of public morals in the new Islamic state of Pakistan had found his story about the young girl who is first abducted by the Hindus and Sikhs during the partition of Punjab and then recovered, raped and left for dead by some of her new Muslim countrymen, obscene, anti-state and degrading.

The case dragged on for months, with Manto under bitter attack from both right and left. He was finally sentenced to a fine and three months in prison by a Lahore magistrate. Manto filed an appeal in the sessions court. He was acquitted and the fine (which had been paid by his equally down-at-heel friends) refunded. The acquitting judge, who had a beard, was to provide the only moment of comic relief in this otherwise sordid trial. After announcing his judgment, he told Manto: 'If I had rejected your appeal, you would have gone around saying that you had been done in by a bearded *Maulvi*.'

The present selection is representative of Manto's best work. Though most of the stories here could be said to relate to the Raj and the Partition of the subcontinent, you will find no princesses or *burra memsahibs* or deputy collectors, only ordinary people trying to keep their humanity intact in a world brutalized and turned upside-down by communal blood-letting.

Thirty years after his death, Manto remains the most widely read author in India and Pakistan, though the official establishment and the guardians of public morals still find him an embarrassment. No posthumous awards have been conferred on him, no literary prizes instituted in his name, no library or university named after him, nor has he been considered good enough to be made part of any academic syllabus. Manto, of course, would have understood this neglect and treated it with the contempt it deserves.

He always wanted to write for the people, but not in the sense in which the term was bandied about by the Stalinist writers with whom he carried on a lifelong running battle, writers whom he accused of trying to turn machines into poems and poems into machines. He said they had ceased to think for themselves. Their only inspiration came from the Kremlin's current party line; they found no vitality or inspiration in their own people and in their own environment. They always told you that such-and-such a Russian intellectual had said this or that, as if their own society had stopped producing intellectuals. To Manto they were nothing more than literary sell-outs who considered themselves progressive while behaving like the worst reactionaries.

Manto wrote his own epitaph, on 18 August 1954, a year before his death. It is brief. And it is not apologetic, because

he was always secure in the knowledge that he was a great
writer:

> Here lies Saadat Hasan Manto. With him lie
> buried all the arts and mysteries of short story
> writing. Under tons of earth he lies, wondering if
> he is a greater short story writer than God.

Khalid Hasan
Vienna, 30 April 1987

Toba Tek Singh

A couple of years after the Partition of the country, it occurred to the respective governments of India and Pakistan that inmates of lunatic asylums, like prisoners, should also be exchanged. Muslim lunatics in India should be transferred to Pakistan and Hindu and Sikh lunatics in Pakistani asylums should be sent to India.

Whether this was a reasonable or an unreasonable idea is difficult to say. One thing, however, is clear. It took many conferences of important officials from the two sides to come to this decision. Final details, like the date of actual exchange, were carefully worked out. Muslim lunatics whose families were still residing in India were to be left undisturbed, the rest moved to the border for the exchange. The situation in Pakistan was slightly different, since almost the entire population of Hindus and Sikhs had already migrated to India. The question of keeping non-Muslim lunatics in Pakistan did not, therefore, arise.

While it is not known what the reaction in India was, when the news reached the Lahore lunatic asylum, it immediately became the subject of heated discussion. One Muslim lunatic, a regular reader of the fire-eating daily newspaper *Zamindar*, when asked what Pakistan was, replied after deep reflection: 'The name of a place in India where cut-throat razors are manufactured.'

This profound observation was received with visible satisfaction.

A Sikh lunatic asked another Sikh: 'Sardarji, why are we being sent to India? We don't even know the language they speak in that country.'

The man smiled: 'I know the language of the *Hindostoras*. These devils always strut about as if they were the lords of the earth.'

One day a Muslim lunatic, while taking his bath, raised the slogan '*Pakistan Zindabad*' with such enthusiasm that he lost his footing and was later found lying on the floor unconscious.

Not all inmates were mad. Some were perfectly normal, except that they were murderers. To spare them the hangman's noose, their families had managed to get them committed after bribing officials down the line. They probably had a vague idea why India was being divided and what Pakistan was, but, as for the present situation, they were equally clueless.

Newspapers were no help either, and the asylum guards were ignorant, if not illiterate. Nor was there anything to be learnt by eavesdropping on their conversations. Some said there was this man by the name Mohamed Ali Jinnah, or the Quaid-e-Azam, who had set up a separate country for Muslims, called Pakistan,

As to where Pakistan was located, the inmates knew nothing. That was why both the mad and the partially mad were unable to decide whether they were now in India or in Pakistan. If they were in India, where on earth was Pakistan? And if they were in Pakistan, then how come that until only the other day it was India?

One inmate had got so badly caught up in this India–Pakistan–Pakistan–India rigmarole that one day, while sweeping the floor, he dropped everything, climbed the nearest tree and installed himself on a branch, from which vantage point he spoke for two hours on the delicate problem of India and Pakistan. The guards asked him to get down; instead he went a branch higher, and when threatened with punishment, declared: 'I wish to live neither in India nor in Pakistan. I wish to live in this tree.'

When he was finally persuaded to come down, he began embracing his Sikh and Hindu friends, tears running down his cheeks, fully convinced that they were about to leave him and go to India.

A Muslim radio engineer, who had an M.Sc. degree, and never mixed with anyone, given as he was to taking long walks by himself all day, was so affected by the current debate that one day he took all his clothes off, gave the bundle to one of the attendants and ran into the garden stark naked.

A Muslim lunatic from Chaniot, who used to be one of the most devoted workers of the All India Muslim League, and obsessed with bathing himself fifteen or sixteen times a day, had suddenly stopped doing that and announced — his name was Mohamed Ali — that he was Quaid-e-Azam Mohamed Ali Jinnah. This had led a Sikh inmate to declare himself Master Tara Singh, the leader of the Sikhs. Apprehending serious communal trouble, the authorities declared them dangerous, and shut them up in separate cells.

There was a young Hindu lawyer from Lahore who had gone off his head after an unhappy love affair. When told that Amritsar was to become a part of India, he went into a depression because his beloved lived in Amritsar, something he had not forgotten even in his madness. That day he abused every major and minor Hindu and Muslim leader who had cut India into two, turning his beloved into an Indian and him into a Pakistani.

When news of the exchange reached the asylum, his friends offered him congratulations, because he was now to be sent to India, the country of his beloved. However, he declared that he had no intention of leaving Lahore, because his practice would not flourish in Amritsar.

There were two Anglo-Indian lunatics in the European ward. When told that the British had decided to go home after granting independence to India, they went into a state of deep shock and were seen conferring with each other in whispers the entire afternoon. They were worried about their changed status after independence. Would there be a European ward or would it be abolished? Would breakfast continue to be served or would they have to subsist on bloody Indian chapati?

There was another inmate, a Sikh, who had been confined for the last fifteen years. Whenever he spoke, it was the same mysterious gibberish: '*Uper the gur gur the annexe the bay dhayana the mung the dal of the laltain.*' Guards said he had not slept a wink in fifteen years. Occasionally, he could be observed leaning against a wall, but the rest of the time, he was always to be found standing. Because of this, his legs were permanently swollen, something that did not appear to bother him. Recently, he had started to listen carefully to discussions about the forthcoming exchange of Indian and Pakistani lunatics. When asked his opinion, he observed solemnly: '*Uper the gur gur the annexe the bay dhayana the mung the dal of the Government of Pakistan.*'

Of late, however, the Government of Pakistan had been replaced by the Government of Toba Tek Singh, a small town in the Punjab which was his home. He had also begun enquiring where Toba Tek Singh was to go. However, nobody was quite sure whether it was in India or Pakistan.

Those who had tried to solve this mystery had become utterly confused when told that Sialkot, which used to be in India, was now in Pakistan. It was anybody's guess what was going to happen to Lahore, which was currently in Pakistan, but could slide into India any moment. It was also possible that the entire subcontinent of India might become Pakistan. And who could say if both India and Pakistan might not entirely vanish from the map of the world one day?

The old man's hair was almost gone and what little was left had become a part of the beard, giving him a strange, even frightening, appearance. However, he was a harmless fellow and had never been known to get into fights. Older attendants at the asylum said that he was a fairly prosperous landlord from Toba Tek Singh, who had quite suddenly gone mad. His family had brought him in, bound and fettered. That was fifteen years ago.

Once a month, he used to have visitors, but since the start of communal troubles in the Punjab, they had stopped coming. His real name was Bishan Singh, but everybody called him Toba Tek Singh. He lived in a kind of limbo, having no idea what day of the week it was, or month, or how many years had passed since his confinement. However, he had developed a sixth sense about the day of the visit, when he used to bathe himself, soap his body, oil and comb his hair and put on clean clothes. He never said a word during these meetings, except occasional outbursts of '*Uper the gur gur the annexe the bay dhayana the mung the dal of the laltain.*'

When he was first confined, he had left an infant daughter behind, now a pretty young girl of fifteen. She would come occasionally, and sit in front of him with tears rolling down her cheeks. In the strange world that he inhabited, hers was just another face.

Since the start of this India–Pakistan caboodle, he had got into the habit of asking fellow inmates where exactly Toba Tek Singh was, without receiving a satisfactory answer, because nobody knew. The visits had also suddenly stopped. He was increasingly restless, but, more than that, curious. The sixth sense, which used to alert him to the day of the visit, had also atrophied.

He missed his family, the gifts they used to bring and the concern with which they used to speak to him. He was sure they would have told him whether Toba Tek Singh was in India or Pakistan. He also had a feeling that they came from Toba Tek Singh, where he used to have his home.

One of the inmates had declared himself God. Bishan

Singh asked him one day if Toba Tek Singh was in India or
Pakistan. The man chuckled: 'Neither in India nor in
Pakistan, because, so far, we have issued no orders in this
respect.'

Bishan Singh begged 'God' to issue the necessary orders,
so that his problem could be solved, but he was disappointed, as 'God' appeared to be preoccupied with more
pressing matters. Finally, he told him angrily: '*Uper the gur
gur the annexe the mung the dal of Guruji da Khalsa and Guruji ki
fateh ... jo boley so nihal sat sri akal.*'

What he wanted to say was: 'You don't answer my
prayers because you are a Muslim God. Had you been a
Sikh God, you would have been more of a sport.'

A few days before the exchange was to take place, one of
Bishan Singh's Muslim friends from Toba Tek Singh came
to see him — the first time in fifteen years. Bishan Singh
looked at him once and turned away, until a guard said to
him: 'This is your old friend Fazal Din. He has come all the
way to meet you.'

Bishan Singh looked at Fazal Din and began to mumble
something. Fazal Din placed his hand on his friend's shoulder and said: 'I have been meaning to come for some time
to bring you news. All your family is well and has gone to
India safely. I did what I could to help. Your daughter
Roop Kaur ...' — he hesitated — 'She is safe too ... in
India.'

Bishan Singh kept quiet. Fazal Din continued: 'Your
family wanted me to make sure you were well. Soon you
will be moving to India. What can I say, except that you
should remember me to bhai Balbir Singh, bhai Vadhawa
Singh and bahain Amrit Kaur. Tell bhai Bibir Singh that
Fazal Din is well by the grace of God. The two brown buffa-
loes he left behind are well too. Both of them gave birth to
calves, but, unfortunately, one of them died after six days.
Say I think of them often and to write to me if there is
anything I can do.'

Then he added: 'Here, I brought you some rice crispies from home.'

Bishan Singh took the gift and handed it to one of the guards. 'Where is Toba Tek Singh?' he asked.

'Where? Why, it is where it has always been.'

'In India or in Pakistan?'

'In India ... no, in Pakistan.'

Without saying another word, Bishan Singh walked away, murmuring: '*Uper the gur gur the annexe the be dhyana the mung the dal of the Pakistan and Hindustan dur fittey moun.*'

Meanwhile, exchange arrangements were rapidly getting finalized. Lists of lunatics from the two sides had been exchanged between the governments, and the date of transfer fixed.

On a cold winter evening, buses full of Hindu and Sikh lunatics, accompanied by armed police and officials, began moving out of the Lahore asylum towards Wagha, the dividing line between India and Pakistan. Senior officials from the two sides in charge of exchange arrangements met, signed documents and the transfer got under way.

It was quite a job getting the men out of the buses and handing them over to officials. Some just refused to leave. Those who were persuaded to do so began to run pell-mell in every direction. Some were stark naked. All efforts to get them to cover themselves had failed because they couldn't be kept from tearing off their garments. Some were shouting abuse or singing. Others were weeping bitterly. Many fights broke out.

In short, complete confusion prevailed. Female lunatics were also being exchanged and they were even noisier. It was bitterly cold.

Most of the inmates appeared to be dead set against the entire operation. They simply could not understand why they were being forcibly removed, thrown into buses and driven to this strange place. There were slogans of '*Pakistan Zindabad*' and '*Pakistan Murdabad*', followed by fights.

When Bishan Singh was brought out and asked to give his name so that it could be recorded in a register, he asked the official behind the desk: 'Where is Toba Tek Singh? In India or Pakistan?'

'Pakistan,' he answered with a vulgar laugh.

Bishan Singh tried to run, but was overpowered by the Pakistani guards who tried to push him across the dividing line towards India. However, he wouldn't move. 'This is Toba Tek Singh,' he announced. '*Uper the gur gur the annexe the be dhyana mung the dal of Toba Tek Singh and Pakistan.*'

Many efforts were made to explain to him that Toba Tek Singh had already been moved to India, or would be moved immediately, but it had no effect on Bishan Singh. The guards even tried force, but soon gave up.

There he stood in no man's land on his swollen legs like a colossus.

Since he was a harmless old man, no further attempt was made to push him into India. He was allowed to stand where he wanted, while the exchange continued. The night wore on.

Just before sunrise, Bishan Singh, the man who had stood on his legs for fifteen years, screamed and as officials from the two sides rushed towards him, he collapsed to the ground.

There, behind barbed wire, on one side, lay India and behind more barbed wire, on the other side, lay Pakistan. In between, on a bit of earth which had no name, lay Toba Tek Singh.

The Dog of Titwal

The soldiers had been entrenched in their positions for several weeks, but there was little, if any, fighting, except for the dozen rounds they ritually exchanged every day. The weather was extremely pleasant. The air was heavy with the scent of wild flowers and nature seemed to be following its course, quite unmindful of the soldiers hiding behind rocks and camouflaged by mountain shrubbery. The birds sang as they always had and the flowers were in bloom. Bees buzzed about lazily.

Only when a shot rang out, the birds got startled and took flight, as if a musician had struck a jarring note on his instrument. It was almost the end of September, neither hot nor cold. It seemed as if summer and winter had made their peace. In the blue skies, cotton clouds floated all day like barges on a lake.

The soldiers seemed to be getting tired of this indecisive war where nothing much ever happened. Their positions were quite impregnable. The two hills on which they were placed faced each other and were about the same height, so no one side had an advantage. Down below in the valley, a stream zigzagged furiously on its stony bed like a snake.

The air force was not involved in the combat and neither of the adversaries had heavy guns or mortars. At night, they would light huge fires and hear each others' voices echoing through the hills.

The last round of tea had just been taken. The fire had gone cold. The sky was clear and there was a chill in the air and a sharp, though not unpleasant, smell of pine cones. Most of the soldiers were already asleep, except Jamadar Harnam Singh, who was on night watch. At two o'clock, he woke up Ganda Singh to take over. Then he lay down, but sleep was as far away from his eyes as the stars in the sky. He began to hum a Punjabi folk song:

> Buy me a pair of shoes, my lover
> A pair of shoes with stars on them
> Sell your buffalo, if you have to
> But buy me a pair of shoes
> With stars on them

It made him feel good and a bit sentimental. He woke up the others one by one. Banta Singh, the youngest of the soldiers, who had a sweet voice, began to sing a lovelorn verse from *Heer Ranjha*, that timeless Punjabi epic of love and tragedy. A deep sadness fell over them. Even the grey hills seemed to have been affected by the melancholy of the song.

This mood was shattered by the barking of a dog. Jamadar Harnam Singh said, 'Where has this son of a bitch materialized from?'

The dog barked again. He sounded closer. There was a rustle in the bushes. Banta Singh got up to investigate and came back with an ordinary mongrel in tow. He was wagging his tail. 'I found him behind the bushes and he told me his name was Jhun Jhun,' Banta Singh announced. Everybody burst out laughing.

The dog went to Harnam Singh who produced a cracker from his kitbag and threw it on the ground. The dog sniffed at it and was about to eat it, when Harnam Singh snatched it away. '... Wait, you could be a Pakistani dog.'

They laughed. Banta Singh patted the animal and said to

Harnam Singh, 'Jamadar sahib, Jhun Jhun is an Indian dog.'

'Prove your identity,' Harnam Singh ordered the dog, who began to wag his tail.

'This is no proof of identity. All dogs can wag their tails,' Harnam Singh said.

'He is only a poor refugee,' Banta Singh said, playing with his tail.

Harnam Singh threw the dog a cracker which he caught in midair. 'Even dogs will now have to decide if they are Indian or Pakistani,' one of the soldiers observed.

Harnam Singh produced another cracker from his kitbag. 'And all Pakistanis, including dogs, will be shot.'

A soldier shouted, '*India Zindabad*!'

The dog, who was about to munch his cracker, stopped dead in his tracks, put his tail between his legs and looked scared. Harnam Singh laughed. 'Why are you afraid of your own country? Here, Jhun Jhun, have another cracker.'

The morning broke very suddenly, as if someone had switched on a light in a dark room. It spread across the hills and valleys of Titwal, which is what the area was called.

The war had been going on for months, but nobody could be quite sure who was winning it.

Jamadar Harnam Singh surveyed the area with his binoculars. He could see smoke rising from the opposite hill, which meant that, like them, the enemy was busy preparing breakfast.

Subedar Himmat Khan of the Pakistan army gave his huge moustache a twirl and began to study the map of the Titwal sector. Next to him sat his wireless operator who was trying to establish contact with the platoon commander to obtain instructions. A few feet away, the soldier Bashir sat on the ground, his back against a rock and his rifle in front of him. He was humming:

Where did you spend the night, my love, my moon?
Where did you spend the night?

Enjoying himself, he began to sing more loudly, savouring the words. Suddenly, he heard Subedar Himmat Khan scream, 'Where did *you* spend the night?'

But this was not addressed to Bashir. It was a dog he was shouting at. He had come to them from nowhere a few days ago, stayed in the camp quite happily and then suddenly disappeared last night. However, he had now returned like a bad coin.

Bashir smiled and began to sing to the dog. 'Where did you spend the night, where did you spend the night?' But he only wagged his tail. Subedar Himmat Khan threw a pebble at him. 'All he can do is wag his tail, the idiot.'

'What has he got around his neck?' Bashir asked. One of the soldiers grabbed the dog and undid his makeshift rope collar. There was a small piece of cardboard tied to it. 'What does it say?' the soldier, who could not read, asked.

Bashir stepped forward and with some difficulty was able to decipher the writing. 'It says Jhun Jhun.'

Subedar Himmat Khan gave his famous moustache another mighty twirl and said, 'Perhaps it is a code. Does it say anything else, Bashirey?'

'Yes sir, it says it is an Indian dog.'

'What does that mean?' Subedar Himmat Khan asked.

'Perhaps it is a secret,' Bashir answered seriously.

'If there is a secret, it is in that word Jhun Jhun,' another soldier ventured in a wise guess.

'You may have something there,' Subedar Himmat Khan observed.

Dutifully, Bashir read the whole thing again. 'Jhun Jhun. This is an Indian dog.'

Subedar Himmat Khan picked up the wireless set and spoke to his platoon commander, providing him with a detailed account of the dog's sudden appearance in their position, his equally sudden disappearance the night before and his return that morning. 'What are you talking about?' the platoon commander asked.

Subedar Himmat Khan studied the map again. Then he tore up a packet of cigarettes, cut a small piece from it and gave it to Bashir. 'Now write on it in Gurmukhi, the language of those Sikhs ...'

'What should I write?'

'Well ...'

Bashir had an inspiration. 'Shun Shun, yes, that's right. We counter Jhun Jhun with Shun Shun.'

'Good,' Subedar Himmat Khan said approvingly. 'And add: This is a Pakistani dog.'

Subedar Himmat Khan personally threaded the piece of paper through the dog's collar and said, 'Now go join your family.'

He gave him something to eat and then said, 'Look here, my friend, no treachery. The punishment for treachery is death.'

The dog kept eating his food and wagging his tail. Then Subedar Himmat Khan turned him round to face the Indian position and said, 'Go and take this message to the enemy, but come back. These are the orders of your commander.'

The dog wagged his tail and moved down the winding hilly track that led into the valley dividing the two hills. Subedar Himmat Khan picked up his rifle and fired in the air.

The Indians were a bit puzzled, as it was somewhat early in the day for that sort of thing. Jamadar Harnam Singh, who in any case was feeling bored, shouted, 'Let's give it to them.'

The two sides exchanged fire for half an hour, which, of course, was a complete waste of time. Finally, Jamadar Harnam Singh ordered that enough was enough. He combed his long hair, looked at himself in the mirror and asked Banta Singh, 'Where has that dog Jhun Jhun gone?'

'Dogs can never digest butter, goes the famous saying,' Banta Singh observed philosophically.

Suddenly, the soldier on lookout duty shouted, 'There he comes.'

'Who?' Jamadar Harnam Singh asked.

'What was his name? Jhun Jhun,' the soldier answered.

'What is he doing?' Harnam Singh asked.

'Just coming our way,' the soldier replied, peering through his binoculars.

Subedar Harnam Singh snatched them from him. 'That's him all right and there's something round his neck. But, wait, that's the Pakistani hill he's coming from, the motherfucker.'

He picked up his rifle, aimed and fired. The bullet hit some rocks close to where the dog was. He stopped.

Subedar Himmat Khan heard the report and looked through his binoculars. The dog had turned round and was running back. 'The brave never run away from battle. Go forward and complete your mission,' he shouted at the dog. To scare him, he fired in his general direction. Harnam Singh fired at the same time. The bullet passed within inches of the dog, who leapt in the air, flapping his ears. Subedar Himmat Khan fired again, hitting some stones.

It soon became a game between the two soldiers, with the dog running round in circles in a state of great terror. Both Himmat Khan and Harnam Singh were laughing boisterously. The dog began to run towards Harnam Singh, who abused him loudly and fired. The bullet caught him in the leg. He yelped, turned around and began to run towards Himmat Khan, only to meet more fire, which was only meant to scare him. 'Be a brave boy. If you are injured, don't let that stand between you and your duty. Go, go, go,' the Pakistani shouted.

The dog turned. One of his legs was now quite useless. He began to drag himself towards Harnam Singh, who picked up his rifle, aimed carefully and shot him dead.

Subedar Himmat Khan sighed, 'The poor bugger has been martyred.'

Jamadar Himmat Singh ran his hand over the still-hot barrel of his rifle and muttered, 'He died a dog's death.'

The Last Salute

This Kashmir war was a very odd affair. Subedar Rab Nawaz often felt as if his brain had turned into a rifle with a faulty safety catch.

He had fought with distinction on many major fronts in the Second World War. He was respected by both his seniors and juniors because of his intelligence and valour. He was always given the most difficult and dangerous assignments and he had never failed the trust placed in him.

But he had never been in a war like this one. He had come to it full of enthusiasm and with the itch to fight and liquidate the enemy. However, the first encounter had shown that the men arrayed against them on the other side were mostly old friends and comrades with whom he had fought in the old British Indian army against the Germans and the Italians. The friends of yesterday had been transformed into the enemies of today.

At times, the whole thing felt like a dream to Subedar Rab Nawaz. He could remember the day the Second World War was declared. He had enlisted immediately. They had been given some basic training and then packed off to the front. He had been moved from one theatre of war to another and, one day, the war had ended. Then had come Pakistan and the new war he was now fighting. So much had happened in these last few years at such breakneck speed. Often it made no sense at all. Those who had planned and executed these great events had perhaps deliberately maintained a dizzying pace so that the participants should get no time to think. How else could one explain one revolution followed by another and then another?

One thing Subedar Rab Nawaz could understand. They were fighting this war to win Kashmir. Why did they want to win Kashmir? Because it was crucial to Pakistan's security and survival. However, sometimes when he sat behind a gun emplacement and caught sight of a familiar face on the other side, for a moment he forgot why they were fighting. He forgot why he was carrying a gun and killing people. At such times, he would remind himself that he was not fighting to win medals or earn a salary, but to secure the survival of his country.

This was his country before the establishment of Pakistan and it was his country now. This was his land. But now he was fighting against men who were his countrymen until only the other day. Men who had grown up in the same village, whose families had been known to his family for generations. These men had now been turned into citizens of a country to which they were complete strangers. They had been told: we are placing a gun in your hands so that you can go and fight for a country which you have yet to know, where you do not even have a roof over your head, where even the air and water are strange to you. Go and fight for it against Pakistan, the land where you were born and grew up.

Rab Nawaz would think of those Muslim soldiers who had moved to Pakistan, leaving their ancestral homes behind, and come to this new country with empty hands. They had been given nothing, except the guns that had been put in their hands. The same guns they had always used, the same make, the same bore, guns to fight their new enemy with.

Before the partition of the country, they used to fight one common enemy who was not really their enemy perhaps but whom they had accepted as their enemy for the sake of employment and rewards and medals. Formerly, all of them were Indian soldiers, but now some were Indian and others were Pakistani soldiers. Rab Nawaz could not unravel this puzzle. And when he thought about Kashmir, he became even more confused. Were the Pakistani soldiers fighting for Kashmir or for the Muslims of Kashmir? If they were being asked to fight in defence of the Muslims of Kashmir, why had they not been asked to fight for the Muslims of the princely states of Junagarh and Hyderabad? And if this was an Islamic war, then why were other Muslim countries of the world not fighting shoulder to shoulder with them?

Rab Nawaz had finally come to the conclusion that such intricate and subtle matters were beyond the comprehension of a simple soldier. A soldier should be thick in the head. Only the thick-headed made good soldiers, but despite this resolution, he couldn't help wondering sometimes about the war he was now in.

The fighting in what was called the Titwal sector was spread across the Kishan Ganga river and along the road which led from Muzaffarabad to Kiran. It was a strange war. Often at night, instead of gunfire, one heard abuse being exchanged in loud voices.

One late evening, while Subedar Rab Nawaz was preparing his platoon for a foray into enemy territory, he heard loud voices from across the hill the enemy was supposed to be on. He could not believe his ears. There was loud laughter followed by abuse. 'Pig's trotters,' he murmured, 'what on earth is going on?'

One of his men returned the abuse in as loud a voice as he could muster, then complained to him, 'Subedar sahib, they are abusing us again, the motherfuckers.'

Rab Nawaz's first instinct was to join the slanging match,

but he thought better of it. The men fell silent also, following his example. However, after a while, the torrent of abuse from the other side became so intolerable that his men lost control and began to match abuse with abuse. He ordered them a couple of times to keep quiet, but did not insist because, frankly, it was difficult for a human being not to react violently.

They couldn't, of course, see the enemy at night, and hardly did so during the day because of the hilly country which provided perfect cover. All they heard was abuse which echoed across the hills and valleys and then evaporated in the air.

Some of the hills were barren, while others were covered with tall pine trees. It was very difficult terrain. Subedar Rab Nawaz's platoon was on a bare, treeless hill which provided no cover. His men were itching to go into attack to avenge the abuse which had been hurled at them without respite for several weeks. An attack was planned and executed with success, though they lost two men and suffered four injuries. The enemy lost three and abandoned the position, leaving behind food and provisions.

Subedar Rab Nawaz and his men were sorry they had not been able to capture an enemy soldier. They could then have avenged the abuse face to face. However, they had captured an important and difficult feature. Rab Nawaz relayed the news of the victory to his commander, Major Aslam, and was commended for gallantry.

On top of most of the hills, one found ponds. There was a large one on the hill they had captured. The water was clear and sweet, and although it was cold, they took off their clothes and jumped in. Suddenly, they heard firing. They jumped out of the pond and hit the ground — naked. Subedar Rab Nawaz crawled towards his binoculars, picked them up and surveyed the area carefully. He could see no one. There was more firing. This time he was able to determine its origin. It was coming from a small hill, lying a few hundred feet below their perch. He ordered his men to open up.

The enemy troops did not have very good cover and Rab Nawaz was confident they could not stay there much longer. The moment they decided to move, they would come in direct range of their guns. Sporadic firing kept getting exchanged. Finally, Rab Nawaz ordered that no more ammunition should be wasted. They should just wait for the enemy to break cover. Then he looked at his still naked body and murmured, 'Pig's trotters. Man does look silly without clothes.'

For two whole days, this game continued. Occasional fire was exchanged, but the enemy had obviously decided to lie low. Then suddenly the temperature dropped several degrees. To keep his men warm, Subedar Rab Nawaz ordered that the tea-kettle should be kept on the boil all the time. It was like an unending tea party.

On the third day — it was unbearably cold — the soldier on the lookout reported that some movement could be detected around the enemy position. Subedar Rab Nawaz looked through his binoculars. Yes, something was going on. Rab Nawaz raised his rifle and fired. Someone called his name, or so he thought. It echoed through the valley. 'Pig's trotters,' Rab Nawaz shouted, 'what do you want?'

The distance that separated their two positions was not great, The voice came back, 'Don't hurl abuse, brother.'

Rab Nawaz looked at his men. The word brother seemed to hang in the air. He raised his hands to his mouth and shouted, 'Brother! There are no brothers here, only your mother's lovers.'

'Rab Nawaz,' the voice shouted.

He trembled. The words reverberated around the hills and then faded into the atmosphere.

'Pig's trotters,' he whispered, 'who was that?'

He knew that the troops in the Titwal sector were mostly from the old 6/9 Jat Regiment, his own regiment. But who was this joker shouting his name? He had many friends in the Regiment, and some enemies too. But who was this man who had called him brother?

Rab Nawaz looked through his binoculars again, but could see nothing. He shouted, 'Who was that? This is Rab Nawaz. Rab Nawaz. Rab Nawaz.'

'It is me ... Ram Singh,' the same voice answered.

Rab Nawaz nearly jumped. 'Ram Singh, oh Ram Singha, Ram Singha, you pig's trotters.'

'Shut your trap, you potter's ass,' came the reply.

Rab Nawaz looked at his men, who appeared startled at this strange exchange in the middle of battle. 'He's talking rot, pig's trotters.' Then he shouted, 'You slaughtered swine, watch your tongue.'

Ram Singh began to laugh. Rab Nawaz could not contain himself either. His men watched him in silence.

'Look, my friend, we want to drink tea,' Ram Singh said.

'Go ahead then. Have a good time,' Rab Nawaz replied.

'We can't. The tea things are lying elsewhere.'

'Where's elsewhere?'

'Let me put it this way. If we tried to get them, you could blow us to bits. We'd have to break cover.'

'So what do you want, pig's trotters?' Rab Nawaz laughed.

'That you hold your fire until we get our things.'

'Go ahead,' Rab Nawaz said.

'You will blow us up, you potter's ass,' Ram Singh shouted.

'Shut your mouth, you crawly Sikh tortoise,' Rab Nawaz said.

'Take an oath on something that you won't open fire.'

'On what?'

'Anything you like.'

Rab Nawaz laughed, 'You have my word. Now go get your things.'

Nothing happened for a few minutes. One of the men

was watching the small hill through his binoculars. He pointed at his gun and asked Rab Nawaz in gestures if he should open fire. 'No, no, no shooting,' Rab Nawaz said.

Suddenly, a man darted forward, running low towards some bushes. A few minutes later he ran back, carrying an armful of things. Then he disappeared. Rab Nawaz picked up his rifle and fired. 'Thank you,' Ram Singh's voice came.

'No mention,' Rab Nawaz answered. 'OK, boys, let's give the buggers one round.'

More by way of entertainment than war, this exchange of fire continued for some time. Rab Nawaz could see smoke going up in a thin blue spiral where the enemy was. 'Is your tea ready, Ram Singha?' he shouted.

'Not yet, you potter's ass.'

Rab Nawaz was a potter by caste and any reference to his origins always enraged him. Ram Singh was the one person who could get away with calling him a potter's ass. They had grown up together in the same village in the Punjab. They were the same age, had gone to the same primary school, and their fathers had been childhood friends. They had joined the army the same day. In the last war, they had fought together on the same fronts.

'Pig's trotters,' Rab Nawaz said to his men, 'he never gives up, that one. Shut up, lice-infested donkey Ram Singha,' he shouted.

He saw a man stand up. Rab Nawaz raised his rifle and fired in his direction. He heard a scream. He looked through his binoculars. It was Ram Singh. He was doubled up, holding his stomach. Then he fell to the ground.

Rab Nawaz shouted, 'Ram Singh' and stood up. There was rapid gunfire from the other side. One bullet brushed past his left arm. He fell to the ground. Some enemy soldiers, taking advantage of this confusion, began to run across open ground to securer positions. Rab Nawaz ordered his platoon to attack the hill. Three were killed, but the others managed to capture the position with Rab Nawaz in the lead.

He found Ram Singh lying on the bare ground. He had been shot in the stomach. His eyes lit up when he saw Rab Nawaz. 'You potter's ass, whatever did you do that for?' he asked.

Rab Nawaz felt as if it was he who had been shot. But he smiled, bent over Ram Singh and began to undo his belt. 'Pig's trotters, who told you to stand up?'

'I was only trying to show myself to you, but you shot me,' Ram Singh said with difficulty. Rab Nawaz unfastened his belt. It was a very bad wound and bleeding profusely.

Rab Nawaz's voice choked, 'I swear upon God, I only fired out of fun. How could I know it was you? You were always an ass, Ram Singha.'

Ram Singh was rapidly losing blood. Rab Nawaz was surprised he was still alive. He did not want to move him. He spoke to his platoon commander Major Aslam on the wireless, requesting urgent medical help.

He was sure it would take a long time to arrive. He had a feeling Ram Singh wouldn't last that long. But he laughed. 'Don't you worry. The doctor is on his way.'

Ram Singh said in a weak voice, 'I am not worried, but tell me, how many of my men did you kill?'

'Just one,' Rab Nawaz said.

'And how many did you lose?'

'Six,' Rab Nawaz lied.

'Six,' Ram Singh said. 'When I fell, they were disheartened, but I told them to fight on, give it everything they'd got. Six, yes.' Then his mind began to wander.

He began to talk of their village, their childhood, stories from school, the 6/9 Jat Regiment, its commanding officers, affairs with strange women in strange cities. He was in excruciating pain, but he carried on. 'Do you remember that madam, you pig?'

'Which one?' Rab Nawaz asked.

'That one in Italy. You remember what we used to call her? Man-eater.'

Rab Nawaz remembered her. 'Yes, yes. She was called Madam Minitafanto or some such thing. And she used to say: no money, no action. But she had a soft spot for you, that daughter of Mussolini.'

Ram Singh laughed loudly, causing blood to gush out of his wound. Rab Nawaz dressed it with a makeshift bandage. 'Now keep quiet,' he admonished him gently.

Ram Singh's body was burning. He did not have the strength to speak, but he was talking nineteen to the dozen. At times, he would stop, as if to see how much petrol was still left in his tank.

After some time, he went into a sort of delirium. Briefly, he would come out of it, only to sink again. During one brief moment of clarity, he said to Rab Nawaz, 'Tell me truthfully, do you people really want Kashmir?'

'Yes, Ram Singha,' Rab Nawaz said passionately.

'I don't believe that. You have been misled,' Ram Singh said.

'No, you have been misled, I swear by the Holy Prophet and his family,' Rab Nawaz said.

'Don't take that oath ... you must be right.' But there was a strange look on his face, as if he didn't really believe Rab Nawaz.

A little before sunset, Major Aslam arrived with some soldiers. There was no doctor. Ram Singh was hovering between consciousness and delirium. He was muttering, but his voice was so weak that it was difficult to follow him.

Major Aslam was an old 6/9 Jat Regiment officer. Ram Singh had served under him for years. He bent over the dying soldier and called his name, 'Ram Singh, Ram Singh.'

Ram Singh opened his eyes and stiffened his body as if he was coming to attention. With one great effort, he raised his arm and saluted. A strange look of incomprehension suddenly suffused his face. His arm fell limply to his side and he murmured, 'Ram Singha, you ass, you forgot this was a war, a war ...' He could not complete the sentence. With half-open eyes, he looked at Rab Nawaz, took one last breath and died.

The Return

The special train left Amritsar at two in the afternoon, arriving at Mughalpura, Lahore, eight hours later. Many had been killed on the way, a lot more injured and countless lost.

It was at 10 o'clock the next morning that Sirajuddin regained consciousness. He was lying on bare ground, surrounded by screaming men, women and children. It did not make sense.

He lay very still, gazing at the dusty sky. He appeared not to notice the confusion or the noise. To a stranger, he might have looked like an old man in deep thought, though this was not the case. He was in shock, suspended, as it were, over a bottomless pit.

Then his eyes moved and, suddenly, caught the sun. The shock brought him back to the world of living men and women. A succession of images raced through his mind. Attack ... fire ... escape ... railway station ... night ... Sakina. He rose abruptly and began searching through the milling crowd in the refugee camp.

He spent hours looking, all the time shouting his daughter's name ... Sakina, Sakina ... but she was nowhere to be found.

Total confusion prevailed, with people looking for lost sons, daughters, mothers, wives. In the end Sirajuddin gave up. He sat down, away from the crowd, and tried to think clearly. Where did he part from Sakina and her mother?

Then it came to him in a flash — the dead body of his wife, her stomach ripped open. It was an image that wouldn't go away.

Sakina's mother was dead. That much was certain. She had died in front of his eyes. He could hear her voice: 'Leave me where I am. Take the girl away.'

The two of them had begun to run. Sakina's *dupatta* had slipped to the ground and he had stopped to pick it up and she had said: 'Father, leave it.'

He could feel a bulge in his pocket. It was a length of cloth. Yes, he recognized it. It was Sakina's *dupatta*, but where was she?

Other details were missing. Had he brought her as far as the railway station? Had she got into the carriage with him? When the rioters had stopped the train, had they taken her with them?

All questions. There were no answers. He wished he could weep, but tears would not come. He knew then that he needed help.

A few days later, he had a break. There were eight of them, young men armed with guns. They also had a truck. They said they brought back women and children left behind on the other side.

He gave them a description of his daughter. 'She is fair, very pretty. No, she doesn't look like me, but her mother. About seventeen. Big eyes, black hair, a mole on the left cheek. Find my daughter. May God bless you.'

The young men had said to Sirajuddin: 'If your daughter is alive, we will find her.'

And they had tried. At the risk of their lives, they had driven to Amritsar, recovered many women and children and brought them back to the camp, but they had not found Sakina.

On their next trip out, they had found a girl on the roadside. They seemed to have scared her and she had started running. They had stopped the truck, jumped out and run after her. Finally, they had caught up with her in a field. She was very pretty and she had a mole on her left cheek. One of the men had said to her: 'Don't be frightened. Is your name Sakina?' Her face had gone pale, but when they had told her who they were, she had confessed that she was Sakina, daughter of Sirajuddin.

The young men were very kind to her. They had fed her, given her milk to drink and put her in their truck. One of them had given her his jacket so that she could cover herself. It was obvious that she was ill-at-ease without her *dupatta*, trying nervously to cover her breasts with her arms.

Many days had gone by and Sirajuddin had still not had any news of his daughter. All his time was spent running from camp to camp, looking for her. At night, he would pray for the success of the young men who were looking for his daughter. Their words would ring in his ears: 'If your daughter is alive, we will find her.'

Then one day he saw them in the camp. They were about to drive away. 'Son,' he shouted after one of them, 'have you found Sakina, my daughter?'

'We will, we will,' they replied all together.

The old man again prayed for them. It made him feel better.

That evening there was sudden activity in the camp. He saw four men carrying the body of a young girl found unconscious near the railway tracks. They were taking her to the camp hospital. He began to follow them.

He stood outside the hospital for some time, then went in. In one of the rooms, he found a stretcher with someone lying on it.

A light was switched on. It was a young woman with a mole on her left cheek. 'Sakina,' Sirajuddin screamed.

The doctor, who had switched on the light, stared at Sirajuddin.

'I am her father,' he stammered.

The doctor looked at the prostrate body and felt for the pulse. Then he said to the old man: 'Open the window.'

The young woman on the stretcher moved slightly. Her hands groped for the cord which kept her *shalwar* tied round her waist. With painful slowness, she unfastened it, pulled the garment down and opened her thighs.

'She is alive. My daughter is alive,' Sirajuddin shouted with joy.

The doctor broke into a cold sweat.

Doing God's Work

I come from Gujarat Kathiawar in the west of India, and am a *bania* by caste, trader by tradition. Last year, when the world went topsy-turvy following the Partition of the country, I was temporarily out of work, except for the odd buck I made through my cocaine deals.

Thousands of refugees had begun moving from here to there, or there to here, so one day I also decided to migrate to Pakistan. There would always be something to do, I said to myself. If not in cocaine, then something else. So I set out. It took me some time to get there, but in the end I managed, even making a little cash as I went along.

Since I had moved to Pakistan to start a business, I began to study the situation carefully. The going thing seemed to be allotment of property left behind by the Hindus. Since I have the gift of the gab and can get round people, I was able to make friends easily in the right quarters and soon a house was allotted in my name. I sold it promptly, making a nice packet in the process. This looked promising and I began to move from city to city, getting property allotted and disposing it of as soon as I had the documents.

All work takes effort. Nothing in life is easy. Well, I could not hope to be an exception. It was a constant struggle. Sometimes flattery would get the necessary done, other times a bribe or a dinner invitation, even a 'good time' in the evening. What I do know is that I was constantly on my feet. I would arrive in a city, survey the residential areas, pick out a nice house and then try to get hold of it.

Hard work always gets rewarded and so it happened that in a year's time, I had managed to pile up a tidy fortune. I now had everything a man needs to live well — a nice house, plenty of cash in the bank, servants, a big car, not to mention commercial property.

But I felt restless. When I was in cocaine, I sometimes used to get this strange depression, but it was nothing compared to what I was going through now. I felt under a kind of weight. What it was I could not define.

I am an intelligent man. If something is bothering me, I always manage to find out what it is. I was determined to get to the bottom of this one as well. What was wrong with me?

Women? Well, I was unencumbered. I had lost my wife in Gujarat. However, there were other women. My gardener's wife, for instance. There is no accounting for taste. I believe that the only thing which matters in a woman is youth. It is not essential that she should have an education or be able to dance or what have you. I can only speak for myself. I like them young. That's all.

As I said, I am an intelligent man and I knew that something was missing in my life. My business was OK, my bank account was growing by the day and I had people working for me. In fact I had reached a stage where money was coming in without much effort on my part. After much reflection, I found the answer. I was restless because I hadn't done a single good deed since coming to Pakistan.

Back in Kathiawar, I had quite a few good deeds to my credit. For example, when my friend Pandorang died, I brought his wife to live in my house and thus was able to prevent her from getting into the oldest profession in the world for at least two years. Another friend, Vinayak, broke his wooden leg and I promptly bought him another. Cost me forty rupees. And so on and so forth. However, I hadn't done anything by way of a virtuous deed since moving to Pakistan, which was perhaps why my heart was restless.

I tried to think how best to go about doing good deeds. Alms? Well, I walked around the city one day and found that it was full of naked and hungry wretches. Could I feed and clothe all of them single-handed? What about setting up a community kitchen? Did not seem practical. It would mean buying huge quantities of foodgrains which could only be had on the black market. What would be the point in doing something morally reprehensible for the sake of a good deed?

I spent hours every day listening to tales of woe and misfortune. Everybody had a sad story to tell: those who slept on the street and those who lived in vast and expensive houses. The pedestrian was unhappy because he did not have a new and comfortable pair of shoes. The man who had the money to be chauffeured around was depressed because he could not afford to buy the latest model of car. In fact, all complaints were genuine and reasonable.

I remembered a *ghazal* I had once heard Amina Bai Chitalkar of Sholapur (may God rest her soul in peace) sing. One of the lines ran: no man can fulfil another's need. So there I was, willing to help, but actually unable to. There were just too many who needed aid. After much reflection, I came to the conclusion that charity was not the answer. I visited many refugee camps and found that because of charity, most of the inmates had become idle. They no longer wanted to work. I found them lolling around in their camps all day, playing cards or just gossiping, waiting all the while to be fed free of charge. How could these wretches do anything for Pakistan? I came to the conclusion that alms-giving was in no way akin to a good deed. So what was I going to do?

Hundreds of inmates were dying in these refugee camps. Epidemics were frequent and the city hospitals were full. I decided to construct a free hospital. I prepared the complete scheme. I would call for tenders, collect a tidy sum in tender fees, set up my own company and give it the contract for, say, a hundred thousand rupees (the building would never cost more than seventy thousand, leaving me a neat thirty thousand) and thus achieve my aim. However, I gave up the idea because what if I managed to save all those lives? Damn it, there would be a population explosion. How would the nation handle that?

Come to think of it, the whole trouble was that there were too many people. While the size of the population kept increasing, the land that grew food remained the same size. The rainfall did not necessarily keep pace with the proliferating numbers. I therefore came to the considered conclusion that it was pointless to build a hospital.

Then I thought of building a mosque. May God keep old Amina Bai Chitalkar of Sholapur in His heavenly peace, for she used to sing something about doing a good deed to keep your name alive after you were gone. And what were the good deeds she used to sing of? Sinking wells and building bridges and constructing mosques. But this kind of thing was no good, because there were far too many mosques in the city as it was. More mosques meant more fights among the believers, more sectarian divisions. I did not wish to add to them.

I decided to go on a pilgrimage to Mecca instead. But before I could embark on my journey, God Himself provided me with an answer. There was a public rally in the city and it broke up in complete pandemonium. Thirty people were killed, trampled underfoot. When the story appeared in the papers the next morning, it was said that they had not been killed but 'martyred'.

This set me thinking. I called on various leading religious scholars in the city and was assured that those who died in accidents were blessed because since it had not been their fault, martyrdom had been conferred on them. And that was the highest state a man could aspire to. I said to myself:

if instead of dying plainly, people could be martyred, wouldn't that be wonderful? What was the point of dying an ordinary death? A complete waste. It was martyrdom alone which could give meaning to a drab life.

I did some more thinking on this very delicate issue. I looked around and what did I see? Hordes of miserable creatures with sunken eyes, their faces yellow with malnutrition, crushed by the weight of poverty, walking about like ghosts in tattered clothes. They looked like junk thrown on the rubbish heap, living in ramshackle huts, crawling about the city bazaars like unclaimed animals. Why were these people alive, I asked myself? What were they living for and how? Nobody knew. There they were, dying by the thousand, dying of hunger and thirst, dying of cold, dying of heat and, what was more, dying unmourned, unremembered.

And when they died, what happened to them? Nothing at all. So I hit upon my great idea. Why should these people not die as martyrs, instead of living in perpetual hunger, sickness and pain? Why should they not win for themselves a place of honour in this world, become the subject of veneration among those who did not even want to look at their ravaged faces today?

The question was, would these people be willing to be martyred? I was confident they would, because they were good Muslims and all good Muslims longed for the exalted state of martyrdom. Even Hindus and Sikhs were now aspiring to martyrdom. I was therefore extremely disappointed when I was told by an emaciated wretch (I had asked him if he wanted to become a martyr) that he had no such ambition.

I just could not understand what this miserable creature was going to get out of being alive. I tried to argue with him. I said: 'Look my friend, you are an old man and you are not likely to live more than a month or a month and a half. As it is, you are so weak you can't even walk. When you go into one of your coughing fits, it is a wonder that you come out of it at all. You haven't a penny to your name. You have never had a day of comfort in your life. There is no question of a future in your case. Why do you want to live? For what? You are too old to join the army; otherwise, you might have had a chance to die fighting for your country. Why not make arrangements to get martyred?'

'How can that be arranged?' he asked. So I explained to him how. 'Lying in front of you on the ground is a banana skin. Supposing you were to slip on it, it is obvious you wouldn't survive the shock and would die and become a martyr.' However, he did not buy my argument. Instead, he said: 'You think I am so out of my mind that I should let myself slip on that banana skin with my eyes open. Don't I love life?' My God! That's what that miserable bag of bones said. He thought he was living life.

His attitude really depressed me. I was even more depressed when I heard a couple of days later that he, who could so easily have attained martyrdom, had died coughing on a bare steel bed in a charity hospital.

Then there was this woman, with no teeth in her mouth and no intestines in her belly. She looked as if she would breathe her last any minute. I felt very sorry for her. All her life had been spent in grief and poverty. I lifted her up in my arms and placed her on the railway track, but as soon as she heard the train approach, she bounced up like a wound-up toy on a spring and ran away.

It broke my heart, but I did not give up. I had seen the straight and narrow path of virtue and I was not going to be deflected so easily.

There was an empty building in the city, dating back to the time of the Mughal kings. There were exactly 151 tiny rooms in it. With my experienced eyes, I estimated at one glance that the first big rain would bring its leaking roof down. I bought the place up for a few thousand rupees and let it out to about one thousand homeless people, charging them no more than a rupee a month. For two months I received rent and, as I had estimated, at the beginning of the third, the first rains came to the city and the roof caved in, martyring seven hundred men, women and children.

My heart felt light. There were now seven hundred less to feed and clothe in the world and, what was more, they had all attained martyrdom and gone to heaven.

My good work has continued. No day passes when two or three people do not drink the sweet cup of martyrdom through my efforts. All work needs labour, and as old Amina Bai Chitalkar of Sholapur used to sing ... but let that pass. I can't recall the words. Suffice it to say that I have had to try very hard to attain my noble objective. There was one miserable creature whom I was unable to dispatch to heaven after having thrown banana skins in his path about ten times. However, like death, martyrdom is pre-ordained and one day he slipped in his bathroom and joined the exalted company of martyrs.

These days I am engaged in constructing a huge residential building. The contract — worth two hundred thousand rupees — is being executed by my own company. I am sure to make a profit of at least seventy-five thousand rupees. I have also had the building insured. I estimate that when the third storey is raised, the whole thing will come tumbling down, for such are the sub-standard materials I have used. And of the three hundred men who are engaged in the construction work, given luck, not one should survive, but immediately attain eternal martyrdom.

And if there are survivors, it would mean that they are sinners, and God, who is merciful and compassionate, is not willing to admit them to the exalted state of martyrdom.

It Happened in 1919

'It happened in 1919. The whole of Punjab was up in arms against the Rowlatt Act. Sir Michael O'Dwyer had banned Gandhiji's entry into the province under the Defence of India rules. He had been stopped at Pulwal, taken into custody and sent to Bombay. I believe if the British had not made this blunder, the Jallianwala Bagh incident would not have added a bloody page to the black history of their rule in India.'

I was on a train and the man sitting next to me had begun talking to me, just like that. I hadn't interrupted him and so he had gone on.

'Gandhiji was loved and respected by the people, Muslims, Hindus and Sikhs alike. When news of the arrest reached Lahore, the entire city went on strike. Amritsar, where the story I am going to narrate happened, followed suit.

'It is said that by the evening of 9 April, the deputy commissioner had received orders for the expulsion from Amritsar of the two leaders, Dr Satyapal and Dr Kitchlew, but was unwilling to implement them because, in his view, there was no likelihood of a breach of the peace. Protest meetings were being organized and no one was in favour of using violent methods.

'I was a witness to a procession taken out to celebrate a Hindu festival, and I can assure you it was the most peaceful thing I ever saw. It faithfully kept to the route marked out by the officials, but this Sir Michael was half-mad. They said he refused to follow the deputy commissioner's advice because he was convinced that Kitchlew and Satyapal were in Amritsar waiting for a signal from Gandhiji before proceeding to topple the government. In his view the protest meetings and processions were all part of this grand conspiracy.

'The new of the expulsion of the two leaders spread like wildfire through the city, creating an atmosphere of uncertainty and fear. One could sense that disaster was about to strike. But, my friend, I can tell you that there was also a great deal of enthusiasm among the people. All businesses were closed. The city was quiet like a graveyard and there was a feeling of impending doom in the air.

'After the first shock of the expulsions had died down, thousands of people gathered spontaneously to go in a procession to the deputy commissioner and call for the withdrawal of the orders. But, my friend, belive me, the times were out of joint. That this extremely reasonable request would be even heard was out of the question. Sir Michael was like a pharaoh and we were not surprised when he declared the gathering itself unlawful.

'Amritsar, which was one of the greatest centres of the liberation struggle and which still proudly carries the wound of Jallianwala Bagh, is now of course changed ... but that is another story. Some people say that what happened in that great city in 1947 was also the fault of the British. But if you want my opinion, we ourselves are responsible for the bloodshed there in 1947. Anyway.

'The deputy commissioner's house was in the Civil Lines. In fact all senior officers and the big toadies of the Raj lived in that exclusive area. If you know your Amritsar, you will recall that bridge which links the city with the Civil Lines. You cross the bridge from the city and you are on the Mall, that paradise on earth created by the British rulers.

'The protest procession began to move towards the Civil Lines. When it reached Hall Gate, word went round that British mounted troops were on guard at the bridge, but the crowd was undeterred and kept moving. I was also among them. We were all unarmed. I mean there wasn't even a stick on any of us. The whole idea was to get to the deputy commissioner's house and protest to him about the expulsion of the two leaders and demand their release. All peacefully.

'When the crowd reached the bridge, the tommies opened fire, causing utter pandemonium. People began to run in all directions. There were no more than twenty to twenty-five soldiers, but they were armed and they were firing. I have never seen anything like it. Some were wounded by gunshot, others were trampled.

'I stood well away from the fray at the edge of a big open gutter and someone pushed me into it. When the firing stopped, I crawled out. The crowd had dispersed. Many of the injured were lying in the road and the tommies on the bridge were having a good laugh. I'm not sure what my state of mind at the time was, but I think it couldn't have been normal. In fact I think I fainted when I fell in. It was only later that I was able to reconstruct the events.

'I could hear angry slogans being chanted in the distance. I began to walk. Going past the shrine of Zahra Pir, I was in Hall Gate in no time, where I found about thirty or forty boys throwing stones at the big clock which sits on top of the gate. They finally shattered its protective glass and the pieces fell on the road.

'"Let's go and smash the Queen's statue," someone shouted.

'"No, let's set fire to the police headquarters."

'"And all the banks too."

'"What would be the point of that? Let's go to the bridge and fight the tommy soldiers," suggested another.

'I recognized the author of the last proposal. He was

Thaila *kanjar* — *kanjar*, because he was the son of a prostitute — otherwise Mohammad Tufail. He was quite notorious in Amritsar. He had got into the habit of drinking and
gambling while still a boy. He had two sisters, Shamshad
and Almas, who were considered the city's most beautiful
singing and dancing girls.

'Shamshad was an accomplished singer and big land-
lords and the like used to travel from great distances to hear
her perform. The sisters were not exactly enamoured of the
doings of their brother Thaila and it was said that they had
practically disowned him. However, through one excuse or
the other, he was always able to get enough money from
them to live in style. He liked to dress and eat well and
drink to his heart's content. He was a great story-teller, but
unlike other people of his type, he was never vulgar. He was
tall, athletic and quite handsome, come to think of it.

'However, the boys did not show much enthusiasm for
his suggestion of taking on the tommies. Instead, they
began to move towards the Queen's statue. Thaila was not
the kind to give up so easily. He said to them: "Why are
you wasting your energy? Why don't you follow me? We'll
go and kill those tommies who have shot and killed so many
innocent people. I swear by God, if we're together, we can
wring their necks with our bare hands."

'Some were already well on their way to the Queen's
statue, but there were still some stragglers who began to
follow Thaila in the direction of the bridge where the
tommies stood guard. I thought the whole thing was
suicidal and I had no desire to be part of it. I even shouted
at Thaila: "Don't do it, *yaar*, why are you bent upon getting
yourself killed?"

'He laughed. "Thaila just wants to demonstrate that he's
not afraid of their bullets," he said cavalierly. Then he told
the few who were willing to follow him: "Those among you
who are afraid can leave now."

'No one left, which is understandable in such situations.

Thaila started to walk briskly, setting the pace for his companions. There seemed to be no question of turning back now.

'The distance between Hall Gate and the bridge is negligible, maybe less than a hundred yards. The approach to the bridge was being guarded by two mounted tommies. I heard the sound of fire as Thaila closed in shouting revolutionary slogans. I thought he'd been hit, but no, he was still moving forward with great resolution. Some of the boys began to run in different directions. He turned and shouted: "Don't run away ... let's go get them."

'I heard more gunfire. Thaila's back was momentarily towards the tommies, since he was trying to infuse some life into his retreating entourage. I saw him veer towards the soldiers and there were big red spots of blood on his silk shirt. He had been hit, but he kept advancing, like a wounded lion. There was more gunfire and he staggered, but then he regained his foothold and leapt at the mounted tommy, bringing him down to the ground.

'The other tommy became panic stricken and began to fire his revolver recklessly. What happened afterwards is not clear, because I fainted.

'When I came to, I found myself home. Some men who knew me had picked me up and brought me back. I heard from them that angry crowds had ransacked the town. The Queen's statue had been smashed and the town hall and three of the city banks had been set on fire. Five or six Europeans had been killed and the crowd had gone on a rampage.

'The British officers were not bothered about damage to property, but the fact that European blood had been shed. And as you know, it was avenged at Jallianwala Bagh. The deputy commissioner handed the city over to General Dyer, so on 12 April the general marched through the streets at the head of columns of armed soldiers. Dozens of innocent people were arrested. On 13 April a protest meeting was organized in Jallianwala Bagh which General Dyer "dispersed" by ordering his Gurkha and Sikh soldiers to open fire on the unarmed crowd.

'However, I was telling you about Thaila and what I saw with my own eyes. Only God is without blemish and Thaila was, let's not forget, the son of a prostitute and he used to practise every evil in the book. But he was brave. I tell you he had already been hit when he exhorted his companions not to run away but to move forward. He was so intoxicated with enthusiasm at the time that he did not realize he had been hit. He was shot twice more, once in the back and then in the chest. They pumped his young body full of molten lead.

'I didn't see it, but I'm told that when Thaila's bullet-ridden body was pulled away, both his hands were dug into the tommy's throat. They just couldn't get his grip to loosen. The tommy had of course been well and truly dispatched to hell.

'Thaila's bullet-torn body was handed over to his family the next day. It seemed the other tommy had emptied the entire magazine of his revolver into him. He must have been dead by then, but the devil had nevertheless gone on.

'It is said that when Thaila's body was brought to his *mohalla*, it was a shattering scene. It's true he wasn't exactly the apple of his family's eye, but when they saw his minced-up remains, there wasn't a dry eye to be seen anywhere. His sisters Shamshad and Almas fainted.

'My friend, I have heard that in the French Revolution, it was a prostitute who was the first to fall. Mohammad Tufail was also a prostitute's son, so whether it was the first bullet of the revolution which hit him or the tenth or the fifth, nobody really bothered to find out because socially he did not matter. I have a feeling that when they finally make a list of those who died in this bloodbath in Punjab, Thaila *kanjar*'s name won't be included. As a matter of fact, I don't think anyone would even bother about a list.

'Those were terrible days. The monster they call martial law held the city in its grip. Thaila was buried amid great hurry and confusion, as if his death was a grave crime which his family should obliterate from the record. What can I say except that Thaila died and Thaila was buried.'

My companion stopped speaking. The train was moving at breakneck speed. Suddenly I felt as if the clickety-clack of its powerful wheels was intoning the words 'Thaila died,· Thaila buried ... Thaila died, Thaila buried ... Thaila died, Thaila buried.' There was no dividing line between his death and his burial. He had died and in the next instant he had been buried. 'You were going to say something,' I said to my companion.

'Yes,' he replied, 'yes ... there is a sad part of the story which I haven't yet come to.'

'And what's that?'

'As I have already told you, he had two sisters, Shamshad and Almas, both very beautiful. Shamshad was tall, with fine features, big eyes, and she was a superb *thumri* singer. They say she had taken music lessons from the great Khan Sahib Fateh Ali Khan. Almas, the other one, was unmusical, but she was a fantastic dancer. When she danced it seemed as if every atom of her body was undulating with the music. Oh! They say there was a magic in her eyes which nobody could resist ...

'Well, my friend, it is said that someone who was trying to make his number with the British told them about Thaila's sisters and how beautiful and gifted they were. So it was decided that to avenge the death of that Englishwoman ... what was the name of that witch? Miss Sherwood I think ... the two girls should be summoned for an evening of pleasure. You know what I mean.'

'Yes.'

'These are delicate matters, but I would say that when it comes to something like this, even dancing girls and prostitutes are like our sisters and mothers. But I tell you, our people have no concept of national honour. So, you can guess what happened.

'The police received orders from the powers that be and an inspector personally went to the house of the girls and said that the sahib *log* had expressed a desire to be entertained by them.

'And to think that the earth on the grave of their brother was still fresh. He hadn't even been dead two days and there were these orders: come and dance in our imperial presence. No greater torture could have been devised! Do you think that it even occurred to those who issued these orders that even women like Shamshad and Almas could have a sense of honour? What do you think?'

But he was speaking more to himself than to me. Nevertheless, I ventured: 'Yes, surely they too have a sense of honour.'

'Quite right. After all, Thaila was their brother. He hadn't lost his life in a gambling brawl or a fit of drunkenness. He had volunteered to drink the cup of martyrdom like a valiant national hero.

'Yes, it's true he was born of a prostitute, but a prostitute is also a mother and Shamshad and Almas were his sisters first and dancing girls later. They had fainted when they had brought Thaila's bullet-ridden body home, and it was heart-breaking to hear them bewail the martyrdom of their brother.'

'Did they go?' I asked.

My companion answered after a pause: 'Yes, yes, they went all right. They were dressed to kill.' There was a note of bitterness in his voice.

'They went to their hosts of the evening and they looked stunning. They say it was quite an orgy. The two sisters displayed their art with fascinating skill. In their silks and brocades they looked like Caucasian fairy queens. There was much drinking and merrymaking and they danced and sang all night.

'And it is said that at two in the morning the guest of honour indicated that the party was over.'

'The party was over, the party was over' the wheels intoned as the train ran headlong along the tracks. I cleared my mind of this intrusion and asked my companion: 'What happened then?'

Taking his eyes away from the passing phantasmagoria of trees and power lines, he said in a determined voice: 'They tore off their silks and brocades and stood there naked and they said ... look at us ... we are Thaila's sisters ... that martyr whose beautiful body you peppered with your bullets because inside that body dwelt a spirit which was in love with this land ... yes, we are his beautiful sisters ... come, burn our fragrant bodies with the red hot irons of your lust ... but before you do that, allow us to spit in your faces once.' He fell silent as if he did not wish to say any more.

'What happened then?'

Tears welled up in his eyes: 'They ... they were shot dead.'

I did not say anything. The train stopped. He sent for a porter and asked him to pick up his bags. As he was about to leave, I said to him: 'I have a feeling that the story you have just told me has a false ending.'

He was startled. 'How do you know?'

'Because there was indescribable agony in your voice when you reached the end.'

He swallowed. 'Yes, those bitches ...' he paused; 'they dishonoured their martyred brother's name.'

He stepped on the platform and was gone.

The Price of Freedom

The year I do not remember, but there was great revolutionary fervour in Amritsar. '*Inqilab Zindabad*' — long live revolution — was the slogan of the day. There was excitement in the air and a feeling of restlessness and youthful abandon. We were living through heady times. Even the fearful memories of the Jallianwala Bagh massacre had disappeared, at least on the surface. One felt intensely alive and on the threshold of something great and final.

People marched through the streets every day raising slogans against the Raj. Hundreds were arrested for breaking the law. In fact, courting arrest had become something of a popular diversion. You were picked up in the morning and quite often released by the evening. A case would be registered, a hearing held and a short sentence awarded. You came out, raised a few more slogans and were put in gaol again.

There was so much to live for in those days. The slightest incident sometimes led to the most violent upheaval. One man would stand on a podium in one of the city squares and call for a strike. A strike would follow. There was of course the movement to wear only Indian-spun cotton with the object of putting the Lancashire textile mills out of business. There was a boycott of all imported cloth in effect. Every street had its own bonfire. People would walk up, take off every imported piece of clothing they were wearing and chuck it into the fire. Sometimes a woman would stand on her balcony and throw down her imported silk sari into the bonfire. The crowd would cheer.

I remember this huge bonfire the boys had lit in front of the town hall and the police headquarters, where in a wild moment my classmate Sheikhoo had taken off his silk jacket and thrown it into the flames. A big cheer had gone up because it was well known that he was the son of one of the richest men of the city, who also had the dubious distinction of being the most infamous 'toady', as government sympathizers were popularly called. Inspired by the applause, Shiekhoo had also taken off his silk shirt and sent it the way of his jacket. It was only later that he had remembered the gold links that had gone with it.

I don't want to make fun of my friend, because in those days, I too was in the same turbulent frame of mind. I used to dream about getting hold of guns and setting up a secret terrorist organization. That my father was a government servant did not bother me. I was restless and did not even understand what I was restless about.

I was never much interested in school, but during those days, I had completely gone off my books. I would spend the entire day at Jallianwala Bagh. Sitting under a tree, I would watch the windows of the houses bordering the park and dream about the girls who lived behind them. I was sure one of these days, one of them would fall in love with me.

Jallianwala Bagh had become the hub of the movement of civil disobedience launched by the Congress. There were small and big tents and colourful awnings everywhere. The largest tent was the political headquarters of the city. Once or twice a week, a 'dictator' — for that was what he was called — would be nominated by the people to 'lead the struggle'. He would be ceremoniously placed in the large tent; volunteers would provide him with a ragtag guard of honour, and for the next few days he would receive delegations of young political workers, all wearing homespun cotton. It was also the 'dictator's' duty to get donations of food and money from the city's big shopkeepers and businessmen. And so it would continue until one day the police would come and pick him up.

I had a friend called Ghulam Ali. Our intimacy can be judged from the fact that both of us had failed our school-leaving examination twice in a row. Once we had run away from home and were on our way to Bombay — from where we planned to sail for the Soviet Union — when our money had run out. After sleeping for a few nights on footpaths, we had written to our parents and promised not to do such a thing again. We were reprieved.

Shahzada Ghulam Ali, as he later came to be called, was a handsome young man, tall and fair as Kashmiris tend to be. He always walked with a certain swagger that one generally associates with 'tough guys'. Actually, he was no Shahzada — which means prince — when we were at school. However, after having become active in the civil dis-obedience movement and run the gamut of revolutionary speeches, public processions, social intercourse with pretty female volunteer workers, garlands, slogans and patriotic songs, he had for some reason come to be known as Shah-zada.

His fame spread like wildfire in the city of Amritsar. It was a small town where it did not take you long to become famous or infamous. The natives of Amritsar, though by nature critical of the general run of humanity, were rather indulgent when it came to religious and political leaders. They always seemed to have this peculiar need for fiery sermons and revolutionary speeches. Leaders had always had a long tenure in our city. The times were advantageous because the established leadership was in gaol and there were quite a few empty chairs waiting to be occupied. The movement needed people like Ghulam Ali who would be seen for a few days in Jallianwala Bagh, make a speech or two and then duly get arrested.

In those days, the German and Italian dictatorships were the new thing in Europe, which is what had perhaps inspired the Indian National Congress to designate certain party workers as 'dictators'. When Shahzada Ghulam Ali's turn came to go to gaol, as many as forty 'dictators' had already been put inside.

When I learnt that Ghulam Ali had been named the current 'dictator', I made my way to the Jallianwala Bagh. There were volunteers outside the big tent. However, since Ghulam Ali had seen me, I was permitted to go in. A white cotton carpet had been laid on the ground and there sat Ghulam Ali, propped up against cushions. He was talking to a group of cotton-clad city shopkeepers about the vegetable trade, I think. After having got rid of them he issued a few instructions to his volunteers and turned to me. He looked too serious, which I thought was funny. When we were alone, I asked him, 'And how is our prince?'

I also realized that he had changed. To my attempt at treating the whole thing as a farce, he said, 'No, Saadat, don't make fun of it. The great honour which has been bestowed on me, I do not deserve. But from now on the movement is going to be my life.'

I promised to return in the evening as he told me that he would be making a speech. When I arrived, there was a large crowd of people around a podium they had set up for the occasion. Then I heard loud applause and there was Shahzada Ghulam Ali. He looked very handsome in his spotless white and his swagger seemed to add to his appeal.

He spoke for an hour or so. It was an emotional speech. Even I was overcome. There were moments when I wished nothing more than to turn into a human bomb and explode for the glory of the freedom of India.

This happened many years ago and memory always plays tricks with detail, but as I write this, I can see Ghulam Ali addressing that turbulent crowd. It was not politics I was conscious of while he spoke, but youth and the promise of revolution. He had the sincere recklessness of a young man who might stop a woman on the street and say to her without any preliminaries, 'Look, I love you.'

Such were the times. I think both the British Raj and the people it ruled were still inexperienced and quite unaware of the consequences of their actions. The government, without really fully comprehending the implications, was putting people in gaol by the thousand, and those who were going to gaol were not quite sure what they were doing and what the results would be.

There was much disorder. I think you could liken the general atmosphere to a spreading fire which leaps out into the air and then just as suddenly goes out, only to ignite again. No longer were people willing to accept the monotony of British rule in India.

As Shahzada Ghulam Ali finished speaking, the entire Jallianwala Bagh came to its feet. I stepped forward to congratulate him, but his eyes were elsewhere. My curiosity was soon satisfied. It was a girl in a white cotton sari, standing behind a flowering bush.

The next day I learnt that Shahzada Ghulam Ali was in love with the girl I had seen the evening earlier. And so was she with him, and just as much. She was a Muslim, an orphan, who worked as a nurse at the local women's hospital. I think she was the first Muslim girl in Amritsar to join the Congress movement against the Raj.

Her white cotton saris, her association with the Congress and the fact that she worked in a hospital had all combined to soften that slight hardness one finds in Muslim girls. She was not beautiful, but she was very feminine. She had acquired that hard-to-describe quality so characteristic of Hindu girls — a mixture of humility, self-assurance and the urge to worship. In her, the beauty of ritualistic Muslim prayer and Hindu devotion to temple gods had been alchemized.

She worshipped Shahzada Ghulam Ali and he loved her to distraction. They had met during a protest march and fallen for each other almost immediately.

Ghulam Ali wanted to marry Nigar before his inevitable and almost eagerly awaited arrest. Why he wanted to do that I am unable to say as he could just as well have married her after his release. Gaol terms in those days varied between three months and a year. There were some who were let out after ten or fifteen days in order to make way for fresh entrants.

All that was really needed was the blessing of Babaji.

Babaji was one of the great figures of the time. He was camped at the splendid house of the richest jeweller in the city, Hari Ram. Normally, Babaji used to live in his village ashram, but whenever he came to Amritsar, he would put up with Hari Ram, and the palatial residence, located outside the city, would turn into a sort of shrine, since the number of Babaji's followers was legion. You could see them standing in line, waiting to be admitted briefly to the great man's presence for what was called *darshan*, or a mere look at him. The old man would receive them sitting cross-legged on a specially constructed platform in a grove of mango trees, accepting donations and gifts for his ashram. In the evening, he would have young women volunteers sing him Hindu devotional songs.

Babaji was known for his piety and scholarship, and his followers included men and women of every faith — Hindus, Muslims, Sikhs and untouchables.

Although on the face of it Babaji had nothing to do with politics, it was an open secret that no political movement in the Punjab could begin or end without his clearance. To the government machinery, he was an unsolved puzzle. There was always a smile on his face which could be interpreted in a thousand ways.

The civil disobedience movement in Amritsar with its daily arrests and processions was quite clearly being

conducted with Babaji's blessing, if not his direct guidance.
He was in the habit of dropping hints about the tactics to be
followed and the next day every major political leader in the
Punjab would be wearing Babaji's wisdom as a kind of
amulet around his neck.

There was a magnetic quality about him and his voice
was soft, persuasive and full of nuances. Not even the most
poisonous criticism could ruffle his composure. To his
enemies he was an enigma because he always kept them
guessing.

Babaji was a frequent visitor to Amritsar, but somehow I
had never seen him. Therefore when Ghulam Ali told me
one day that he planned to call on the great man to obtain
his blessing for his intended marriage to Nigar I told him to
take me along. The next day, Ghulam Ali arranged for a *tonga*,
and the three of us — Ghulam Ali, Nigar and I — found ourselves at Hari Ram's magnificent house.

Babaji had already had his ritualistic morning bath —
ashnan — and his devotions were done. He now sat in the
mango grove listening to a stirring nationalistic song,
courtesy of a young beautiful Kashmiri Pandit girl. He sat
cross-legged on a mat made from date-palm leaves, and
though there were plenty of cushions around, he did not
seem to want any. He was in his seventies but his skin was
without blemish. I wondered if it was the result of his
famous olive oil massage every morning.

He smiled at Ghulam Ali and asked us to join him on the
floor. It was obvious to me that Ghulam Ali and Nigar were
less interested in the revolutionary refrain of the song,
which seemed to have Babaji in a kind of trance, than their
own symphony of young love. At last the girl finished,
winning in the bargain Babaji's affectionate approval, indicated with a subtle nod of his head, and he turned to us.

Ghulam Ali was about to introduce Nigar and himself,
but he never got an opportunity, thanks to Babaji's excep-
tional memory for names and faces. In his low, soothing

voice he enquired, 'Prince, so you have not yet been arrested?'

'No sir,' Ghulam Ali replied, his hands folded as a mark of respect.

Playing with a pencil which he had pulled out from somewhere, he said, 'But I think you have already been arrested.' He looked meaningfully at Nigar: 'She has already arrested our prince.'

Babaji's next remark was addressed to the girl who had earlier been singing. 'These children have come to seek my blessing. Tell me, when are you going to get married, Kamal?'

Her pink face turned even pinker. 'But how can I? I am already at the ashram.'

Babaji sighed, turned to Ghulam Ali and said, 'So you two have made up your minds.'

'Yes,' they answered together. Babaji smiled.

'Decisions can sometimes be changed,' he said.

And despite the reverence-laden atmosphere, Ghulam Ali answered, 'This decision can be put off, but it can never be changed.'

Babaji closed his eyes and asked in a lawyer's voice, 'Why?'

Ghulam Ali did not hesitate. 'Because we are committed to it as we are committed to the freedom of India, and while circumstances may change the timing of that event, it is final and immutable.'

Babaji smiled. 'Nigar,' he said, 'why don't you join our ashram because Shahzada is going to gaol in a few days anyway?'

'I will,' she whispered.

Babaji changed the subject and began to ask us about political activities in Jallianwala Bagh. For the next hour or so, the conversation revolved around arrests, processions and even the price of vegetables. I did not join in these pleasantries, but I did wonder why Babaji had been so reluctant to accord his blessing to the young couple. Was he not quite sure that they were in love? Why had he asked Nigar to join the ashram? Was it to help her not think of Ghulam Ali being in gaol, or did it mean that if she joined the ashram, she would not be allowed to marry?

And what was going to happen to Kamal once she was admitted to the rarefied surroundings of the ashram? Would she spend her time intoning devotional and patriotic songs for the spiritual and political enlightenment of Babaji? Would she be happy? I had seen many ashram inmates in my time. There was something lifeless and pallid about them, despite their early morning cold bath and long walks. With their pale faces and sunken eyes, they somehow always reminded me of cows' udders. I couldn't see Kamal living among them, she who was so young and fresh, made up entirely, it seemed to me, of honey, milk and saffron. What had ashrams got to do with India's freedom?

I had always hated ashrams, seminaries, saints' shrines and orphanages. There was something unnatural about these places. I had often seen young boys walking in single file on the street, led by men who administered these institutions. I had visited religious seminaries and schools with their pious inmates. The older ones always wore long beards and the adolescents walked around with sparse, ugly hair sprouting out of their chins. Despite their five prayers a day, their faces never showed any trace of that inner light prayer is supposed to bring about.

Nigar was a woman, not a Muslim, Hindu, Sikh or Christian, but a woman. I simply could not see her praying like a machine every morning at the ashram. Why should she, who was herself pure as a prayer, raise her hands to heaven?

When we were about to leave, Babaji told Ghulam Ali and Nigar that they had his blessing and he would perform the marriage the next day in (where else?) Jallianwala Bagh. He arrived as promised. He was accompanied by his usual entourage of volunteers, with Hari Ram the jeweller in tow. A much-bedecked podium had been put up for the ceremony. The girls had taken charge of Nigar and she made a lovely bride. Ghulam Ali had made no special arrangements. All day long, he had been doing his usual chores, raising donations for the movement and the like. Both of them had decided to hoist the Congress flag after it was all over.

Just before Babaji's arrival, I had been telling Ghulam Ali that we must never forget what had happened in Jallianwala Bagh a few years earlier, in 1919 to be exact. There was a well in the park, which people say was full of dead bodies after General Dyer had ordered his soldiers to stop firing at the crowd. Today, I had told him, the well was used for drinking water which was still sweet. It bore no trace of the blood which had been spilt so wantonly by the British general and his Gurkha soldiers. The flowers still bloomed and were just as beautiful as they had been on that day.

I had pointed out to Ghulam Ali a house which overlooked the park. It was said that a young girl, who was standing at her window watching the massacre, had been shot through the heart. Her blood had left a mark on the wall below. If you looked carefully, you could still perhaps see it. I remember that six months after the massacre, our teacher had taken the entire class to Jallianwala Bagh and, picking up a piece of earth from the ground, had said to us, 'Children, never forget that the blood of our martyrs is part of this earth.'

Bababji was given a military-style salute by the volunteers. He and Ghulam Ali were taken around the camp, and as the evening was falling, the girls had begun to sing a devotional song and Babaji had sat there listening to it with his eyes closed.

The song had ended and Babaji had opened his eyes and said, 'Children, I am here to join these two freedom lovers in holy wedlock.' A cheer had gone up from the crowd. Nigar was in a sari which bore the three colours of the flag of the Indian National Congress — orange, green and white. The ceremony was a combination of Hindu and Muslim rituals.

Then Babaji had stood up and begun to speak: 'These two children will now be able to serve the nation with even greater enthusiasm. The true purpose of marriage is comradeship. What is being sanctified today will serve the cause of India's freedom. A true marriage should be free of lust because those who are able to exorcise this evil from their lives deserve our respect.'

Babaji spoke for a long time about his concept of marriage. According to him, the true bliss of marriage could only be experienced if the relationship between man and wife was something more than the physical enjoyment of each other's bodies. He did not think the sexual link was as important as it was made out to be. It was like eating. There were those who ate out of indulgence and there were those who ate to stay alive. The sanctity of marriage was more important than the gratification of the sexual instinct.

Ghulam Ali was listening to Babaji's rambling speech as if in a trance. He whispered something to Nigar as soon as Babaji had finished. Then, standing up on the podium, he said in a voice trembling with emotion, 'I have a declaration to make. As long as India does not win freedom, Nigar and I will live not as husband and wife but as friends.' He looked at his wife. 'Nigar, would you like to mother a child who would be a slave at the moment of his birth? No, you wouldn't.'

Ghulam Ali then began to ramble, going from subject to subject, but basically confining his emotional remarks to the freedom of India from the British Raj. At one point, he looked at Nigar and stopped speaking. To me he looked like a drunken man who realizes too late that he has no money left in his wallet. But he recovered his composure and said to Babaji, 'Both of us need your blessing. You have our solemn word of honour that the vow made today shall be kept.'

The next morning Ghulam Ali was taken in because he had threatened to overthrow the Raj and had declared publicly that he would father no children as long as India was ruled by a foreign power. He was given eight months and sent to the distant Multan gaol. He was Amritsar's fortieth 'dictator' to be gaoled and the forty thousandth prisoner of the civil disobedience movement against the Raj.

At that time most of us were convinced that the ousting of the British from India was a matter of days away. However, the Raj was cleverer than we were prepared to give it credit for. It let the movement come to the boil, then made a deal with the leaders, and everything simmered down.

When the workers began to come out of gaol, they realized that the atmosphere had changed. Wisely, most of them decided to resume their normal humdrum lives. Shahzada Ghulam Ali was let out after seven months, and while it is true the old popular enthusiasm had gone, yet he was received by a large crowd at the Amritsar railway station from where he was taken out in a procession through the city. A number of public meetings were also held in his honour, but it was evident that the fire and passion had died out. There was a sense of fatigue among the people. It was as if they were runners in a marathon who had been told by the organizers to stop running, return to the starting point, and begin again.

Years went by, but that heady feeling never returned. In my own life, a number of small and big revolutions came and went. I joined college, but failed my exams twice. My father died and I had to run from pillar to post looking for a job. I finally found a translator's position with a third-class newspaper, but I soon became restless and left. For a time, I joined the Aligarh Muslim University, but fell ill and was

sent to the more salubrious climate of Kashmir to recover.
After three months there, I moved to Bombay. Disgusted
with its frequent Hindu–Muslim riots, I made my way to
Delhi, but found it too slow and dull and returned to
Bombay, despite its impersonal inhabitants who seemed to
have no time for strangers.

It was now eight years since I had left Amritsar. I had no
idea what had happened to my old friend or the streets and
squares of my early youth. I had never written to anyone
and the fact was that I was not interested in the past or the
future. I was living in the present. The past, it seemed to
me, was like a sum of money you had already spent, and to
think about it was like drawing up a ledger account of
money you no longer had.

One afternoon — I had both time and some money — I
decided to go looking for a pair of shoes. Once, while passing by the Army & Navy Store, I had noticed a small shop
which had a very attractive display window. I didn't find
that shop, but I noticed another which looked quite reasonable.

'Show me a pair of shoes with rubber soles,' I told the
shop assistant.

'We don't stock them,' he replied.

Since the monsoons were expected any time, I asked him
if he could sell me rubber ankle-boots.

'We don't stock those either,' he said. 'Why don't you try
the store on the corner? We don't carry any rubber or part-
rubber footwear at all.'

'Why?' I asked, surprised.

'It's the boss's orders,' he answered.

As I stepped out of this strange place which did not sell
rubber shoes, I saw a man carrying a small child. He was
trying to buy oranges from a vendor.

'Ghulam Ali,' I screamed excitedly.

'Saadat,' he shouted, embracing me. The child didn't
like it and began to cry. He went into the shop and told the

assistant with whom I had just been talking to take the child home.

'It's been years, hasn't it?' he said.

He had changed. He was no longer the cotton-clad revolutionary who used to make fiery speeches in Jallianwala Bagh. He looked like a normal homely man.

My mind went back to his last speech. 'Nigar, would you like to mother a child who would be a slave at birth?'

'Whose child was that?' I asked.

'Mine. I have another one who is older. How many children do you have?' he answered without hesitation.

What had happened? Had he forgotten the vow he had taken that day? Was politics no longer a part of his life? What had happened to his passion for the freedom of India? Where was that firebrand revolutionary I used to know? What had happened to Nigar? What had induced her to beget slave children? Had Ghulam Ali married a second time?

'Let us talk,' he said. 'We haven't seen each other for ages.'

I didn't know where to begin, but he didn't put me to the test.

'This shop belongs to me. I've been living in Bombay for the last two years. I'm told you are a big-time story writer now. Do you remember the old days, how we ran away from home to come to Bombay? God, how time flies!'

We went into the shop. A customer who wanted a pair of tennis shoes was told that he would have to go to the shop on the corner.

'Why don't you stock them? You know I also came here looking for a pair,' I asked.

Ghulam Ali's face fell. 'Let's say I just don't like those things,' he replied.

'What things?'

'Those horrible rubber things. But I'll tell you why,' he said.

The anxious look which had clouded his handsome face suddenly cleared. 'That life was rubbish. Believe me, Saadat, I have forgotten about those days when the demon of politics was in my head. I'm very happy. I have a wife and two children and my business is going well.'

He took me to a room at the back of the store. The assistant had come back. Then he began to talk. I will let him tell his story.

'You know how my political life began. You also know what sort of person I was. I mean we grew up together and we were no angels. I wasn't a strong person and yet I wanted to accomplish something in my life. I swear upon God that I was prepared then, as I am prepared today, to sacrifice even my life for the freedom of India. However, after much reflection, I've come to the conclusion that both the politics of India and its political leadership are immature. There are sudden storms and then all is quiet. There is no spontaneity.

'Look, man may be good or evil, but he should remain the way God made him. You can be virtuous without having your head shaved, without donning saffron robes or covering yourself with ash. Those who advocate such things forget that these external manifestations of virtue, if that be indeed what they are, will only get lost on those who follow them. Only ritual will survive. What led to the ritual will be overlooked. Look at all the great prophets. Their teachings are no longer remembered, but we still have their legacy of crosses, holy threads and unshaven armpit hair. They tell you to kill your baser self. Well, if everyone went ahead and did it, what sort of a world would it be?

'You have no idea what hell I went through because I decided to violate human nature. I made a pledge that I would not produce children. It was made in a moment of euphoria. As time passed, I began to feel that the most vital part of my being was paralysed. What was more, it was my own doing. There were moments when I felt proud of my

great vow, but they passed. As the pores of my consciousness began to open, reality seemed to want to defeat my
resolve. When I met Nigar after my release, I felt that she
had changed. We lived together for one year and we kept
our promise to Babaji. It was hell. We were being
consumed by the futility of our married life.

'The world outside had changed too. Spun cotton, tricolour flags and revolutionary slogans had lost their power.
The tents had disappeared from Jallianwala Bagh. There
were only holes in the ground where those grand gatherings
used to take place. Politics no longer sent the blood cruising
through my veins as it used to.

'I spent most of my time at home and we never spoke our
minds to each other. I was afraid of touching her. I did not
trust myself. One day, as we sat next to each other, I had a
mad urge to take her in my arms and kiss her. I let myself
go, but I stopped just in time. It was a tremendous feeling
while it lasted. However, in the days that followed, I
couldn't get rid of a feeling of guilt.

'There had to be a way out of this absurd situation. One
day we hit upon a compromise. We would not produce
children. We would take the necessary steps, but we would
live like husband and wife.

'Thus began a new chapter in our lives. It was as if a blind
man had been given back the sight of one eye. But our
happiness did not last. We wanted our full vision restored.
We felt unhappy and it seemed that everything in our lives
had turned into rubber. Even my body felt blubbery and
unnatural. Nigar's agony was even more evident. She
wanted to be a mother and she couldn't be. When there
was a child born in the neighbourhood, she would shut
herself in a room.

'I wasn't so keen on children myself because, come to
think of it, one did not really have to have them. There were
millions of people in the world who seemed to be able to get
by without them. I could well be one of them. However,

what I could no longer stand was this clammy sensation in my hands. When I ate, it felt as if I was eating rubber. My hands always felt as if they had been soaped and then left unrinsed.

'I began to hate myself. All my sensations had atrophied except this weird, unreal sense of touch which made everything feel like rubber. All I needed to do was to peel off my terrible affliction with the help of two fingers and throw it as far as possible. But I didn't have the courage.

'I was like a drowning man who clutches at straws. And one day I found the straw I was looking for. I was reading a religious text and there it was. I almost jumped. It said: "If a man and woman are joined in wedlock, it is obligatory for them to procreate." And that day I peeled off my curse and have never looked back.'

At this moment, a servant entered the room. He was carrying a child who was holding a balloon. Like a madman, Ghulam Ali pounced on the balloon. There was a bang and all the child was left with was a piece of string with a shrivelled piece of ugly rubber dangling at the other end.

With two fingers, Ghulam Ali carefully picked up the deflated balloon and threw it away as if it were a particularly disgusting piece of filth.

The Woman in the Red Raincoat

This dates back to the time when both East and West Punjab were being ravaged by bloody communal riots between Hindus and Muslims. It had been raining hard for many days and the fire which men had been unable to put out had been extinguished by nature, However, there was no let-up in the murderous attacks on the innocent, nor was the honour of young women safe. Gangs of young men were still on the prowl and abductions of helpless and terrified girls were common.

On the face of it, murder, arson and looting are really not so difficult to commit as some people think. However, my friend 'S' had not found the going so easy.

But before I tell you his story, let me introduce 'S'. He's a man of ordinary looks and build and is as much interested in getting something for nothing as most of us are. But he isn't cruel by nature. It is another matter that he became the perpetrator of a strange tragedy, though he did not quite realize at the time what was happening.

He was just an ordinary student when we were in school, fond of games, but not very sporting. He was always the first to get into a fight when an argument developed during a game. Although he never quite played fair, he was an honest fighter.

He was interested in painting, but he had to leave college after only one year. Next we knew, he had opened a bicycle shop in the city.

When the riots began, his was one of the first shops to be

burnt down. Having nothing else to do, he joined the roaming bands of looters and arsonists, nothing extraordinary at the time. It was really more by way of entertainment and diversion than out of a feeling of communal revenge, I would say. Those were strange times. This is his story and it is in his own words.

'It was really pouring down. It seemed as if the skies would burst. In my entire life, I had never seen such rain. I was at home, sitting on my balcony, smoking a cigarette. In front of me lay a large pile of goods I had looted from various shops and houses with the rest of the gang. However, I was not interested in them. They had burnt down my shop but, believe me, it did not really seem to matter, mainly because I had seen so much looting and destruction that nothing made any sense any longer. The noise of the rain was difficult to ignore but, strangely enough, all I was conscious of was a dry and barren silence. There was a stench in the air. Even my cigarette smelt unpleasant. I'm not sure I was thinking even. I was in a kind of daze, very difficult to explain. Suddenly a shiver ran down my spine and a powerful desire to run out and pick up a girl took hold of me. The rain had become even heavier. I got up, put on my raincoat, and fortifying myself with a fresh tin of cigarettes from the pile of loot, went out in the rain.

'The roads were dark and deserted. Not even soldiers — a common sight in those days — were around. I kept walking about aimlessly for hours. There were many dead bodies lying on the streets, but they seemed to have no effect on me. After some time, I found myself in the Civil Lines area. The roads were without any sign of life. Suddenly I heard the sound of an approaching car. I turned. It was a small Austin being driven at breakneck speed. I don't know what came over me, but I placed myself in the middle of the road and began to wave frantically for the driver to stop.

'The car did not slow down. However, I was not going to move. When it was only a few yards away, it suddenly swerved to the left. In trying to run after it, I fell down, but got up immediately. I hadn't hurt myself. The car braked, then skidded and went off the road. It finally came to a stop, resting against a tree. I began to move towards it. The door was thrown open and a woman in a red raincoat jumped out. I couldn't see her face, but her shimmering raincoat was visible in the murky light. A wave of heat gripped my body.

'When she saw me moving towards her, she broke into a run. However, I caught up with her after a few yards. "Help me," she screamed as my arms enveloped her tightly, more her slippery raincoat than her, come to think of it.

'"Are you a Englishwoman?" I asked her in English, realizing too late that I should have said *an*, not *a*.

'"No," she replied.

'I hated Englishwomen, so I said to her, "Then it's all right."

'She began to scream in Urdu: "You're going to kill me. You're going to kill me."

'I said nothing. I was only trying to guess her age and what she looked like. The hood of her raincoat covered her face. When I tried to remove it, she put both her hands in front of her face. I didn't force her. Instead, I walked towards the car, opened the rear door and pushed her in. I started the car and the engine caught. I put it in reverse and it responded. I steered it carefully back onto the road and took off.

'I switched off the engine when we were in front of my house. My first thought was to take her to the balcony, but I changed my mind, not being sure if she would willingly walk up all those stairs. I shouted for the houseboy. "Open the living room door," I told him. After he had done that, I pushed her into the room. In the dark, I caught hold of her and gently pushed her onto the sofa.

'"Don't kill me. Don't kill me please," she began to scream.

'It sounded funny. In a mock-heroic voice I said, "I won't kill you. I won't kill you, darling."

'She began to cry. I sent the servant, who was still hanging around, out of the house. I pulled out a box of matches from my pocket, but the rain had made it damp. There hadn't been any power for weeks. I had a torch upstairs but I didn't really want to bother. "I'm not exactly going to take pictures that I should need a light," I said to myself. I took off my raincoat and threw it on the floor. "Let me take yours," I suggested to her.

'I fumbled for her on the sofa but she wasn't there. However, I wasn't worried. She had to be in the room somewhere. Methodically, I began to comb the place and in a few minutes I had found her. In fact we had a near collision on the floor. I touched her on the throat by accident. She screamed. "Stop that," I said, "I'm not going to kill you."

'I ignored her sobbing and began to unbutton her raincoat, which was made of some plastic material and was very slippery. She kept wailing and trying to struggle free, but I managed to get her free of that silly coat of hers. I realized that she was wearing a sari underneath. I touched her knee and it felt solid. A violent electric current went through my entire body. But I didn't want to rush things.

'I tried to calm her down. "Darling, I didn't bring you here to murder you. Don't be afraid. You are safer here than you would be outside. If you want to leave, you are free to do so. However, I would suggest that as long as these riots last, you should stay here with me. You're an educated girl. Out there, people have become like wild beasts. I don't want you to fall into the hands of those savages."

'"You won't kill me?" she sobbed.

'"No sir," I said.

'She burst out laughing because I had called her sir. However, her laughter encouraged me. "Darling, my

English is rather weak," I said with a laugh.

'She did not speak for some time. Then she said, "If you don't want to kill me, why have you brought me here?"

'It was an awkward question. I couldn't think of an answer, but I heard myself saying, "Of course, I don't want to kill you for the simple reason that I don't like killing people. So why have I brought you here? Well, I suppose because I'm lonely."

'"But you have your live-in servant."

'"He is only a servant. He doesn't matter."

'She fell silent. I began to experience a sense of guilt, so I got up and said, "Let's forget about it. If you want to leave, I won't stop you."

'I caught hold of her hand, then I thought of her knee which I had touched. Violently, I pressed her against my breast. I could feel her warm breath under my chin. I put my lips on hers. She began to tremble. "Don't be afraid, darling. I won't kill you," I whispered.

'"Please let me go," she said in a tremulous voice.

'I gently pulled my arms away, but then on an impulse, I lifted her off the ground. The flesh on her hips was extremely soft, I noticed. I also found that she was carrying a small handbag. I laid her down on the sofa and took her bag away. "Believe me, if it contains valuables, they will be quite safe. In fact, if you like, there are things I can give you," I told her by way of reassurance.

'"I don't need anything," she said.

'"But there is something I need," I replied.

'"What?" she asked.

'"You," I answered.

'She didn't say anything. I began to rub her knee. She offered no resistance. Feeling that she might think I was taking advantage of her helplessness, I said, "I don't want to force you. If you don't want it, you can leave, really."

'I was about to get up, when she grabbed my hand and put it on her breast. Her heart was beating violently. I became excited. "Darling," I whispered, taking her into my arms again.

'We began to kiss each other with reckless abandon. She kept cooing "darling" and God knows what nonsense I myself spoke during that mad interlude.

' "You should take those things off," I suggested.

' "Why don't you take them off yourself?" she answered in an emotional voice.

'I began to caress her. "Who are you?" she asked.

'I was in no mood to tell her, so I said, "I am yours, darling."

' "You're a naughty boy," she said coquettishly, while pressing me close to her. I was now trying to take off her blouse, but she said to me, "Please don't make me naked."

' "What does it matter? It's dark," I said.

' "No, no!"

'She lifted my hands and began to kiss them. "No, please no. I just feel shy."

' "Forget about the blouse," I said. "It's all going to be fine."

'There was a silence, which she broke. "You're not annoyed, are you?"

' "No, why should I be? You don't want to take off your blouse, so that's fine, but ..." I couldn't complete the sentence, but then, with some effort, I said, "But anyway something should happen. I mean, take off your sari."

' "I am afraid." Her throat seemed to have gone dry.

' "Who are you afraid of?" I asked flirtatiously.

' "I am afraid," she replied and began to weep.

' "There is nothing to be afraid of," I said in a consoling voice. "I won't hurt you, but if you are really afraid, then let's forget about it. You stay here for a few days and when you begin to feel at home and are not afraid of me any longer, then we'll see."

' "No, no," she said, putting her head on my thighs. I began to comb her hair with my fingers. After some time, she calmed down, then suddenly she pulled me to her with such force that I was taken aback. She was also trembling violently.

'There was a knock at the door and streaks of light began to filter into the dark room from outside.

'It was the servant. "I have brought a lantern. Would you please take it?"

'"All right," I answered.

'"No, no," she said in a terrified, muffled voice.

'"Look, what's the harm? I will lower the wick and place it in a corner," I said.

'I went to the door, brought the lantern in and placed it in a corner of the room. Since my eyes were not yet accustomed to the light, for a few seconds I could see nothing. Meanwhile, she had moved into the furthest corner.

'"Come on now," I said, "we can sit in the light and chat for a few minutes. Whenever you wish, I will put the lantern out."

'Picking up the lantern, I took a few steps towards her. She had covered her face with her sari. "You're a strange girl," I said, "after all, I'm like your bridegroom."

'Suddenly, there was a loud explosion outside. She rushed forward and fell into my arms. "It's only a bomb," I said, "Don't be afraid. It's nothing these days."

'My eyes were now beginning to get used to the light. Her face began to come into focus. I had a feeling that I had seen it before, but I still couldn't see it clearly.

'I put my hands on her shoulders and pulled her closer. God, I can't explain to you what I saw. It was the face of an old woman, deeply painted and yet lined with creases. Because of the rain, her make-up had become patchy. Her hair was coloured, but you could see the roots which were white. She had a band of plastic flowers across her forehead. I stared at her in a state bordering on shock. Then I put the lantern down and said, "You may leave if you wish."

'She wanted to say something, but when she saw me

picking up her raincoat and handbag, she decided not to. Without looking at her, I handed her things to her. She stood for a few minutes staring at her feet, then opened the door and walked out.'

After my friend had finished his story, I asked him, 'Did you know who that woman was?'

'No,' he answered.

'She was the famous artist Miss "M",' I told him.

'Miss "M",' he screamed, 'the woman whose paintings I used to try to copy at school?'

'Yes. She was the principal of the art college and she used to teach her women students how to paint still lifes. She hated men.'

'Where is she now?' he asked suddenly.

'In heaven,' I replied.

'What do you mean?' he asked.

'That night when you let her out of your house, she died in a car accident. You are her murderer. In fact, you are the murderer of two women. One, who is known as a great artist, and the other who was born from the body of the first woman in your living room that night and whom you alone know.'

My friend said nothing.

The New Constitution

Mangu the *tongawala* was considered a man of great wisdom among his friends. He had never seen the inside of a school, and in strictly academic terms was no more than a cipher, but there was nothing under the sun he did not know something about. All his fellow *tongawalas* at the *adda*, or *tonga* stand, were well aware of his versatility in worldly matters. He was always able to satisfy their curiosity about what was happening.

One day he overheard a couple of his fares discussing yet another outbreak of communal violence between Hindus and Muslims.

That evening when he returned to the *adda*, he looked perturbed. He sat down with his friends, took a long drag on the hookah, removed his khaki turban and said in a worried voice: 'It is no doubt the result of a holy man's curse that Hindus and Muslims keep slashing each other up every other day. I have heard it said by one of my elders that Akbar Badshah once showed disrespect to a saint, who cursed him in these words: "Get out of my sight! And, yes, your Hindustan will always be plagued by riots and disorder." And you can see for yourselves. Ever since the end of Akbar's raj, what else has India known but riots!'

He took a deep breath, drew on his hookah reflectively and said: 'These Congressites want to get India its freedom. Well, you take my word, they will get nowhere even if they try for a thousand years. At the most, the Angrez will leave, but then you will get maybe the Italywala or the Russian. I have heard that the Russiawala is tough. Hindustan, I can assure you, will always remain enslaved. Yes, I forgot to tell you that part of the saint's curse on Akbar was that India will always be ruled by foreigners.'

Ustad Mangu hated the British. He used to tell his friends that he hated them because they were ruling Hindustan against the will of the Indians and missed no opportunity to commit atrocities. However, the fact was that it was the *gora* soldiers of the cantonment who were responsible for Ustad Mangu's rather low opinion of the British. They used to treat him as if he were some lower creation of God, even worse than a dog. Nor was Ustad Mangu overly fond of their fair complexions. He used to experience near nausea when confronted by a white and ruddy *gora* soldier. 'Their red faces remind me of decaying carcasses,' he was fond of saying.

After a violent quarrel with a drunken *gora*, he used to remain depressed for days. He would return to his *adda* and curse them while smoking his hookah or his favourite brand of cigarettes with the picture of a plough on the packet.

'Look at them,' he would say, shaking his head, 'came to the house to fetch a candle and before you knew, they had taken it over. I can't stand the sight of them, these human monkeys. The way they order you around as if one was their father's slave!'

Sometimes, even after having abused them for hours, he would continue to feel enraged. And he would say to someone sitting next to him, 'Look at them ... don't they seem like lepers? Something dead and rotting. I could knock them all out with one blow, but what can you do about their arrogance? Yesterday, there was one I ran into. I was so sick of his *gitpit* that I nearly smashed his head in, but then I restrained myself. I mean it would have been below my dignity to hit the wretch.'

He would wipe his nose with his sleeve and continue his diatribe. 'As God is my witness, I'm sick of humouring these *Lat* sahibs. Every time I look at their blighted faces, my blood begins to boil. Maybe we need a new law to get rid of these people. Only that can save us, I swear on your life.'

One day Ustad Mangu picked up two fares from the district courts. He gathered from their conversation that there was going to be a new Act for India. They were discussing the soon-to-be-introduced Government of India Act 1935.

'It is said that from 1 April, there's going to be this new constitution. Do you think it will change everything?'

'Not everything, but they say a lot will change. The Indians would be free.'

'What about interest?' asked one. They were probably moneylenders who were in town for litigation.

'Well, frankly I don't know. Will have to ask a lawyer,' replied his friend.

Ustad Mangu was already in seventh heaven. Normally, he was in the habit of abusing his horse for being slow and was not averse to using the whip, but not today. Every now and then, he would look back at his two passengers, caress his moustache and loosen the reins affectionately. 'Come on son, let's show them what you can do. Let's go.'

After dropping his fares, he stopped at the Anarkali shop of his friend, Dino the sweetmeat vendor. He ordered a large glass of lassi, drank it down in one gulp, belched with satisfaction and shouted, 'The hell with 'em.'

When he returned to the *adda* in the evening, none of his friends seemed to be around. He felt bitterly disappointed because he had been looking forward to sharing the great news with his audience. He had to tell someone that there was going to be a new constitution soon which would change everything.

For about half an hour, he paced around restlessly, his whip under his arm. His mind was on many things, good

things that lay in the future. The news that a new constitution was to be given to the country had suddenly opened
new possibilities. He had switched on all the lights in his
brain to examine carefully the implications of the 1 April
change in India. He felt thrilled. He even smiled to himself
when he thought about the fears of those wretched moneylenders about interest. 'The new constitution is going to be
like boiling hot water which will destroy these bugs who
suck the blood of the poor,' he said to himself.

He was very happy. The new constitution was going to
force these white mice (for that was his name for the British)
once and for all back into their miserable holes. No longer
would they infest the earth.

When Nathoo, the bald-headed *tongawala*, ambled in a
while later, his turban tucked under his arm, Ustad Mangu
shook his hand vigorously and said: 'I have great news for
you. It's so good that it might make your hair grow back.'

He then went into a detailed description of the changes
the new constitution was going to bring to India. 'You just
wait and see. Things are going to happen. You have my
word, this Russian king is bound to show them his paces.'

Ustad Mangu had heard many stories about the
Communist system over the years. There were many things
he liked about it, such as their new laws and even newer
ideas. That was why he'd decided to link the king of Russia
with the India Act. He was convinced that the changes
being brought in on 1 April were a direct result of the
influence of the Russian king. He was of course quite
convinced that every country in the world was ruled by a
king.

For some years, the Red Shirt movement in Peshawar
had been much in the news. To Ustad Mangu, this movement had something to do with 'the king of Russia' and,
naturally, with the new Government of India Act. There
were also frequent reports of bomb blasts in various Indian
cities. Whenever Ustad Mangu heard that so many had

been caught for possessing explosives or so many were going to be tried by the government on treason charges, he interpreted it all as a curtain-raiser for the new constitution.

One day he had two barristers at the back of his *tonga*. They were arguing loudly about the new constitution. One of them was saying: 'It is section two of the Act that I still can't make sense of. It relates to the federation of India. Well, no such federation exists in the world. From a political angle, it will amount to a disaster. As a matter of fact, what is being proposed is anything but a federation.'

Since most of this conversation was being carried on in English, Ustad Mangu was unable to follow it. However, it was his impression that these two barristers were opposed to the new Act and did not want India to be free. 'Toadies,' he muttered under his breath.

Three days after this incident, he picked up three students from the Government College who wanted to be taken to Mozang. They were talking about the new constitution.

'I think things are going to open up with the new Act. Just imagine, we are going to have elected assemblies and if Mr ... gets elected, I'm bound to get a government job.'

'Oh! There are going to be many openings and much confusion, of course. I'm sure all of us will be able to lay our hands on something.'

'I couldn't agree more.'

'And, naturally, there's going to be a reduction in the number of all these thousands of unemployed graduates.'

This conversation was most thrilling as far as Ustad Mangu was concerned. The new constitution now appeared to him to be something bright and full of promise. The only thing he could compare the new constitution with was the splendid brass and gilt paraphernalia he had purchased a couple of years ago for his *tonga* from Chaudhry Khuda Bux. The new constitution gave him the same nice, warm feeling.

In the weeks following, Ustad Mangu heard much about the changes, both for and against. However, his mind was quite made up. He was secure in his belief that come 1 April, everything would change.

At last the thirty-one days of March came to an end. There was a chill in the air as Ustad Mangu rose earlier than usual. He went to the stable, set up his *tonga* and took to the road. He was extraordinarily happy today because he was going to witness with his own eyes the coming of the new constitution.

In the morning fog, he went round the broad and narrow streets of the city but everything had the same old and worn-out look. He wanted to see colour and light. There was nothing. He had bought a special new plume for his horse to celebrate the big day and it seemed to be the only bit of colour he could see. It had cost him a bit of money too.

The road lay black under his horse's hooves. The lamp-posts looked the same. The shop signs had not changed. People moved about as if nothing new had happened. Perhaps it was too early in the morning. Most of the shops were closed. He consoled himself with the thought that the courts did not open until nine, and it was there the new constitution would be launched.

He was in front of the Government College when the tower clock struck nine, almost imperiously. The students walking in through the main entrance were all nicely dressed, but somehow they looked shabby to Ustad Mangu. He wanted to see something colourful and dramatic.

He moved his *tonga* towards the main shopping centre, the Anarkali. Half the shops were already open. There were crowds of people at sweetmeat stalls, and general traders were busy with their customers, their wares displayed invitingly in their windows. However, none of this had any interest whatsoever for Ustad Mangu. He wanted to see the new constitution as clearly as he could see his horse.

Ustad Mangu was one of those people who cannot stand the suspense of waiting. When he was going to get his first child, he had been unable to sit still. He wanted to see the child even before it was born. Many times, he had put his ear over his wife's pregnant belly in an attempt to find out when the child was coming or what he was like, but of course he had found nothing. One day he had shouted at his wife in exasperation.

'What's the matter with you? All day long you're in bed like you were dead. Why don't you get yourself out, walk around, gain some strength to help the child be born? He won't come this way, I can tell you.'

Ustad Mangu was always in a hurry. He just couldn't wait for things to take shape. He wanted everything to happen immediately. Once his wife Gangawatti had said to him: 'You haven't even begun digging the well and already you're impatient to have a drink of water.'

This morning he was not as impatient as he normally should have been. He had come out early to view the new constitution with his own eyes, the same way he used to wait for hours to catch a glimpse of Gandhiji and Pandit Jawaharlal Nehru.

Great leaders, in Ustad Mangu's view, were those who were profusely garlanded when taken out in procession. And if there were a few scuffles with the police during the proceedings, the man went up even further in Ustad's estimation. He wanted to see the new constitution brought out with the same razzle-dazzle.

From Anarkali he moved back to the Mall. In front of the motor showroom, he found a fare for the cantonment. They settled the price and were soon on their way. Ustad Mangu was now hopeful that he might learn something about the new constitution in the cantonment.

His fare got down from the *tonga* and Ustad Mangu stretched himself on the rear seat. He lit a cigarette and started thinking. This was one way he relaxed when he had the time. He wasn't looking for a new fare. He was only curious as to what had overtaken the new constitution.

Ustad Mangu was trying to work out if the present system of allotting *tonga* number plates would change with the new dispensation, when he saw a *gora* soldier standing next to a lamp-post.

His first instinct was not to take him. He hated these monkeys. However, it occurred to him that to refuse to take their money wouldn't be very wise either. 'Might as well recover what I've spent on the new plume,' he said to himself.

He turned round and without moving from his comfortable perch, asked in a leisurely manner: 'Sahib bahadur, where do you wish to be taken?'

He had spoken these words with undisguised irony. There was a smile on his face and he wished nothing better than the immediate demise of this impertinent *gora*.

The *gora*, who was trying to light a cigarette against the wind, turned and began to walk towards the *tonga*. They looked at each other, and Ustad Mangu felt as if they were two guns firing from point-blank range.

Finally he stepped down from his *tonga* all the while eyeing the soldier with mute fury.

'Do you want to go or are you going to make trouble?' the *gora* asked in his pidgin Urdu.

'This swine I know,' Ustad Mangu said to himself. He was quite sure that it was the same man with whom he had had a quarrel the year before. The fellow had been drunk and had abused Ustad Mangu, who had borne the insults in silence. He wanted to smash the bastard's skull in but he knew that if the case went to court, it was he, the humble *tongawala*, who would get it in the neck.

'Where do you want to go?' Ustad Mangu asked, not unforgetful of the fact that there was a new constitution in force in India now.

'Hira Mandi, the dancing girls' bazaar,' the *gora* answered.

'It will cost you five rupees,' Ustad Mangu said, and his thick moustache trembled.

'Five rupees! Are you out of your mind?' the gora screamed in disbelief.

'Yes, you heard me,' Ustad Mangu said, clenching his fist. 'Are you interested or do you merely want to waste my time?'

The *gora* remembered their last encounter and had chosen to pay no attention to Ustad Mangu's barrel-chested stance. He was determined to teach the man another lesson for his insolence. He took a couple of steps towards him, his swagger stick brushing past the Indian's thigh.

Ustad Mangu looked down on the short-statured soldier with great contempt. Then he raised his arm and hit him heavily on the chin. He followed this with a merciless beating of the Englishman.

The *gora* couldn't believe it was actually happening. He tried to ward off the descending blows, but without much luck. He could see that his assailant was in a rage bordering on madness. In desperation, he began to shout for help. This seemed to enrage Ustad Mangu even more, and the blows got harder. He was screaming with fury: 'The same old cockiness even on 1 April! Well, son, it is we who are the Raj now.'

A crowd had gathered. Two policemen appeared from somewhere and with great difficulty managed to rescue the hapless Englishman. It was quite a sight. There stood Ustad Mangu with one policeman to his left and one to his right, his broad chest thrown out in defiance. He was foaming at the mouth, but there was a strange light in his eyes. To the astonished crowd, Ustad Mangu was saying: 'Those days are gone, friends, when we were just good for nothing. There is a new constitution, a new constitution. Understand?'

The Englishman's face was swollen and he looked extremely foolish. He still couldn't understand what had happened.

Ustad Mangu was taken by the two constables to the local police station. All the time, even when he was inside the station, he kept screaming, 'New constitution, new constitution!'

'What rubbish are you talking? What new constitution? It's the same old constitution, you fool,' he was told.

Then they locked him up.

Free for All

In every city, town and village of the newly independent state, word went forth that anyone found begging on the street would be sent to gaol. Arrests began immediately, causing a lot of public joy because the curse of beggary had at last been abolished.

Only the wandering minstrel Kabir was grief-stricken.

'What is the matter with you, weaver?' — because that is what he was by caste — asked the citizens.

'I am sad because cloth is woven with two threads. One runs horizontally, the other vertically. The arrests are horizontal, but feeding the hungry is vertical. How are you going to weave this fabric?'

A refugee from India, a lawyer by profession, was given ownership of two hundred abandoned handlooms. Kabir passed that way and began to weep.

'Are you crying because I've been given what by right should have been yours?' asked the lawyer.

'No, what made me cry was the knowledge that these looms will never weave cloth again, because you'll sell the thread for a profit. You have no patience with the clickety-clack of a loom, but that noise is a weaver's only reason to live.'

On the street a man was turning the printed leaves of a book into paper bags.

Kabir picked one up and as he began to read the print, tears welled up in his eyes.

'What troubles you?' the astonished bag-maker asked.

'Inscribed on the paper out of which you have fashioned these bags is the mystic poetry of the blind Hindu saint, Bhagat Sur Das,' answered Kabir.

The bag-maker didn't know any Hindi, but he did know that in his native Punjabi, Sur Das did not mean the blind devotee, but a pig.

'How can a pig be a saint?' he said.

One of the most magnificent buildings in the city was adorned with a statue of the Hindu goddess of good fortune, Lakshmi. However, the new occupants, refugees from across the border, had covered it with an ugly length of cloth made from jute fibre. Kabir saw it and began to cry.

'Our religion forbids idolatry,' they told him.

'Does it not forbid the degradation of beauty?' Kabir asked.

A general was addressing his troops: 'We are short of food because our crops have been destroyed, but there's no cause for anxiety. My soldiers will fight the enemy on empty stomachs.'

Slogans of the impending victory were raised.

'My valiant general, who will fight hunger?' Kabir asked.

'Dear brothers in faith, grow beards, shave off your sinful whiskers and wear your trousers as ordained — an inch above the ankle. Dear sisters in faith, don't paint your faces and cover yourselves with a veil. That is the divine command.'

Tears came to Kabir's eyes.

'You have neither brother nor sister and your beard is not black, but dyed. Don't you like to show your white hair?' Kabir said.

A heated intellectual argument was in progress.

'Art for art's sake.'

'Nonsense, art for life.'

'To hell with you!'

'To hell with your Stalin!'

'Shut up. Today art is another form of propaganda.'

'To hell with the reactionaries of the world and their Flauberts and Baudelaires!'

Kabir began to weep.

'He is undergoing a bourgeois trauma,' said one of the intellectuals.

'No, I weep because I want you to understand what art is for,' Kabir said.

'He is a proletariat joker.'

'No, he is a bourgeois clown.'

A new law was proclaimed requiring the city's prostitutes to get married within thirty days. When Kabir looked at their ravaged and anxiety-ridden faces, he wept.

A religious leader said to him, 'Why do you weep, my good man?'

'Who will find them husbands?' Kabir asked.

The religious leader began to laugh. It was the funniest thing he had ever heard.

A politician was addressing a crowd: 'My dear brothers, our greatest problem is the recovery of our women abducted by our enemies across the border. If we do nothing, I fear they will all end up in the prostitutes' quarter. We must save them from this fate. I call on you to take them into your homes. When you next think of a match for a member of your family, you should bear these unfortunate creatures in mind.'

When Kabir heard these words, he wept inconsolably.

'Look at this good man,' the leader told the crowd. 'How deeply my appeal has moved him.'

'No, your call did not move me,' Kabir said: 'I wept because I know that you have remained unmarried because you haven't yet found a rich bride.'

'Throw this lunatic out,' the crowd hissed.

Mohamed Ali Jinnah, the father of the nation, died. The country went into mourning. Everyone went round with black armbands.

Kabir watched them in silence with tears rolling down his cheeks.

'So much cloth for so many armbands. It could have covered the hungry and the naked,' he said to the mourners.

'You are a Communist,' they said.

'You are a fifth columnist.'

'You are a traitor to Pakistan.'

And for the first time, Kabir laughed that day. 'But my friends, I am wearing no armband, black, green or red.'

Mozail

Tarlochan stepped out on the balcony and looked up at the pre-dawn sky. It occurred to him that he hadn't done something like that for years. He felt tired and listless and in need of fresh air.

It was clear, with not a cloud in the sky under whose vast, spotless tent lay the city of Bombay. He could see the lights, twinkling like little stars which had somehow fallen to earth and got lodged in thousands of residential high-rise buildings.

Like most residents of Bombay, Tarlochan was a flat-dweller who hardly ever came outdoors, but standing there under the open sky, he felt good. It was almost like a new experience. He felt as if he had kept himself imprisoned in his flat for four years.

It was well past midnight. The breeze which blew from the sea was light and pleasant after the heavy, mechanically-stirred air of the fan under which he always slept. His agitation was gone. All alone, in the open air, he felt calm. He could think clearly.

Karpal Kaur and her entire family lived in a *mohalla* which was predominantly and ferociously Muslim. Many non-Muslim houses had been set on fire since the start of the city's communal riots. Many people had died. Tarlochan would have brought Karpal Kaur and her family to his flat — which was safer— except that a 48-hour curfew had been imposed by the authorities.

The Muslims of the area were greatly agitated. Reports were pouring in from Punjab about atrocities committed on the Muslims by the Sikhs. He shuddered to think what an enraged Muslim could do to Karpal Kaur to avenge Muslim massacres in Punjab.

Karpal Kaur's mother was blind and her father was a cripple. There was a brother, Naranjan, who lived in another suburb because of a construction contract he had recently been given.

Tarlochan had been trying to persuade Naranjan for weeks to move with his family to his flat. He had told him: 'Forget about your business for the time being. We are passing through difficult times. You should stay with your family, or better, move to my flat. I know there isn't enough space, but these are not normal times. We'll manage somehow.'

Naranjan had smiled through his thick beard and said: 'This is not Amritsar or Lahore. I have seen many communal riots in Bombay. They always pass. And remember, you have only known the city for four years. I've been around for twelve. I know what I'm talking about.'

Tarlochan wasn't convinced. He knew it in his bones. He had reached a point where were he to read in the morning papers that Karpal Kaur and her parents had been massacred the night before, he would not have been in the least surprised.

He did not care much for Karpal Kaur's blind mother and her crippled father. If they were killed and Karpal survived, it would make things even easier for him. He couldn't give a damn what happened to her stupid brother either. He was only worried about Karpal Kaur. The others didn't matter.

The breeze felt good on his face. Tarlochan thought of Karpal Kaur again. She had grown up in the village, but she was delicate, completely unlike normal village girls who

have to do hard labour in the fields and become masculine.
Karpal Kaur was all woman.

She had very fine features and her breasts were small,
still growing. She was fairer than most Sikh girls are, and
compared with most of them, she was shy and withdrawn.

Tarlochan originally came from the same village, but he
had left it years ago to go to school in the city. And though
he had gone back several times in between, he had never
met Karpal Kaur, though he knew the family. He had got
to know her only in Bombay.

The building he lived in was called Advani Chambers
and as he stood on the balcony looking at the pre-morning
sky, he thought of Mozail, the Jewish girl who had a flat
here. He used to be in love with her 'up to his knees' as he
liked to say. Never in his thirty-five years had he felt that
way about a woman.

He had run into her the very day he had moved into
Advani Chambers. His first impression was that she was
slightly mad. Her brown hair was cut short and always
looked dishevelled. She wore thick lipstick and a loose white
dress, cut so low at the neck that you could see three-
quarters of her big, bouncing breasts, tinged with faint blue
veins.

Her lips were not as thick as they appeared, but it was
the liberal quantities of lipstick she plastered on them that
gave them the appearance of beefsteaks.

Her flat faced Tarlochan's, divided by a narrow corridor.

He remembered their first encounter. He was trying to
slip the key into his front door when she had appeared,
wearing wooden sandals which made a big racket when she
walked. She had looked at him unabashedly and laughed.
Suddenly she had slipped and fallen over him. It was very
funny, with her legs pinning him to the ground in a scissor-
like grip and her gown trussed up to reveal her generous
thighs.

He had tried to get up and, in so doing, brushed against

every revealed and unrevealed part of her body. He had apologized profusely and Mozail had straightened her dress and smiled: 'These wooden slippers are always slipping.' Then she had carefully rethreaded her big toes in them and walked away.

Tarlochan was afraid it might not be easy to get to know her, but he was wrong. In a few days they had become great friends. She was both headstrong and unpredictable. She would make him take her out to dinner, the cinema or the beach, but whenever he tried to go beyond holding her hand, she would tell him to lay off.

Tarlochan had never before been in love — or was it infatuation? In Lahore, Burma, Singapore — where he had lived for the last ten years — he had found it convenient to pick up a girl and pay for the service. It would never have occurred to him that one day he would fall 'up to the knees' in love with a Jewish girl from Bombay.

Mozail was totally unpredictable. They would be in a cinema and she would suddenly spot a friend in the back row and, without saying a word, go and sit next to him for the duration of the show.

The same sort of thing had happened in restaurants. He would order a nice meal for her and then watch in agonized silence as she abruptly rose to join an acquaintance at the next table. When he protested she would stop meeting him for days and when he insisted she would pretend that she had a headache or her stomach was upset.

Or she would say: 'Your are a Sikh. You are incapable of understanding anything subtle.'

'Such as your lovers?' he would taunt her.

She would put her hands on her hips, spread out her legs and say: 'Yes, my lovers, but why does it burn you up?'

'We cannot carry on like this,' Tarlochan would say.

And Mozail would laugh. 'You're not only a real Sikh, you're also an idiot. In any case, who asked you to carry on with me? I have a suggestion. Go back to your Punjab and marry a Sikhni.' In the end Tarlochan would always give in because Mozail had become his weakness and he wanted to be around her all the time. Often she would humiliate him in front of some young 'Kristan' lout she had picked up that day from somewhere. He would get angry, but not for long.

This cat-and-mouse thing with Mozail continued for two years, but he was steadfast. One day when she was in one of her high and happy moods, he took her in his arms and asked: 'Mozail, don't you love me?'

Mozail freed herself, sat down in a chair, gazed intently at her dress, then raised her big Jewish eyes, batted her thick eyelashes and said: 'I cannot love a Sikh.'

'You always make fun of me. You make fun of my love,' he said in an angry voice.

She got up, swung her brown head of hair from side to side and said coquettishly: 'If you shave off your beard and let down your long hair which you keep under your turban, I promise you many men will wink at you suggestively, because you are very dishy.'

Tarlochan felt as if his hair was on fire. He dragged Mozail towards him, squeezed her in his arms and put his bearded lips on hers.

She pushed him away. 'Phew!' she said, 'I brushed my teeth this morning. You don't have to bother.'

'Mozail!' Tarlochan screamed.

She paid no attention, but took out her lipstick from the bag she always carried and began to touch up her lips which looked havoc-stricken after contact with Tarlochan's beard and moustache.

'Let me tell you something,' she said without looking up. 'You have no idea how to use your hirsute assets properly. They would be perfect for brushing dust off my navy-blue skirt.'

She came and sat next to him and began to unpin his beard. It was true he was very good-looking, but being a practising Sikh he had never shaved a single hair off his body and, consequently, he had come to assume a look which was not natural. He respected his religion and its customs and he did not wish to change any of its ritual formalities.

'What are you doing?' he asked Mozail. By now his beard, freed of its shackles, was hanging over his chest in waves.

'You have such soft hair, so I don't think I would use it to brush my navy-blue skirt. Perhaps a nice, soft woven handbag,' she said, smiling flirtatiously.

'I have never made fun of your religion. Why do you always mock mine? It's not fair. But I have suffered these insults silently because I love you. Did you know I love you?'

'I know,' she said, letting go of his beard.

'I want to marry you,' he declared, while trying to repin his beard.

'I know,' she said with a slight shake of her head. 'In fact, I have nearly decided to marry you.'

'You don't say,' Tarlochan nearly jumped.

'I do,' she said.

He forgot his half-folded beard and embraced her passionately. 'When ... when?'

She pushed him aside. 'When you get rid of your hair.'

'It will be gone tomorrow,' he said without thinking.

She began to do a tap dance around the room. 'You're talking rubbish, Tarloch. I don't think you have the courage.'

'You will see,' he said defiantly.

'So I will,' she said, kissing him on the lips, followed by her usual 'Phew!'

He could hardly sleep that night. It was not a small decision. However, next day he went to a barber in the Fort area and had him cut his hair and shave off his beard. While this operation was in progress, he kept his eyes closed. When it was finished, he looked at his new face in the mirror. It looked good. Any girl in Bombay would have found it difficult not to take a long, second look at him.

He did not leave the flat his first hairless day, but sent word to Mozail that he was not well and if she would mind dropping in for a minute. She stopped dead in her tracks when she saw him. 'My darling Tarloch,' she cried and fell into his arms. She ran her hands over his smooth cheeks and combed his short hair with her fingers. She laughed so much that her nose began to run. She had no handkerchief and calmly she lifted her skirt and wiped it. Tarlochan blushed: 'You should wear something underneath.'

'Gives me a funny feeling. That's how it is,' she replied.

'Let's get married tomorrow,' he said.

'Of course,' she replied, rubbing his chin.

They decided to get married in Poona, where Tarlochan had many friends.

Mozail worked as a salesgirl in one of the big department stores in the Fort area. She told Tarlochan to wait for her at a taxi stand in front of the store the next day, but she never turned up. He learnt later that she had gone off with an old lover of hers who had recently bought a new car. They had moved to Deolali and were not expected to return to Bombay 'for some time'.

Tarlochan was shattered, but in a few weeks he had got over it.

And it was at this point that he had met Karpal Kaur and fallen in love with her.

He now realized what a vulgar girl Mozail was and how totally heartless. He thanked his stars that he hadn't married her.

But there were days when he missed her. He remembered that once he had decided to buy her some gold earrings and had taken her to a jeweller's, but all she wanted was some cheap baubles. That was the way she was.

She used to lie in bed with him for hours and let him kiss and fondle her as much as he wanted, but she would never let him make love. 'You're a Sikh,' she would laugh, 'and I hate Sikhs.'

One argument they always had was over her habit of not wearing any underclothes. Once she said to him: 'You're a Sikh and I know that you wear some ridiculous shorts under your trousers because that is the Sikh religious requirement, but I think it's rubbish that religion should be kept tucked under one's trousers.'

Tarlochan looked at the gradually brightening sky.

'The hell with her,' he said loudly and decided not to think about her at all. He was worried about Karpal Kaur and the danger which loomed over her.

A number of communal incidents had already taken place in the locality. The place was full of orthodox Muslims and, curfew or no curfew, they could easily enter her house and massacre everyone.

Since Mozail had left him, he had decided to grow his hair. His beard had flourished again, but he had come to a compromise. He would not let it grow too long. He knew a barber who could trim it so skilfully that it would not appear trimmed.

The curfew was still in force, but you could walk about in the street, as long as you did not stray too far. He decided to do so. There was a public tap in front of the building. He sat down under it and began to wash his hair and freshen up his face.

Suddenly, he heard the sound of wooden sandals on the cobblestones. There were other Jewish women in that building, all of whom for some reason wore the same kind of sandals. He thought it was one of them.

But it was Mozail. She was wearing her usual loose gown under which he could see her breasts dancing. It disturbed him. He coughed to attract her attention, because he had a feeling she might just pass him by. She came towards him, examined his beard and said: 'What do we have here, a twice-born Sikh?'

She touched his beard: 'Still good enough to brush my navy-blue skirt with, except that I left it in that other place in Deolali.'

Tarlochan said nothing. She pinched his arm: 'Why don't you say something, Sardar sahib?'

He looked at her. She had lost weight. 'Have you been ill?' he asked.

'No.'

'But you look run down.'

'I am dieting. So you are once again a Sikh?' She sat down next to him, squatting on the ground.

'Yes,' he replied.

'Congratulations. Are you in love with some other girl?'

'Yes.'

'Congratulations. Does she live here, I mean, in our building?'

'No.'

'Isn't that awful?'

She pulled at his beard. 'Is this grown on her advice?'

'No.'

'Well, I promise you that if you get this beard of yours shaved off, I'll marry you. I swear.'

'Mozail,' he said, 'I have decided to marry this simple girl from my village. She is a good observing Sikh, which is why I am growing my hair again.'

Mozail got up, swung herself in a semi-circle on her heel and said: 'If she's a good Sikh, why should she marry you? Doesn't she know that you once broke all the rules and shaved your hair off?'

'No, she doesn't. I started growing a beard the very day you left me — as a gesture of revenge, if you like. I met her some time later, but the way I tie my turban, you can hardly tell that I don't have a full head of hair.'

She lifted her dress to scratch her thigh. 'Damn these mosquitoes,' she said. Then she added: 'When are you getting married?'

'I don't know.' The anxiety in his voice showed.

'What are you thinking, Tarlochan?' she asked. He told her.

'You are a first-class idiot. What's the problem? Just go and get her here where she would be safe.'

'Mozail, you can't understand these things. It's not that simple. You don't really give a damn and that is why we broke up. I'm sorry,' he said.

'Sorry? Come off it, you silly idiot. What you should be thinking of now is how we can get ... whatever her name is ... to your flat. And here you go talking about your sorrow at losing me. It could never have worked. Your problem is that you are both stupid and cautious. I like my men to be reckless. OK, forget about that, let's go and get your whatever Kaur from wherever she is.'

Tarlochan looked at her nervously. 'But there's a curfew in the area,' he said.

'There's no curfew for Mozail. Let's go,' she said, almost dragging him.

She looked at him and paused. 'What's the matter?' he asked.

'Your beard, but it's not that long. However, take that turban off, then nobody will take you for a Sikh.'

'I won't go bareheaded,' he said.

'Why not?'

'You don't understand. It is not proper for me to go to their house without my turban.'

'And why not?'

'Why don't you understand? She has never seen me except in a turban. She thinks I am a proper Sikh. I daren't let her think otherwise.'

Mozail rattled her wooden sandals on the floor. 'You are not only a first-class idiot, you are also an ass. It is a question of saving her life, whatever that Kaur of yours is called.'

Tarlochan was not going to give up. 'Mozail, you've no idea how religious she is. Once she sees me bareheaded, she'll start hating me.'

'Your love be damned. Tell me, are all Sikhs as stupid as you? On the one hand, you want to save her life and at the same time you insist on wearing your turban, and perhaps even those funny knickers you are never supposed to be without.'

'I do wear my knickers — as you call them — all the time,' he said.

'Good for you,' she said. 'But think, you're going to go in that awful area full of those bloodthirsty Muslims and their big *Maulanas*. If you go in a turban, I promise you they will take one look at you and run a big, sharp knife across your throat.'

'I don't care, but I must wear my turban. I can risk my life, but not my love.'

'You're an ass,' she said exasperatedly. 'Tell me, if you're bumped off, what use will that Kaur be to you? I swear, you're not only a Sikh, you are an idiot of a Sikh.'

'Don't talk rot,' Tarlochan snapped.

She laughed, then she put her arms around his neck and swung her body slightly. 'Darling,' she said, 'then it will be the way you want it. Go put on your turban. I will be waiting for you in the street.'

'You should put on some clothes,' Tarlochan said.

'I'm fine the way I am,' she replied.

When he joined her, she was standing in the middle of the street, her legs apart like a man, and smoking. When he came close, she blew the smoke in his face. 'You're the most terrible human being I've ever met in my life,' Tarlochan said. 'You know we Sikhs are not allowed to smoke.'

'Let's go,' she said.

The bazaar was deserted. The curfew seemed to have affected even the usually brisk Bombay breeze. It was hardly noticeable. Some lights were on but their glow was sickly. Normally at this hour the trains would start running and shops begin to open. There was absolutely no sign of life anywhere.

Mozail walked in front of him. The only sound came from the impact of her wooden sandals on the road. He almost asked her to take the stupid things off and go barefoot, but he didn't. She wouldn't have agreed.

Tarlochan felt scared, but Mozail was walking ahead of him nonchalantly, puffing merrily at her cigarette. They came to a square and were challenged by a policeman: 'Where are you going?' Tarlochan fell back, but Mozail moved towards the policeman, gave her head a playful shake and said: 'It's you! Don't you know me? I'm Mozail. I'm going to my sister's in the next street because she's sick. That man there is a doctor.'

While the policeman was still trying to make up his mind, she pulled out a packet of cigarettes from her bag and offered him one. 'Have a smoke,' she said.

The policeman took the cigarette. Mozail helped him light it with hers. He inhaled deeply. Mozail winked at him with her left eye and at Tarlochan with her right and they moved on.

Tarlochan was still very scared. He looked left and right as he walked behind her, expecting to be stabbed any moment. Suddenly she stopped. 'Tarloch dear, it is not good to be afraid. If you're afraid, then something awful always happens. That's my experience.'

He didn't reply.

They came to the street which led to the *mohalla* where Karpal Kaur lived. A shop was being looted. 'Nothing to worry about,' she told him. One of the rioters who was carrying something on his head ran into Tarlochan and the object fell to the ground. The man stared at Tarlochan and knew he was a Sikh. He slipped his hand under this shirt to pull out his knife.

Mozail pushed him away as if she was drunk. 'Are you mad, trying to kill your own brother? This is the man I'm going to marry.' Then she said to Tarlochan: 'Karim, pick this thing up and help put it back on his head.'

The man gave Mozail a lecherous look and touched her breasts with his elbow. 'Have a good time, *sali*,' he said.

They kept walking and were soon in Karpal Kaur's *mohalla*. 'Which street?' she asked.

'The third on the left. That building in the corner,' he whispered.

When they came to the building, they saw a man run out of it into another across the street. After a few minutes, three men emerged from that building and rushed into the one where Karpal Kaur lived. Mozail stopped. 'Tarloch dear, take off your turban,' she said.

'That I'll never do,' he replied.

'Just as you please, but I hope you do notice what's going on.'

Something terrible was going on. The three men had re-emerged, carrying gunny-bags with blood dripping from them. Mozail had an idea. 'Look, I'm going to run across the street and go into that building. You should pretend that you're trying to catch me. But don't think. Just do it.'

Without waiting for his response, she rushed across the street and ran into Karpal Kaur's building, with Tarlochan in hot pursuit. He was panting when he found her in the front courtyard.

'Which floor?' she asked.

'Second.'

'Let's go,' and she began to climb the stairs, her wooden sandals clattering on each step. There were large blood-stains everywhere.

They came to the second floor, walked down a narrow corridor, and Tarlochan stopped in front of a door. He knocked. Then he called in a low voice, 'Mehnga Singh ji, Mehnga Singh ji.'

A girl's voice answered. 'Who is it?'

'Tarlochan.'

The door opened slightly. Tarlochan asked Mozail to follow him in. Mozail saw a very young and very pretty girl standing behind the door trembling. She also seemed to have a cold. Mozail said to her: 'Don't be afraid. Tarlochan has come to take you away.'

Tarlochan said: 'Ask Sardar sahib to get ready, but quickly.'

There was a shriek from the flat upstairs. 'They must have got him,' Karpal Kaur said, her voice hoarse with terror.

'Whom?' Tarlochan asked.

Karpal Kaur was about to say something, when Mozail pushed her in a corner and said: 'Just as well they got him. Now take off your clothes.'

Karpal Kaur was taken aback, but Mozail gave her no time to think. In one movement, she divested her of her loose shirt. The young girl frantically put her arms in front of her breasts. She was terrified. Tarlochan turned his face. Then Mozail took off the kaftan-like gown she always wore and asked Karpal Kaur to put it on. She was now stark naked herself.

'Take her away,' she told Tarlochan. She untied the girl's hair so that it hung over her shoulders. 'Go.'

Tarlochan pushed the girl towards the door, then turned back. Mozail stood there, shivering slightly because of the cold.

'Why don't you go?' she asked.

'What about her parents?' he said.

'They can go to hell. You take her.'

'And you?'

'Don't worry about me.'

They heard men running down the stairs. Soon they were banging at the door with their fists. Karpal Kaur's parents were moaning in the other room. 'There's only one thing to do now. I'm going to open the door,' Mozail said.

She addressed Tarlochan: 'When I open the door, I'll rush out and run upstairs. You follow me. These men will be so flabbergasted that they will forget everything and come after us.'

'And then?' Tarlochan asked.

'Then, this one here, whatever her name is, can slip out. The way she's dressed, she'll be safe. They'll take her for a Jew.'

Mozail threw the door open and rushed out. The men had no time to react. Involuntarily, they made way for her. Tarlochan ran after her. She was storming up the stairs in her wooden sandals with Tarlochan behind her.

She slipped and came crashing down, head first. Tarlochan stopped and turned. Blood was pouring out of her mouth and nose and ears. The men who were trying to break into the flat had also gathered round her in a circle, forgetting temporarily what they were there for. They were staring at her naked, bruised body.

Tarlochan bent over her. 'Mozail, Mozail.'

She opened her eyes and smiled. Tarlochan undid his turban and covered her with it.

'This is my lover. He's a bloody Muslim, but he's so crazy that I always call him a Sikh,' she said to the men.

More blood poured out of her mouth. 'Damn it!' she said.

Then she looked at Tarlochan and pushed aside the turban with which he had tried to cover her nakedness.

'Take away this rag of your religion. I don't need it.'

Her arm fell limply on her bare breasts and she said no more.

The Assignment

Beginning with isolated incidents of stabbing, it had now developed into full-scale communal violence, with no holds barred. Even home-made bombs were being used.

The general view in Amritsar was that the riots could not last long. They were seen as no more than a manifestation of temporarily inflamed political passions which were bound to cool down before long. After all, these were not the first communal riots the city had known. There had been so many of them in the past. They never lasted long. The pattern was familiar. Two weeks or so of unrest and then business as usual. On the basis of experience, therefore, the people were quite justified in believing that the current troubles would also run their course in a few days. But this did not happen. They not only continued, but grew in intensity.

Muslims living in Hindu localities began to leave for safer places, and Hindus in Muslim majority areas followed suit. However, everyone saw these adjustments as strictly temporary. The atmosphere would soon be clear of this communal madness, they told themselves.

Retired judge Mian Abdul Hai was absolutely confident that things would return to normal soon, which was why he wasn't worried. He had two children, a boy of eleven and a girl of seventeen. In addition, there was an old servant who was now pushing seventy. It was a small family. When the troubles started, Mian sahib, being an extra cautious man, stocked up on food ... just in case. So on one count, at least, there were no worries.

His daughter Sughra was less sure of things. They lived in a three-storey house with a view over almost the entire city. Sughra could not help noticing that whenever she went on the roof, there were fires raging everywhere. In the beginning, she could hear fire engines rushing past, their bells ringing, but this had now stopped. There were too many fires in too many places.

The nights had become particularly frightening. The sky was always lit by conflagrations like giants spitting out flames. Then there were the slogans which rent the air with terrifying frequency — Allaho Akbar, Har Har Mahadev.

Sughra never expressed her fears to her father, because he had declared confidently that there was no cause for anxiety. Everything was going to be fine. Since he was generally always right, she had initially felt reassured.

However, when the power and water supplies were suddenly cut off, she expressed her unease to her father and suggested apologetically that, for a few days at least, they should move to Sharifpura, a Muslim locality, to where many of the old residents had already moved. Mian sahib was adamant: 'You're imagining things. Everything is going to be normal very soon.'

He was wrong. Things went from bad to worse. Before long there was not a single Muslim family to be found in Mian Abdul Hai's locality. Then one day Mian sahib suffered a stroke and was laid up. His son Basharat, who used to spend most of his time playing self-devised games, now stayed glued to his father's bed.

All the shops in the area had been permanently boarded up. Dr Ghulam Hussian's dispensary had been shut for weeks and Sughra had noticed from the roof-top one day that the adjoining clinic of Dr Goranditta Mall was also closed. Mian sahib's condition was getting worse day by day. Sughra was almost at the end of her wits. One day she took Basharat aside and said to him, 'You've got to do something. I know it's not safe to go out, but we must get some help. Our father is very ill.'

The boy went, but came back almost immediately. His face was pale with fear. He had seen a blood-drenched body lying in the street and a group of wild-looking men looting shops. Sughra took the terrified boy in her arms and said a silent prayer, thanking God for his safe return. However, she could not bear her father's suffering. His left side was now completely lifeless. His speech had been impaired and he mostly communicated through gestures, all designed to reassure Sughra that soon all would be well.

It was the month of Ramadan and only two days to Id. Mian sahib was quite confident that the troubles would be over by then. He was again wrong. A canopy of smoke hung over the city, with fires burning everywhere. At night the silence was shattered by deafening explosions. Sughra and Basharat hadn't slept for days.

Sughra, in any case, couldn't because of her father's deteriorating condition. Helplessly, she would look at him, then at her young frightened brother and the seventy-year-old servant Akbar, who was useless for all practical purposes. He mostly kept to his bed, coughing and fighting for breath. One day Sughra told him angrily, 'What good are you? Do you realize how ill Mian sahib is? Perhaps you are too lazy to want to help, pretending that you are suffering from acute asthma. There was a time when servants used to sacrifice their lives for their masters.'

Sughra felt very bad afterwards. She had been unnecessarily harsh on the old man. In the evening when she took his food to him in his small room, he was not there. Basharat looked for him all over the house, but he was nowhere to be found. The front door was unlatched. He was gone, perhaps to get some help for Mian sahib. Sughra prayed for his return, but two days passed and he hadn't come back.

It was evening and the festival of Id was now only a day away. She remembered the excitement which used to grip the family on this occasion. She remembered standing on the roof-top, peering into the sky, looking for the Id moon and praying for the clouds to clear. But how different everything was today. The sky was covered in smoke and on distant roofs one could see people looking upwards. Were they trying to catch sight of the new moon or were they watching the fires, she wondered?

She looked up and saw the thin sliver of the moon peeping through a small patch in the sky. She raised her hands in prayer, begging God to make her father well. Basharat, however, was upset that there would be no Id this year.

The night hadn't yet fallen. Sughra had moved her father's bed out of the room onto the veranda. She was sprinkling water on the floor to make it cool. Mian sahib was lying there quietly looking with vacant eyes at the sky where she had seen the moon. Sughra came and sat next to him. He motioned her to get closer. Then he raised his right arm slowly and put it on her head. Tears began to run from Sughra's eyes. Even Mian sahib looked moved. Then with great difficulty he said to her, 'God is merciful. All will be well.'

Suddenly there was a knock on the door. Sughra's heart began to beat violently. She looked at Basharat, whose face had turned white like a sheet of paper. There was another knock. Mian sahib gestured to Sughra to answer it. It must be old Akbar who had come back, she thought. She said to Basharat, 'Answer the door. I'm sure it's Akbar.' Her father shook his head, as if to signal disagreement.

'Then who can it be?' Sughra asked him.

Mian Abdul Hai tried to speak, but before he could do so, Basharat came running in. He was breathless. Taking Sughra aside, he whispered, 'It's a Sikh.'

Sughra screamed, 'A Sikh! What does he want?'

'He wants me to open the door.'

Sughra took Basharat in her arms and went and sat on her father's bed, looking at him desolately.

On Mian Abdul Hai's thin, lifeless lips, a faint smile appeared. 'Go and open the door. It is Gurmukh Singh.'

'No, it's someone else,' Basharat said.

Mian sahib turned to Sughra. 'Open the door. It's him.'

Sughra rose. She knew Gurmukh Singh. Her father had once done him a favour. He had been involved in a false legal suit and Mian sahib had acquitted him. That was a long time ago, but every year on the occasion of Id, he would come all the way from his village with a bag of home-made noodles. Mian sahib had told him several times, 'Sardar sahib, you really are too kind. You shouldn't inconvenience yourself every year.' But Gurmukh Singh would always reply, 'Mian sahib, God has given you everything. This is only a small gift which I bring every year in humble acknowledgement of the kindness you did me once. Even a hundred generations of mine would not be able to repay your favour. May God keep you happy.'

Sughra was reassured. Why hadn't she thought of it in the first place? But why had Basharat said it was someone else? After all, he knew Gurmukh Singh's face from his annual visit.

Sughra went to the front door. There was another knock. Her heart missed a beat. 'Who is it?' she asked in a faint voice.

Basharat whispered to her to look through a small hole in the door.

It wasn't Gurmukh Singh, who was a very old man. This was a young fellow. He knocked again. He was holding a bag in his hand, of the same kind Gurmukh Singh used to bring.

'Who are you?' she asked, a little more confident now.

'I am Sardar Gurmukh Singh's son Santokh.'

Sughra's fear had suddenly gone. 'What brings you here today?' she asked politely.

'Where is judge sahib?' he asked.

'He is not well,' Sughra answered.

'Oh, I'm sorry,' Santokh Singh said. Then he shifted his bag from one hand to the other. 'These are home-made noodles.' Then after a pause, 'Sardar ji is dead.'

'Dead!'

'Yes, a month ago, but one of the last things he said to me was, "For the last ten years, on the occasion of Id, I have always taken my small gift to judge sahib. After I am gone, it will become your duty." I gave him my word that I would not fail him. I am here today to honour the promise made to my father on his death-bed.'

Sughra was so moved that tears came to her eyes. She opened the door a little. The young man pushed the bag towards her. 'May God rest his soul,' she said.

'Is judge sahib not well?' he asked.

'No.'

'What's wrong?'

'He had a stroke.'

'Had my father been alive, it would have grieved him deeply. He never forgot judge sahib's kindness until his last breath. He used to say, "He is not a man, but a god." May God keep him under his care. Please convey my respects to him.'

He left before Sughra could make up her mind whether or not to ask him to get a doctor.

As Santokh Singh turned the corner, four men, their faces covered with their turbans, moved towards him. Two of them held burning oil torches, the others carried cans of kerosene oil and explosives. One of them asked Santokh, 'Sardar ji, have you completed your assignment?'

The young man nodded.

'Should we then proceed with ours?' he asked.

'If you like,' he replied and walked away.

Colder than Ice

As Ishwar Singh entered the room, Kalwant Kaur rose from the bed and locked the door from the inside. It was past midnight. A strange and ominous silence seemed to have descended on the city.

Kalwant Kaur returned to the bed, crossed her legs and sat down in the middle. Ishwar Singh stood quietly in a corner, holding his *kirpan* absent-mindedly. Anxiety and confusion were writ large on his handsome face.

Kalwant Kaur, apparently dissatisfied with her defiant posture, moved to the edge and sat down, swinging her legs suggestively. Ishwar Singh still had not spoken.

Kalwant Kaur was a big woman with generous hips, fleshy thighs and unusually high breasts. Her eyes were sharp and bright and over her upper lip, there was a faint bluish down. Her chin suggested great strength and resolution.

Ishwar Singh had not moved from his corner. His turban, which he always kept smartly in place, was loose and his hands trembled from time to time. However, from his strapping manly figure, it was apparent that he had just what it took to be Kalwant Kaur's lover.

More time passed. Kalwant Kaur was getting restive. 'Ishr Sian,' she said in a sharp voice.

Ishwar Singh raised his head, then turned it away, unable to deal with Kalwant Kaur's fiery gaze.

This time she screamed: 'Ishr Sian', then she lowered her voice and added: 'Where have you been all this time?'

Ishwar Singh moistened his parched lips and said: 'I don't know.'

Kalwant Kaur lost her temper: 'What sort of a mother-fucking answer is that!'

Ishwar Singh threw his *kirpan* aside and slumped on the bed. He looked unwell. She stared at him and her anger seemed to have left her. Putting her hand on his forehead, she asked gently: 'Jani, what's wrong?'

'Kalwant.' He turned his gaze from the ceiling and looked at her. There was pain in his voice and it melted all of Kalwant Kaur. She bit her lower lip: 'Yes, jani.'

Ishwar Singh took off his turban. He slapped her thigh and said, more to himself that to her: 'I feel strange.'

His long hair came undone and Kalwant Kaur began to run her fingers through it playfully. 'Ishr Sian, where have you been all this time?'

'In the bed of my enemy's mother,' he said jocularly. Then he pulled Kalwant Kaur towards him and began to knead her breasts with both hands. 'I swear by the Guru, there's no other woman like you.'

Flirtatiously, she pushed him aside: 'Swear over my head. Did you go to the city?'

He gathered his hair in a bun and replied: 'No.'

Kalwant Kaur was irritated. 'Yes, you did go to the city and you looted a lot more money and you don't want to tell me about it.'

'May I not be my father's son if I lie to you,' he said.

She was silent for a while, then she exploded: 'Tell me what happened to you the last night you were here. You were lying next to me and you had made me wear all those gold ornaments you had looted from the houses of the Muslims in the city and you were kissing me all over and then, suddenly, God only knows what came over you, you put on your clothes and walked out.'

Ishwar Singh went pale. 'See how your face has fallen,' Kalwant Kaur snapped. 'Ishr Sian,' she said, emphasizing every word, 'you're not the man you were eight days ago. Something has happened.'

Ishwar Singh did not answer, but he was stung. He suddenly took Kalwant Kaur in his arms and began to hug and kiss her ferociously. 'Jani, I'm what I always was. Squeeze me tighter so that the heat in your bones cools off.'

Kalwant Kaur did not resist him, but she kept asking: 'What went wrong that night?'

'Nothing.'

'Why don't you tell me?'

'There's nothing to tell.'

'Ishr Sian, may you cremate my body with your own hands if you lie to me!'

Ishwar Singh did not reply. He dug his lips into hers. His moustache tickled her nostrils and she sneezed. They burst out laughing.

Ishwar Singh began to take off his clothes, ogling Kalwant Kaur lasciviously. 'It's time for a game of cards.'

Beads of perspiration appeared over her upper lip. She rolled her eyes coquettishly and said: 'Get lost.'

Ishwar Singh pinched her lip and she leapt aside. 'Ishr Sian, don't do that. It hurts.'

Ishwar Singh began to suck her lower lip and Kalwant Kaur melted. He took off the rest of his clothes. 'Time for a round of trumps,' he said.

Kalwant Kaur's upper lip began to quiver. He peeled her shirt off, as if he was skinning a banana. He fondled her naked body and pinched her arm. 'Kalwant, I swear by the Guru, you're not a woman, you're a delicacy,' he said between kisses.

Kalwant Kaur examined the skin he had pinched. It was red. 'Ishr Sian, you're a brute.'

Ishwar Singh smiled through his thick moustache. 'Then let there be a lot of brutality tonight.' And he began to prove what he had said.

He bit her lower lip, nibbled at her earlobes, kneaded her breasts, slapped her glowing hips resoundingly and planted big wet kisses on her cheeks.

Kalwant Kaur began to boil with passion like a kettle on high fire.

But there was something wrong.

Ishwar Singh, despite his vigorous efforts at foreplay, could not feel the fire which leads to the final and inevitable act of love. Like a wrestler who is being had the better of, he employed every trick he knew to ignite the fire in his loins, but it eluded him. He felt cold.

Kalwant Kaur was now like an overtuned instrument. 'Ishr Sian,' she whispered languidly, 'you have shuffled me enough, it is time to produce your trump.'

Ishwar Singh felt as if the entire deck of cards had slipped from his hands on to the floor.

He laid himself against her, breathing irregularly. Drops of cold perspiration appeared on his brow. Kalwant Kaur made frantic efforts to arouse him, but in the end she gave up.

In a fury, she sprang out of bed and covered herself with a sheet. 'Ishr Sian, tell me the name of the bitch you have been with who has squeezed you dry.'

Ishwar Singh just lay there panting.

'Who was that bitch?' she screamed.

'No one, Kalwant, no one,' he replied in a barely audible voice.

Kalwant Kaur placed her hands on her hips: 'Ishr Sian, I'm going to get to the bottom of this. Swear to me on the Guru's sacred name, is there a woman?'

She did not let him speak. 'Before you swear by the Guru, don't forget who I am. I am Sardar Nihal Singh's daughter. I will cut you to pieces. Is there a woman in this?'

He nodded his head in assent, his pain obvious from his face.

Like a wild and demented creature, Kalwant Kaur picked up Ishwar Singh's *kirpan*, unsheathed it and plunged it in his neck. Blood spluttered out of the deep gash like water out of a fountain. Then she began to pull at his hair and scratch his face, cursing her unknown rival as she continued tearing at him.

'Let go, Kalwant, let go now,' Ishwar Singh begged.

She paused. His beard and chest were drenched in blood. 'You acted impetuously,' he said, 'but what you did I deserved.'

'Tell me the name of that woman of yours,' she screamed.

A thin line of blood ran into his mouth. He shivered as he felt its taste.

'Kalwant, with this *kirpan* I have killed six men ... with this *kirpan* with which you ...'

'Who was the bitch, I ask you?' she repeated.

Ishwar Singh's dimming eyes sparked into momentary life. 'Don't call her a bitch,' he implored.

'Who was she?' she screamed.

Ishwar Singh's voice was failing. 'I'll tell you.' He ran his hand over his throat, then looked at it, smiling wanly. 'What a motherfucking creature man is!'

'Ishr Sian, answer my question,' Kalwant Kaur said.

He began to speak, very slowly, his face coated with cold sweat.

'Kalwant, jani, you can have no idea what happened to me. When they began to loot Muslim shops and houses in the city, I joined one of the gangs. All the cash and ornaments that fell to my share, I brought back to you. There was only one thing I hid from you.'

He began to groan. His pain was becoming unbearable, but she was unconcerned. 'Go on,' she said in a merciless voice.

'There was this house I broke into ... there were seven people in there, six of them men ... whom I killed with my *kirpan* one by one ... and there was one girl ... she was so beautiful ... I didn't kill her ... I took her away.'

She sat on the edge of the bed, listening to him.

'Kalwant jani, I can't even begin to describe to you how beautiful she was ... I could have slashed her throat but I didn't ... I said to myself ... Ishr Sian, you gorge yourself on Kalwant Kaur every day ... how about a mouthful of this luscious fruit!

'I thought she had gone into a faint, so I carried her over my shoulder all the way to the canal which runs outside the city ... then I laid her down on the grass, behind some bushes and ... first I thought I would shuffle her a bit ... but then I decided to trump her right away ...'

'What happened?' she asked.

'I threw the trump ... but, but ...'

His voice sank.

Kalwant Kaur shook him violently: 'What happened?'

Ishwar Singh opened his eyes. 'She was dead ... I had carried a dead body ... a heap of cold flesh ... jani, give me your hand.'

Kalwant Kaur placed her hand on his. It was colder than ice.

The Dutiful Daughter

The country had been divided. Hundreds of thousands of Muslims and Hindus were moving from India to Pakistan and from Pakistan to India in search of refuge. Camps had been set up to give them temporary shelter, but they were so overcrowded that it seemed quite impossible to push another human being into them, and yet more refugees were being brought in every day. There wasn't enough food to go round and basic facilities were almost non-existent. Epidemics and infections were common, but it didn't bother anybody. Such were the times.

The year 1948 had begun. Hundreds of volunteers had been assigned the task of recovering abducted women and children and restoring them to their families. They would go in groups to India from Pakistan and from Pakistan to India to make their recoveries.

It always amused me to see that such enthusiastic efforts were being made to undo the effects of something which had been perpetrated by more or less the same people. Why were they trying to rehabilitate the women who had been raped and taken away when they had let them be raped and taken away in the first place?

It was all very confusing, but one still admired the devotion of these volunteers.

It was not a simple task. The difficulties were enormous. The abductors were not easy to trace. To avoid discovery they had devised various means of eluding their pursuers. They were constantly on the move, from this locality to that, from one city to another. One followed a tip and often found nothing at the end of the trail.

One heard strange stories. One liaison officer told me that in Saharanpur, two abducted Muslim girls had refused to return to their parents who were in Pakistan. Then there was this Muslim girl in Jullandar who was given a touching farewell by the abductor's family as if she was a daughter-in-law leaving on a long journey. Some girls had committed suicide on the way, afraid of facing their parents. Some had lost their mental balance as a result of their traumatic experiences. Others had become alcoholics and used abusive and vulgar language when spoken to.

When I thought about these abducted girls, I only saw their protruding bellies. What was going to happen to them and what they contained? Who would claim the end result? Pakistan or India?

And who would pay the women the wages for carrying those children in their wombs for nine months? Pakistan or India? Or would it all be put down in God's great ledger, if there were still any pages left?

The abducted women were being moved from this side to that and that side to this all the time.

Why were they being described as abducted women? I had always thought that when a woman ran away from home with her lover — the police always called it 'abduction' — it was the most romantic act in the world. But these women had been taken against their will and violated.

They were strange, illogical times. I had boarded up all the doors and windows of my mind, shuttered them up. It was difficult to think straight.

Sometimes it seemed to me that the entire operation was being conducted like import-export trade.

One liaison officer said to me: 'Why do you look lost?'

I didn't answer his question.

Then he told me a story.

'We were looking for abducted women from town to town, village to village, street to street, and days would go by sometimes before we would have any success.

'And almost every time I went across to what was now India, I would notice an old woman, the same old woman. The first time it was in the suburbs of Jullandar. She looked distracted, almost unaware of her surroundings. Her eyes had a desolate look, her clothes had turned to rags and her hair was coated with dust. The only thing that struck me about her was that she was looking for someone.

'I was told by one of the women volunteers that she had lost her mind because her only daughter had been abducted during the riots in Patiala. She said they had tried for months to find the girl but had failed. In all probability, she had been killed, but that was something the old woman was not prepared to believe.

'The next time I ran into her at Saharanpur. She was at the bus stop and she looked much worse than she had the first time I had seen her. Her lips were cracked and her hair looked matted. I spoke to her. I said she should abandon her futile search; and to induce her to follow my advice, I told her — it was brutal — that her daughter had probably been murdered.

'She looked at me. "Murdered? No. No one can murder my daughter. No one can murder my daughter."

'And she walked away.

'It set me thinking. Why was this crazy woman so confident that no one could murder her daughter, that no sharp, deadly knife could slash her throat? Did she think her daughter was immortal or was it her motherhood which would not admit defeat, not entertain the possibility of death?

'On my third visit, I saw her again in another town. She looked very old and ragged. Her clothes were now so threadbare that they hardly covered her frail body. I gave her a change of dress, but she didn't want it. I said to her: "Old woman, I swear to you that your daughter was killed in Patiala."

'"You are lying," she said. There was steely conviction in her voice.

'To convince her, I said: "I assure you I'm telling the truth. You've suffered enough. It's time to go to Pakistan. I'll take you."

'She paid no attention to what I had said and began muttering to herself. "No one can murder my daughter," she suddenly declared in a strong, confident voice.

'"Why?" I asked.

'"Because she's beautiful. She's so beautiful that no one can kill her. No one could even dream of hurting her," she said in a low whisper.

'I wondered if her daughter was really as beautiful as she said. I thought: all children are beautiful to their mother. It's also possible that the old woman is right. Who knows? But in this holocaust nothing has survived. This mad old woman is deceiving herself. There are so many ways of escape from unpleasant reality. Grief is like a roundabout which one intersects with an infinite number of roads.

'I made many other trips across the border to India and almost every time I somehow ran into the old woman. She was no more than a bag of bones now. She could hardly see and tottered about like a blind person, a step at a time. Only one thing hadn't changed — her faith that her daughter was alive and that no one could kill her.

'One of the women volunteers said to me: "Don't waste your time over her. She's raving mad. It would be good if you could take her to Pakistan with you and put her in an asylum."

'Suddenly, I didn't want to do that. I didn't want to divest her of her only reason for living. As it was, she was in a vast asylum where nothing made any sense. I didn't wish to confine her within the four walls of a regular one.

'The last time I met her was in Amritsar. She looked so broken that it almost brought tears to my eyes. I decided that I would make one last effort to take her to Pakistan.

'There she stood in Farid Chowk, peering around with her half-blind eyes. I was talking to a shopkeeper about an abducted Muslim girl, who, we had been informed, was being kept in the house of a Hindu moneylender.

'After my exchange with the shopkeeper, I crossed the street, determined to persuade the old woman to come with me to Pakistan.

'I noticed a couple. The woman's face was partly covered by her white *chaddur*. The man was young and handsome — a Sikh.

'As they went past the old woman, the man suddenly stopped. He even fell back a step or two. Nervously, he caught hold of the woman's hand. I couldn't see her full face, but one glimpse had been enough to show that she was beautiful beyond words.

'"Your mother," he said to her.

'The girl looked up, but only for a second. Then, covering her face with her *chaddur*, she grabbed her companion's arm and said: "Let's get away from here."

'They crossed the road, taking long, brisk steps.

'The old woman shouted: "Bhagbari, Bhagbari."

'I rushed towards her. "What is the matter?" I asked.

'She was trembling. "I have seen her . . . I have seen her."

'"Whom have you seen?" I asked.

'"I have seen my daughter . . . I have seen Bhagbari." Her eyes were like burnt-out lights.

'"Your daughter is dead," I said.

'"You're lying," she screamed.

'"I swear on God your daughter is dead."

'The old woman fell in a heap on the road.'

Three Simple Statements

Not far from Congress House and Jinnah Hall in Bombay
is a urinal, called *mootri* by the locals, who also have made a
habit of dumping all their rubbish outside this facility. The
stink it produces is so revolting that you cannot walk past it
without covering your nose with your handkerchief.

He was once constrained to go into this hell-hole, his
nose protected by a handkerchief, while trying all the time
not to breathe. The floor was wet and filthy. The walls were
covered with crude representations of human genitalia and
in one corner someone had scribbled in charcoal the words:
'Ram Pakistan up the you-know-what of the Muslims.'

He felt revolted and stepped out as quickly as he could.

Both Congress House and Jinnah Hall were under the
control of the government, but the *mootri* was free, free to
spread its stink far and wide, free to receive the garbage of
the local community at its doorstep.

A few days later, he found himself visiting the *mootri* once
again to answer the call of nature. He had his face covered
and his breath held in his lungs. There was more filth on
the floor than the last time and more murals on the wall
depicting the engines of human procreation.

Under the words 'ram Pakistan up the you-know-what of
the Muslims,' someone had scrawled with a thick pencil:
'ram Akhand Bharat up the you-know-what of the Hindus.'
He left hurriedly, feeling as if he had been sprayed with
acid.

Some time later, Mahatma Gandhi was granted unconditional release by the British Indian government. Mr Jinnah was defeated in the Punjab. As for Congress House and Jinnah Hall, they were neither defeated nor released. And the *mootri*, which was only a short distance from these imposing buildings, continued to remain under the occupation of malodorous filth. Only the pile of garbage ouside had grown larger.

He went for the third time to the *mootri* — but not to answer the call of nature.

He covered his nose and held his breath as he entered. The floor was crawling with vermin. No further space was left on the wall to draw more human genitalia.

The words 'ram Pakistan up the you-know-what of the Muslims' and 'ram Akhand Bharat up the you-know-what of the Hindus' were now somewhat faded.

When he left, a new line had appeared under the two declarations: 'ram Mother India up the you-know-what of both Muslims and Hindus.'

For a moment, these words seemed to dispel the stink of the *mootri* like a light fragrance dancing in the wind — but only for a moment.

Babu Gopi Nath

I think it was in 1940 that I first met Babu Gopi Nath. I was the editor of a weekly magazine in Bombay. One day, while I was busy writing something, Abdul Rahim Sando burst into my office, followed by a short, nondescript man. Greeting me in his typical style, Sando introduced his friend. 'Manto Sahib, meet Babu Gopi Nath.'

I rose and shook hands with him. Sando was in his element. 'Babu Gopi Nath, you are shaking hands with India's number one writer.' He had a talent for coining words which, though not to be found in any dictionary, somehow always managed to express his meaning. 'When he writes,' Sando continued, 'it is *dharan takhta*. Nobody can get people's "continuity" together like him. Manto Sahib, what did you write about Miss Khurshid last week? "Miss Khurshid has bought a car. Verily, God is the great carmaker." Well, Babu Gopi Nath, if that's not the "anti" of *pantipo*, then what is, I put it to you!'

Abdul Rahim Sando was an original. Most of the words he used in ordinary conversation were strictly of his own authorship. After this introduction, he looked at Babu Gopi Nath, who appeared to be impressed. 'This is Babu Gopi Nath from Lahore, but now of Bombay, accompanied by a "pigeonette" from Kashmir.'

Babu Gopi Nath smiled.

Abdul Rahim Sando continued: 'If you are looking for the

world's number one innocent, this is your man. Everyone
cheats him out of his money by saying nice things to him.
Look at me. All I do is talk and he rewards me with two
packets of Poulson's smuggled butter every day. Manto
sahib, he is a genuine "antifloojustice" fellow, if ever there
was one. We are expecting you at Babu Gopi Nath's flat
this evening.'

Babu Gopi Nath, whose mind seemed to be elsewhere,
now joined the conversation. 'Manto sahib, I insist that you
come.' Then he looked at Sando. 'Sando, is Manto sahib . . .
well, fond of . . . you know what?'

Abdul Rahim Sando laughed. 'Of course, he is fond of
that and of many other things as well. Is it all settled then?
May I add that I have also started drinking because it can
now be done free of cost.'

Sando wrote out the address and, at six o'clock, I
presented myself at the flat. It was nice and clean. Three
rooms, good furniture, all in order. Besides Sando and
Babu Gopi Nath, there were four others — two men and
two women — to whom I was presently introduced by
Sando.

There was Ghaffar Sain, a typical Punjabi villager in a
loose *tehmad*, wearing a huge necklace of beads and
coloured stones. 'He is Babu Gopi Nath's legal adviser,
you know what I mean?' Sando said. 'In Punjab, every
lunatic is a man of God. Our friend here is either already a
man of God, or about to be admitted to that divine order.
He has accompanied Babu Gopi Nath from Lahore,
because he had run out of suckers in that city. Here, he
drinks Scotch whisky, smokes Craven A cigarettes and
prays for the good of Babu Gopi Nath's soul.'

Ghaffar Sain heard this colourful description in silence, a
smile playing on his lips.

The other man was called Ghulam Ali, tall and athletic
with a pockmarked face. About him Sando provided the following information: 'He is my *shagird*, my true apprentice.

A famous singing girl of Lahore fell in love with him. She brought all manner of "continuities" in play to ensnare him, but the only response she received from Ghulam Ali was: "Women are not my cup of tea." Ran into Babu Gopi Nath at a Lahore shrine and has never left his side since. He receives a tin of Craven A cigarettes daily and all the food he can eat.'

Ghulam Ali smiled good-naturedly.

I looked at the women. One of them was young, fair and round-faced, the Kashmiri 'pigeonette' Sando had mentioned. She had short hair, which first appeared to be cropped, but was not. Her eyes were large and bright and her expression suggested that she was raw and inexperienced. Sando introduced her.

'Zeenat Begum, called Zeno, a love-name given by Babu sahib. This apple, plucked from Kashmir, was brought to Lahore by one of the city's most formidable madams. Babu Gopi Nath's private intelligence sources relayed the news of this arrival to him and, overnight, he decamped with her. There was litigation and for about two months the city police had a ball, thanks to Babu Gopi Nath's generosity. Naturally, Babu Gopi Nath won the suit. And so here she is. "*Dharan takhta*".'

The other woman, who was quietly smoking, was dark and red-eyed. Babu Gopi Nath looked at her. 'Sando, and this one?' Sando slapped her thigh and declaimed: 'Ladies and gentlemen, this is "*mutton tippoti, fulful booti*", Mrs Abdul Rahim Sando, alias Sardar Begum. Fell in love with me in 1936 and inside of two years, I was done for — "*dharan takhta*". I had to run away from Lahore. However, Babu Gopi Nath sent for her the other day to keep me out of harm's way. Her daily rations consist of one tin of Craven A cigarettes and two rupees eight annas every evening for her morphine shot. She may be dark, but, by God, she is a tit-for-tat lady.'

'What rubbish you talk,' Sardar said. She sounded like

the hardened professional woman she was.

Having finished with the introductions, Sando began a lecture highlighting my greatness. 'Cut it out, Sando,' I said. 'Let's talk of something else.'

Sando shouted: 'Boy, whisky and soda. Babu Gopi Nath, out with the cash.'

Babu Gopi Nath reached in his pocket, pulled out a thick bundle of money, peeled a note off and gave it to Sando. Sando stared at it reverently, raised his eyes to heaven and said: 'Dear God of the universe, bring unto me the day when I put my hand in my pocket and fish out a thick wad of money like this. Meanwhile, I am asking Ghulam Ali to run to the store and return post-haste with two bottles of Johnny Walker Still-Going-Strong.'

The whisky arrived and we began to drink, with Sando continuing to monopolize the conversation. He downed his glass in one go. '*Dharan takhta,*' he shouted, 'Manto sahib, this is what I call honest-to-goodness whisky, inscribing "Long Live Revolution" as it blazes its way through the gullet into the stomach. Long live Babu Gopi Nath.'

Babu Gopi Nath did not say much, occasionally nodding to express agreement with Sando's opinions. I had a feeling that the man had no views of his own. His superstitious nature was evident from the presence of Ghaffar Sain, his legal adviser, in Sando's words. What it really meant was that Babu Gopi Nath was a born devotee of real and fake holy men. I learnt during the conversation that most of his time in Lahore was spent in the company of fakirs, mendicants, sadhus and the like.

'What are you thinking?' I asked him.

'Nothing, nothing at all.' Then he smiled, glanced at Zeenat amorously. 'Just thinking about these beautiful creatures. What else do people like us think about?'

Sando explained, 'Manto sahib, Babu Gopi Nath is a great man. There is hardly a singing girl or a courtesan worth the name in Lahore he has not had a "continuity" with.'

'Manto sahib, one no longer has the fire of youth in one's loins,' Babu Gopi Nath said modestly.

Then followed a long discussion about the leading families of courtesans and singing girls of Lahore. Family trees were traced, genealogy analysed, not to speak of how much Babu Gopi Nath had paid for the ritual deflowering of which woman in what year. These exchanges remained confined to Sando, Sardar, Ghulam Ali and Ghaffar Sain. The jargon of Lahore's *kothas* was freely employed, not all of it comprehensible to me, though the general drift of the conversation was clear.

Zeenat never said a word. Off and on, she smiled. It was quite clear that she was not interested in these things. She drank a rather diluted glass of whisky, and I noticed that she smoked without appearing to enjoy it. Strangely enough, she smoked the most. I could find no visible indication that she was in love with Babu Gopi Nath, but it was obvious that he was with her. However, one could sense a tension between the two, despite their physical closeness.

At about eight o'clock, Sardar left to get her morphine shot. Ghaffar Sain, three drinks ahead, lay on the floor, rosary in hand. Ghulam Ali was sent out to get some food. Sando had got tired of talking. Babu Gopi Nath, now quite tipsy, looked at Zeenat longingly and said: 'Manto sahib, what do you think about my Zeenat?'

I did not know how to answer that, so I said: 'She is nice.' Babu Gopi Nath was pleased. 'Manto sahib, she is a lovely girl and so simple. She has no interest in ornaments and things like that. Many times I have offered to buy her a house of her own and you know what her answer has been? "What will I do with a house? Who do I have in the world?"'

'What does a motor car cost, Manto sahib?' he asked suddenly.

'I've no idea.'

'I don't believe it, Manto sahib. I'm sure you know. You

must help me buy Zeno a car. I've come to the conclusion that one must have a car in Bombay.'

Zeenat's face was devoid of expression.

Babu Gopi Nath was quite drunk now and getting more sentimental by the minute. 'Manto sahib, you are a man of learning. I am nothing but an ass. Please let me know if I can be of some service to you. It was only by accident that Sando brought up your name yesterday. I immediately sent for a taxi and asked him to take me to meet you. If I have shown you any discourtesy, you must forgive me. I am nothing but a sinner, a man full of faults. Should I get you some more whisky?'

'No, we've all had much too much to drink,' I said.

He became even more sentimental. 'You must drink some more, Manto sahib.' He produced his bundle of money, but before he could peel some off, I thrust it back into his pocket. 'You gave a hundred rupees to Ghulam Ali earlier, didn't you?' I asked.

The fact was that I had begun to feel sorry for Babu Gopi Nath. He was surrounded by so many leeches and he was such a simpleton. Babu Gopi Nath smiled. 'Manto sahib, whatever is left of those hundred rupees will slip through Ghulam Ali's pocket.'

The words were hardly out of his mouth, when Ghulam Ali entered the room with the doleful announcement that some scoundrel had picked his pocket on the street. Babu Gopi Nath looked at me, smiled, and gave another hundred rupees to Ghulam Ali. 'Get some food quickly.'

After five or six meetings, I got to know a great deal more about Babu Gopi Nath's personality. First of all, my initial view that he was a fool and a sucker had turned out to be wrong. He was perfectly aware of the fact that Sando, Ghulam Ali and Sardar, his inseparable companions, were all selfish opportunists, but you could never guess his inner thoughts from his behaviour.

Once he said to me: 'Manto sahib, in my entire life, I

have never rejected advice. Whenever someone offers it to me, I accept it with gratitude. Perhaps they consider me a fool, but I value their wisdom. Look at it like this. They have the wisdom to see that I am the sort of man who can be made a fool of. The fact is that I have spent most of my life in the company of fakirs, holy men, courtesans and singing girls. I love them. I just couldn't do without them. I have decided that when my money runs out, I would like to settle down at a shrine. There are only two places where my heart finds peace: prostitutes' *kothas* and saints' shrines. It's only a matter of time before I shall be unable to afford the former, because my money is running out, but there are thousands of saints' shrines in India. I will go to one.'

'Why do you like *kothas* and shrines?' I asked.

'Because both establishments are an illusion. What better refuge can there be for someone who wants to deceive himself?'

'You are fond of singing girls. Do you understand music?' I asked.

'Not at all. It doesn't matter in the least. I can spend an entire evening listening to the most flat-voiced woman in the world and still feel happy. It is the little things which go with these evenings that I love. She sings, I flash a hundred-rupee note in front of her. She moves languorously towards me, and instead of letting her take it from my hand, I stick it in my sock. She bends and gently pulls it out. It's the sort of nonsense that people like us enjoy. Everybody knows, of course, that in a *kotha* parents prostitute their daughters and in shrines men prostitute their God.'

I learnt that Babu Gopi Nath was the son of a miserly moneylender and had inherited ten lakh rupees, which he had been frittering away ever since. He had come to Bombay with fifty thousand rupees, and though those were inexpensive times, his daily outgoings were heavy.

As promised, he bought a car for Zeno — a Fiat — for three thousand rupees. A chauffeur was also employed —

an unreliable ruffian — but they were the sort of people Babu Gopi Nath felt happy with.

Our meetings had become more frequent. Babu Gopi Nath interested me. In turn, he treated me with great respect and devotion.

One evening, I found among Babu Gopi Nath's regulars a man I had known for a long time — Mohammed Shafiq Toosi. Widely regarded as a singer and a wit, Shafiq had another unusual side to his character. He was the known lover of the most famous singing girls of the time. It was not so commonly known, however, that he had had affairs, one after the other with three sisters, belonging to one of the most famous singing families of Patiala.

Even less known was the fact that their mother, when she was young, was his mistress. His first wife, who died a few years after their marriage, he did not care for, because she was too housewifely and did not act like a woman of pleasure. He had no use for housewives. He was about forty and though he had gone through scores of famous courtesans and singing girls, he was not known to have spent a penny of his own on them. He was one of nature's gigolos.

Courtesans had always found him irresistible. When I walked into the flat, I found him engrossed in conversation with Zeenat. I couldn't understand who had introduced him to Babu Gopi Nath. I knew that Sando was a friend of his, but they had not been on speaking terms for some time. In the end, it turned out that the two had made up and it was actually Sando who had brought him here today.

Babu Gopi Nath sat in a corner, smoking his hookah. He never smoked cigarettes. Shafiq was telling stories, most of them ribald and all of them about courtesans and singing girls. Zeenat looked uninterested, but Sardar was all ears. 'Welcome, welcome,' Shafiq said to me, 'I did not know you too were a wayfarer of this valley.'

Sando shouted: 'Welcome to the angel of death. *Dharan takhta.*'

One could not fail to notice that Mohammed Shafiq Toosi and Zeenat were exchanging what could only be described as amorous glances. This troubled me. I had become quite fond of Zeenat, who had begun to call me Manto bhai.

I didn't like the way Shafiq was ogling at Zeenat. After some time, he left with Sando. I am afraid I was a bit harsh with Zeenat, because I expressed strong disapproval of the goings-on between Shafiq and her. She burst into tears and ran into the next room, followed by Babu Gopi Nath. A few minutes later, he came out and said: 'Manto sahib, come with me.'

Zeenat was sitting on her bed. When she saw us, she covered her face with both hands and lay down. Babu Gopi Nath was very sombre. 'Manto sahib, I love this woman. She has been with me for two years, and I swear by the Saint Hazrat Ghaus Azam Jilani that she has never given me cause for complaint. Her other sisters, I mean women of her calling, have robbed me without compunction over the years, but she is a girl without greed or love of money. Sometimes, I go away for weeks, maybe to be with another woman, without leaving her any money. You know what she does? She pawns her ornaments to manage until I return.

'Manto sahib, as I told you once, I don't have long to go. My money has almost run out. I don't want her life to go to waste after I am gone. So often have I said to her: "Zeno, look at other women and learn something from them. Today, I have money, tomorrow, I'll be a beggar. Women can't do with just one rich lover in their lives; they need several. If you don't find a rich patron after I leave, your life will be ruined. You act like a housewife, confined at home all day. That won't do."

'But Manto sahib, this woman is hopeless. I consulted Ghaffar Sain in Lahore and he advised me to take her to Bombay. He knows two famous actresses here who used to be singing girls in Lahore. I sent for Sardar from Lahore to teach Zeno a few tricks of the trade. Ghaffar Sain is also very capable in these matters.

'Nobody knows me in Bombay. She was afraid she would bring me dishonour, but I said to her: "Don't be silly. Bombay is a big city, full of millionaires. I have bought you a car. Why don't you find yourself a rich man who could look after you?"

'Manto sahib, I swear on God that it is my sincere wish that Zeno should stand on her own feet. I am prepared to put ten thousand rupees in a bank for her, but I know that within ten days, that woman Sardar will rob her of the last penny. Manto sahib, you should try to persuade her to become worldly-wise. Since she has had the car, Sardar takes her out for a drive every evening to the Apollo Bandar beach, which is frequented by fashionable people. But there has been no success so far. Sando brought Mohammed Shafiq Toosi this evening, as you saw. What is your opinion about him?'

I decided to offer no opinion, but Babu Gopi Nath said: 'He appears to be rich, and he is good-looking. Zeno, did you like him?'

Zeno said nothing.

I simply could not believe what he was telling me: that he had brought Zeenat to Bombay so that she could become the mistress of a rich man, or, at least, learn to live off rich men. But that's the way it was. Had he wanted to get rid of her, it would have been the easiest thing in the world, but his intentions were exactly what he said they were. He had tried to get her into films, Bombay being India's movie capital. For her sake, he had entertained men who claimed to be film directors, but were no such thing. He even had had a phone installed in the flat. None of these things had produced the man he was looking for.

Mohammed Shafiq Toosi, a regular visitor for a month or so, suddenly disappeared one day. True to style, he had used the opportunity to seduce Zeenat. Babu Gopi Nath said to me: 'Manto sahib, it is so sad. Shafiq sahib was all show and no substance. Not only did he do nothing to help Zeno, but he cheated her out of many valuables and two hundred rupees. Now I am told he is having an affair with a girl called Almas.'

This was true. Almas was the youngest daughter of the famous courtesan Nazir Jan of Patiala. She was the fourth sister he had seduced in a row. Zeno's money had been spent on her, but like all his liaisons, this too had turned out to be short-lived. It was later rumoured that Almas had tried to poison herself after being abandoned.

However, Zeenat had not given up on Mohammed Shafiq Toosi. She often phoned me, asking me to find Toosi and bring him to her. One day I accidentally ran into him at the radio station. When I gave him Zeenat's message, he said: 'This is not the first one. I have had several. The truth is that while Zeenat is a nice woman, she is too nice for my taste. Women who behave like wives are of no interest to me.'

Disappointed in Toosi, Zeenat resumed her visits to the beach in the company of Sardar. After two weeks of effort, Sardar was able to get hold of two men who appeared to be just the kind of gentlemen of leisure being sought. One of them, who owned a silk mill, even gave four hundred rupees to Zeenat and promised to marry her, but that was the last she heard from him.

One day, while on an errand on Hornsby Road, I saw Zeenat's parked car, with Mohammed Yasin, owner of the Nagina Hotel, occupying the back seat. 'Where did you get this car?' I asked.

'Do you know who it belongs to?'

'I do.'

'Then you can put two and two together.' He winked meaningfully.

A couple of days later, Babu Gopi Nath told me the

story. Sardar had met someone at the beach and they had
decided to go to Nagina Hotel to spend the evening. There
was a quarrel and the man had walked out, which is how
Yasin, the hotel's owner, had come into the picture.

Zeenat's affair with Yasin appeared to be progressing
well. He had bought her some expensive gifts, and Babu
Gopi Nath was mentally prepared to return to Lahore,
because he was certain Yasin was the man Zeno could be
entrusted to. Unfortunately, things did not work out that
way.

A mother and daughter had recently moved into Nagina
Hotel and Yasin was quick to see that Muriel, the daughter,
was looking for someone to while away the time. So, while
Zeenat sat in the hotel all day long, waiting for him, the two
of them could be seen driving around Bombay in Zeenat's
car. Babu Gopi Nath was hurt.

'What sort of men are these, Manto sahib?' he asked me.
'I mean if one has had one's fill of a woman, one just says so
honestly. I no longer understand Zeenat. She knows what is
going on, but she wouldn't even tell him that if he must
carry on with that Christian *chokri*, then at least he should
have the decency not to use her car. What am I to do,
Manto sahib? She is such a wonderful girl, but she is so
naïve. She has to learn how to survive in this world.'

The affair with Yasin finally ended, but it seemed to have
left no untoward effect on Zeenat. One day I phoned the
flat and learnt that Babu Gopi Nath had returned to
Lahore, along with Ghulam Ali and Ghaffar Sain. His
money had run out, but he still had some property left
which he was planning to sell before returning to Bombay.

Sardar needed her morphine and Sando his Poulson's
butter. They had therefore decided to turn the flat into a
whorehouse. Two or three men were roped in every day to
receive Zeenat's sexual favours. She had been told to co-
operate until Babu Gopi Nath's return. The daily takings
were around a hundred rupees or so, half of them Zeenat's.

'You do realize what you are doing to yourself?' I said to her one day.

'I don't know, Manto bhai,' she answered innocently. 'I merely do what these people tell me.'

I wanted to say that she was a fool and the two of them would not even hesitate to auction her off, if it came to that. However, I said nothing. She was a woman without ambition and unbelievably naive. She simply had no idea of her own value or what life was all about. If she was being made to sell her body, she could at least have done so with some intelligence and style, but she was simply not interested in anything, drinking, smoking, eating, or even the sofa on which she was to be found lying most of the time, and the telephone which she was so fond of using.

A month later, Babu Gopi Nath returned from Lahore. He went to the flat, but found some other people living there. It turned out that on the advice of Sando and Sardar, Zeenat had rented the top portion of a bungalow in the Bandara area. When Babu Gopi Nath came to see me, I told him of the new arrangement, but I said nothing about the establishment Sando and Sardar were running, thanks to Zeenat.

Babu Gopi Nath had come back with ten thousand rupees this time. Ghaffar Sain and Ghulam Ali had been left behind in Lahore. When we met, he insisted that I should come with him to Zeenat's place. He had left a taxi waiting on the street.

It took us an hour to get to Bandara. As we were driving up Pali Hill, we saw Sando. 'Sando, Sando,' Babu Gopi Nath shouted. '*Dharan takhta*,' Sando exclaimed when he saw who it was.

Babu Gopi Nath wanted him to get into the taxi, but Sando wouldn't. 'There is something I have to tell you,' he said.

I stayed in the taxi. The two of them talked for some time, then Babu Gopi Nath came back and told the driver to return to town.

He looked happy. As we were approaching Dawar, he said: 'Manto sahib, Zeno is about to be married.'

'To whom?' I asked, somewhat astonished.

'A rich landlord from Hyderabad, Sind. May God keep both of them happy. The timing is perfect. The money I have can be used to buy Zeno her dowry.'

I was a bit sceptical about the story. I was sure it was another of Sardar's and Sando's tricks to cheat Babu Gopi Nath. However, it all turned out to be true. The man was a rich Sindhi landlord who had been introduced to Zeno through the good offices of a Sindhi music teacher who had failed to teach her how to sing.

One day he had brought Ghulam Hussain — for that was the landlord's name — to Zeenat's place and she had received him with her usual hospitality. She had even sung something for him which he had liked. Ghulam Hussain was stricken. One thing had led to another and now they were going to get married.

Babu Gopi Nath was ecstatic. He had managed to meet Ghulam Hussain, having had himself introduced as Sando's friend. He told me later: 'Manto sahib, he is handsome and he is intelligent. Before leaving Lahore, I went and prayed at the shrine of Data Ganj Baksh for Zeno and my prayer has been answered. May Bhagwan keep both of them happy.'

Babu Gopi Nath made all the wedding arrangements. Four thousand rupees was spent on ornaments and clothes and five thousand was to be given in cash to Zeenat.

The wedding guests from Zeenat's side were myself, Mohammed Shafiq Toosi and Mohammed Yasin, proprietor of the Nagina Hotel. After the ceremony, Sando whispered: '*Dharan takhta.*'

Ghulam Hussain was a handsome man. He was dressed in a blue suit and was graciously acknowledging the congratulations being offered to him. Babu Gopi Nath looked like a little bird in his presence.

There was a wedding dinner, with Babu Gopi Nath very much the host. At one point, he said to me: 'Manto sahib, you must see how lovely Zeno looks in her bridal dress.'

I went into the next room. There sat Zeenat, dressed in expensive, silver-embroidered red silk. She was lightly made up, but was wearing too much lipstick. She greeted me by bowing her head slightly. She did look lovely, I thought. However, when I looked in the other corner, I found a bed profusely bedecked with flowers. I just could not contain my laughter. 'What is this farce?' I asked her. 'You are making fun of me, Manto bhai,' Zeno said, tears welling up in her eyes.

I was still wondering how to react, when Babu Gopi Nath came in. Lovingly, he dried Zeno's tears with his handkerchief and said to me in a heartbroken voice: 'Manto sahib, I had always considered you a wise and sensitive man. Before making such cruel fun of Zeno, you should at least have weighed your words.'

I suddenly had the feeling that the devotion he had always shown me had suffered a setback, but before I could apologize to him, he placed his hand affectionately over Zeenat's head and said: 'May God keep you happy.'

When he left the room, his eyes were wet and there was a look of disillusionment on his face.

A Question of Honour

If you happen to be on Faras Road, Bombay, and turn into the street called Sufaid Gulli, you run into a cluster of cafés and restaurants. Nothing special about that, Bombay being a city of cafés and restaurants. However, there is something special about Sufaid Gulli. It is the city's red light district where prostitutes of every race and description can be found.

If you went past Sufaid Gulli, you came to Playhouse, a noisy all-day cinema.

There were actually four cinemas in the area, each with its bell-ringing barker. 'Walk in, walk in. First class show for only two annas.' Sometimes, unwilling passers-by were physically pushed inside by these enterprising salesmen.

Street masseurs were always around. Getting your head massaged was a popular pastime in Bombay. I would watch men contentedly getting their skulls reconditioned. It never failed to amuse me.

If you felt like a massage at three in the morning, a *malashia* could easily be sent for, no matter in what part of the city you lived. These fellows were omnipresent, yelling 'pi, pi, pi' — short for *champi* or massage.

The name Faras Road was used to describe the entire prostitutes' quarter. The small side-streets had their own names, but collectively they were referred to as Faras Road or Sufaid Gulli.

The women sat in small rooms behind bamboo screens. The price varied from eight annas to eight rupees, and from eight rupees to eight hundred rupees. You could find your choice in this versatile buyers' market.

There was also a small Chinatown. It was not clear what occupations its residents engaged in, though some certainly ran restaurants, their names scrawled in funny insect-like letters outside.

Another street in the area was called Arab Gulli, with about twenty to twenty-five Arabs living there, all apparently in the pearl trade. Others were Punjabis or Rampuris.

It was in Arab Gulli that I had a rented room which was so dark that the light had to be kept on at all times. The monthly rent was exactly nine rupees, eight annas.

If you have never lived in Bombay, you would find it hard to believe that its people simply do not interfere in each other's business. If you are dying in your room — *kholi* in Bombayese — nobody is going to give a damn. If a murder takes place in the neighbourhood, nobody is going to bring you the news.

However, there was one man in Arab Gulli who was informed about every single resident of the area. His name was Mammad Bhai. He came from Rampur and had the reputation of being the master of every known martial art. I was told many stories about him when I first moved in, but it was a long time before I got an opportunity to meet him.

I used to leave my *kholi* early in the morning and return late at night. However, this character Mammad Bhai had begun to fascinate me. It was said, for instance, that, single-handed, he could fight off twenty-five men armed with *lathis*. One by one, he could fell them to the ground. It was also said that a knifer of his dexterity was hard to find in Bombay. He could slash an adversary with demonic speed. His victims were said to walk away without noticing anything amiss and then suddenly crumble to the ground — stone dead. 'Nobody has Mammad Bhai's touch,' it was whispered.

My curiosity to meet Mammad Bhai grew every day. You were always conscious of his presence in the area. He was the *dada*, the *burra badmash*, but everyone swore that he was a puritan as far as women were concerned, or, as the local expression went, he was 'wedded to the sanctity of his loincloth'. He was also a sort of local Robin Hood.

Not only in Arab Gulli, but in the surrounding streets, every poor woman without means knew Mammad Bhai. He used to help them regularly. It was always one of his apprentices — a *shagird*, as they were called — who was sent over. He never went himself.

I did not know what means of income Mammad Bhai had. He was said to dress well, eat well and drive himself around in a dandy pony *tonga*, invariably accompanied by two or three *shagirds*. They would make a round of the bazaar, stop at a local shrine briefly, then trot back into Arab Gulli, get into one of its Iranian cafés for a long session, with Mammad Bhai holding forth on the intricacies of martial arts.

Next to my *kholi* was the *kholi* of a male dancer from Marwar who had told me hundreds of stories about Mammad Bhai. He once said: 'Mammad Bhai is simply peerless. Once I came down with cholera. Somebody informed Mammad Bhai and he got every Faras Road doctor into my *kholi*, warning them that if something went wrong with Ashiq Hussain, he would bump them off personally.'

Then Ashiq Hussain added in an emotional voice: 'Manto sahib, Mammad Bhai is an angel. When he threatened the doctors, you could see them trembling. Then they really got down to the treatment and I was bouncing about like a ball in two days flat.'

There were other stories I had heard about Mammad Bhai in the filthy and third class cafés of Arab Gulli. One man, probably a *shagird*, told me that Mammad Bhai always carried a razor-sharp steel dagger tucked against his thigh, so sharp that he could shave himself with it. It was kept unsheathed and was so lethal that had Mammad Bhai not been a careful man, he could have seriously injured himself with it.

So, with each passing day, my keenness to meet this man increased. I would try to imagine him. A tall, muscular, formidable figure, the kind of man they used as a model to advertise the Hercules bicycle.

Tired after my long day, I would generally hit my bed and fall asleep immediately. There was never time to meet Mammad Bhai. I often thought of skipping work one day to catch a glimpse of him. Unfortunately, I was never able to do that. I had a ridiculous job.

One day, I suddenly came down with high fever. I am hardy by nature and have never required care, but God knows what kind of a fever it was. It felt as if someone was slowly crushing my spine. For the first time in my life, I felt in need of help, but I had nobody around.

For two days I lay in agony all alone. There were no visitors, not that I had expected any. I hardly knew anyone. The few friends I had lived in far-flung areas. If I had died, for instance, they would never have even come to know and, in any case, who cared in Bombay whether you lived or died.

I was in terrible shape. Ashiq Hussain the dancer had gone back home because his wife was ill, according to the tea boy — *chokra* — from the Iranian cafe.

One day, I decided to try the impossible — get up from my bed and go to one of the bazaar doctors. Suddenly, there was a knock at the door. I thought it was the *chokra*. In a barely audible voice, I said, 'Come in.'

The door opened to reveal a man of slight build. The first thing I noticed about him was his moustache. It was his entire personality, and without it, one would hardly have noticed him.

He walked in, giving his Emperor Kaiser Wilhelm moustache a twirl. He was followed by three or four men I did not know.

The man with the Kaiser Wilhelm moustache said to me in a very soft voice: 'Vimto sahib, this is no good. Why didn't you send me word you were ill?'

That I had been called Vimto instead of Manto was nothing new, nor was I in the mood to correct him. All I could say in my weak, feverish voice to the moustache was: 'Who are you?'

'Mammad Bhai,' came the cryptic answer.

I almost rose from my bed. 'Mammad Bhai ... Mammad Bhai, the famous *dada*?'

It was a bit tactless, but he ignored it. With his little finger he gave his moustache a slight lift and smiled. 'That's right, Vimto bhai, I am Mammad, the famous *dada*. It was the *chokra* who told me how sick you were. This is no *sala* good. You should have sent me word. When something like this happens, Mammad Bhai *sala* loses his cool.'

I was about to say something, when he ordered one of his companions, 'Hey, what's your name. Go run to what's his name that *sala* doctor. Tell him Mammad Bhai wants him here double quick. Tell him to run. Drop whatever he is doing. And let the *sala* not forget to bring his stuff with him.'

The man whom Mammad Bhai had commissioned for the errand disappeared. I looked at him and remembered the stories I had heard about him, but all I could see was his moustache. It was a terrifying sight — and an impressive one. His features were soft and it seemed he had grown a moustache to give himself a macho touch.

Since there was no chair, I invited Mammad Bhai to sit on my bed, an offer he refused, saying drily, 'Never mind.'

He began to pace around, although the room was hardly capable of offering such luxury. Presently, he produced his famous dagger from somewhere. It was a dazzling sight. At first I thought it was made of silver. He ran it gently over his wrist and any hair that came in its path was instantly shaved away. This seemed to please him and he began to trim his nails with it.

His mere arrival had brought my fever down several degrees, or so it seemed. 'Mammad Bhai,' I said, 'this dagger that you carry is awfully sharp. Aren't you afraid you'll hurt yourself?'

Neatly slicing off another nail, he said: 'Vimto bhai, this dagger is meant for my enemies. How can it hurt me?'

He sounded like a father speaking fondly of his child. 'How can my own child hurt me?'

Finally, the doctor came. His name was Pinto — and I was Vimto. He greeted Mammad Bhai respectfully and asked what the matter was. 'I'll tell you what the matter is,' he replied sternly. 'If you don't get Vimto bhai well, *sala* you're going to pay for it.'

Obediently, Dr Pinto began to examine me. He took my pulse, put his stethoscope on my chest, tapped my back, checked my blood pressure and asked me how and when I had fallen ill. Then he said to Mammad Bhai — not me — 'Nothing to worry. It is only malaria. I'll give him a shot.'

Mammad Bhai shaved some more hair off his wrist and said: 'I know nothing about these things. If you want to give him a shot, then give him a *sala* shot, but if anything happens to him, remember . . .'

'No, Mammad Bhai, everything is going to be fine. Now let me give him a shot.' He opened his bag and took out a syringe.

'Wait, wait,' Mammad Bhai screamed. Pinto put the syringe back into the bag and looked at Mammad Bhai nervously.

'I just cannot watch anybody getting the needle,' he said and walked out, followed by his entourage.

Dr Pinto gave me a quinine injection neatly, although normally it is a very painful affair. When he was done, I asked him what I owed him. 'Ten rupees,' he said. I reached for my wallet, which lay under my pillow, and had just paid him when Mammad Bhai entered the room.

'What's going on?' he screamed. 'I was only paying the doctor his fee,' I said. '*Sala*, what do you think you are doing?' he screamed at Pinto. 'Mammad Bhai, I swear I didn't ask for it,' Pinto replied meekly.

'*Sala*, if you want your fee, you get it from me. Give Vimto sahib back his money.' It was immediately returned.

Mammad Bhai twirled his moustache and smiled: 'Vimto sahib. How can a doctor from my area take money from you? Had he done that, I swear I would have had my moustache shaved off. Everyone here is your slave.'

I asked Mammad Bhai how he knew me.

'How do I know you? Is there anyone here whom Mammad Bhai doesn't know? My friend, Mammad Bhai is the king and looks after his people. My detectives keep me informed about everything. Arrivals, departures, who is doing what.'

Then he added: 'I know everything about you.'

'Is that so?' I asked.

'*Sala* ... don't I know? You come from Amritsar. You are a Kashmiri. You work here for newspapers. You owe ten rupees to the Bismillah Hotel in the bazaar, which is why you no longer pass that way. In Bhindi Bazaar there is a *panwala* who curses you day and night. You owe him twenty rupees ten annas for the cigarettes he sold you on credit.'

It was humiliating.

Mammad Bhai patted his moustache and smiled.

'Vimto bhai, you are not to worry. All your debts have been paid. You can start with a clean slate. I have warned these *salas* never to bother you. You have Mammad Bhai's word.'

That was nice of him, but since I was not feeling too good after my shot, all I could manage to murmur was, 'Mammad Bhai, may God bless you.'

Mammad Bhai gave his moustache another twirl and left.

Dr Pinto came twice a day, but when asked what he was owed, he would say: 'No, Mr Manto, it is between Mammad Bhai and me. I wouldn't dream of charging you.'

It was comical. The doctor was paying for my treatment.

Mammad Bhai himself came daily, sometimes in the morning, sometimes later, but never without five or six of his *shagirds*. 'You are going to get better. It is only *sala* malaria,' he would console me.

In about two weeks, I was back on my feet. By now, I had come to know Mammad Bhai quite well. He was between twenty-five and thirty and a fast mover. Arab Gulli residents swore that when he threw his dagger at an enemy, it went straight through the unfortunate man's heart.

One day, I ran into him outside one of the Chinese restaurants in Arab Gulli.

I said to him: 'Mammad Bhai, this is the age of guns and revolvers. Why do you go around with this dagger?'

Mammad Bhai touched his moustache and replied: 'Vimto bhai, guns are boring. Even a child can fire them. What is the point? All you do is press the trigger and bang they go. But daggers and knives ... by God it is fun using them. What was that you once said? Yes, art. It is an art.

'What is a revolver? Nothing but a toy. But look at this dagger and how sharp it is.' He wet his thumb and ran it lovingly over the edge. 'It makes no sound. Just push it into the belly and the *sala* doesn't even so much as squirm. Guns are rubbish.'

Whenever I tried to thank him for what he had done for me, he would say: 'What favour are you talking about?'

In the eyes of the law, he was a *dada*, a *goonda*, but what I could not understand then — and do not understand now — was why he was considered dangerous. There was nothing dangerous about him, except his moustache.

Somebody once told me that Mammad Bhai always massaged his moustache after each meal with butter, because it was guaranteed to provide nourishment to the hair. So, the real Mammad Bhai was either the moustache or the dagger?

The prostitutes of the area treated him like a *pir*, and as he was the acknowledged *dada*, it was only natural for him to have a mistress or two among them, but my enquiries had failed to reveal any such liaison.

One morning, while I was on my way to work, I heard in the Chinese restaurant that Mammad Bhai had been arrested. This was surprising because he had influence with the local police.

I asked around and was told that an Arab Gulli woman, Shirin Bai, who had a young daughter, had gone to Mammad Bhai the day before in a distraught state. Her daughter had been raped. 'You are the *dada* and my daughter has been raped. What are you going to do about it? Sit at home?' she had screamed.

Mammad Bhai had first abused the old woman, then asked, 'What do you want me to do? Go rip open that bastard's stomach?'

Finally, he had pulled out his dagger, run his finger along the sharp, glittering edge and said, 'Go home. The necessary will be done.'

The necessary was done within half an hour. The man who had raped the old woman's daughter was stabbed to death.

Mammad Bhai was arrested, but he had done the job so quickly and with such care that no witnesses could be found. And in any case, even if there had been witnesses, none would have testified against Mammad Bhai in court. He was bailed out.

He had spent two days in the lockup, but had been kept in comfort. The police constables and the inspectors knew him well. However, when he came out, one noticed that his brush with the law had been a big shock to him. Even his moustache looked somewhat droopy.

I met him in the Chinese restaurant. His clothes, normally so neat, looked shabby.

I did not mention the murder to him, but he himself said: 'Vimto sahib, I am sorry the *sala* took such a long time dying. It was all my fault. I did not stab him cleanly. I botched it.'

You can imagine my reaction. He was not sorry the man had died, but that he had not been able to dispatch him neatly and forthwith.

The court case was soon to come up and Mammad Bhai was worried. He had never seen the inside of a court in his life. I don't know if he had committed any murders before, but what I do know is that he simply had no idea what sort of birds magistrates, lawyers and witnesses were. They had never entered his life before.

One could see that he was worried. When the date for the first hearing was announced, Mammad Bhai said to me: 'Vimto sahib, I would sooner die than appear in court. I don't know what kind of a place it is.'

His Arab Gulli friends assured him that there was nothing to it. There were no witnesses and the only thing which might go against him would be his moustache. It might prejudice the magistrate.

As I have said, had it not been for his moustache, Mammad Bhai could never have been mistaken for a *dada*.

As the date approached, Mammad Bhai began to show unmistakable signs of anxiety. When I met him in the Iranian café, his agitation was obvious. His friends had told him: 'Mammad Bhai, if you have to go to court, then for God's sake do something about that moustache. One look and the magistrate will jail you.'

One day, while we were sitting in the Iranian café, he pulled out his dagger and threw it into the street. 'Mammad Bhai,' I exclaimed, 'what have you done?'

'Vimto bhai, everything is going downhill. I have to appear in court. Everybody tells me that one look at my moustache and the *sala* magistrate would convict me. What do I do?'

I could not help feeling what a criminal his moustache made him look. Finally, I said: 'Mammad Bhai, your moustache is most likely to affect your chances in court. The decision will not be so much against you as your moustache.'

'Should I then get rid of it?' he asked, running his hand lovingly over the offending feature.

'If you want to,' I replied.

'It is not what I want, it is what everybody seems to think I should do to make a good impression on the *sala* magistrate. What do you think, Vimto bhai?'

'Well, get it over and done with then,' I replied.

The next day Mammad Bhai had his moustache shaved off, since that had been the universal advice.

His case was heard in the court of Mr F.H. Tail. He appeared without his moustache. There were no prosecution witnesses, but the magistrate nevertheless declared him a dangerous *goonda* and ordered him out of the province of Bombay. He was given just one day to settle his affairs.

When we got out of the court, we said nothing to each other. Involuntarily, his fingers rose to his face, but there was no longer anything there to caress.

In the evening, we met in the Iranian café. About twenty of his *shagirds* sat around him drinking tea. He did not greet me when I entered. He looked very harmless. And he was depressed.

'What's on your mind?' I asked.

He swore loudly, then added thoughtfully, 'The Mammad Bhai you knew is dead.'

'What does it matter, Mammad Bhai — one has to live. If not in Bombay, then elsewhere,' I said.

He began to abuse everything under the sun. '*Sala*, I am not bothered where I live. What bothers me is why I got my moustache shaved off.'

Then he began to abuse everyone who had persuaded him to get rid of his moustache. 'If I had to be exiled from the province anyway, I should have gone with, not without, my moustache.'

I couldn't help laughing. '*Sala*, what sort of a man are you, Vimto? God is my witness, I wouldn't have cared if they'd hanged me. But look at me now. *Sala*. I got terrified of my own moustache.'

Then he beat his breast with both hands and cried: 'A curse on you, *sala* Mammad Bhai. Scared of your own moustache. Go sleep with your mother.'

Tears welled up in his eyes, an odd sight on an egg-smooth face.

Siraj

There was a small park facing the Nagpara police post and an Iranian teahouse next to it. Dhondoo was always to be found in this area, leaning against a lamp-post, waiting for custom.

Nobody knew his real name, but everyone called him Dhondoo — the one who searches and finds — which was most appropriate because his business consisted of procuring women of every type and description for his clients.

He had been in the trade for the last ten years and during this period hundreds of women had passed through his hands, women of every religion, race and temperament.

This had always been his hang-out, the lamp-post facing the Iranian teahouse which stood in front of the Nagpara police headquarters. The lamp-post had become his trade mark. Often, when I passed that way and saw the lamp-post, I felt as if I was actually looking at Dhondoo, besmeared like him with betel juice and much the worse for wear.

The lamp-post was tall, and so was Dhondoo. A number of power lines ran in various directions from the top of this ugly steel column into adjoining buildings, shops and even other lamp-posts.

The telephone department had tagged on a small terminal to the post and technicians could be seen checking it out from time to time. Sometimes I felt that Dhondoo was also a kind of terminal, attached to the lamp-post to verify the sexual signals of his customers. He not only knew the locals, but even some of the big *seths* of the city would come to him of an evening to get their sexual cables straightened out.

He knew almost all the women in the profession. He had intimate knowledge of their bodies, since they constituted the wares he transacted, and he was familiar with their temperaments. He knew exactly which woman would please which customer. But there was one exception — Siraj. He just had not been able to fathom her out.

Dhondoo had often said to me: 'Manto sahib, this one is off her rocker. I just cannot make her out. Never seen a *chokri* like her. She is so changeable. When you think she is happy and laughing her head off, just as suddenly she bursts into tears. She simply cannot get along with anyone. Fights with every "passenger". I have told her a million times to sort herself out, but it has had absolutely no effect on her. Many times I have had to tell her to go back to wherever she first came from to Bombay. Have you seen her? She has practically nothing to wear and not a penny to her name, and yet she simply will not play ball with the men I bring her. What an obstinate, mixed-up piece of work!'

I had seen Siraj a few times. She was slim and rather pretty. Her eyes were like outsize windows in her oval face. You simply could not get away from them. When I saw her for the first time on Clare Road, I felt like saying to her eyes: 'Would you please step aside for a minute so that I can see this girl?'

She was slight and yet there was so much of her. She reminded me of a glass goblet which had been filled to the brim with strong, under-diluted spirits, and the restlessness showed. I say strong spirits because there was something sharp and tangy about her personality. And yet I felt that in this heady mixture someone had added a bit of water to soften the fire. Her femininity was strong, despite her somewhat irate manner. Her hair was thick and her nose was aquiline. Her fingers reminded me of the sharpened pencils draughtsmen use. She gave the impression of being slightly annoyed with everything, with Dhondoo and the lamp-post he always stood against, with the gifts he brought her and even with her big eyes which ran away with her face.

But these are the impressions of a story-teller. Dhondoo had his own views. One day he said to me: 'Manto sahib, guess what that *sali* Siraj did today? Boy, am I lucky! Had it not been for God's mercy and the fact that the Nagpara police are always kind to me, I would have found myself in the jug. And that could have been one big, blooming disaster.'

'What happened?'

'The usual. I don't know what the matter with me is. I must be off my head. It is not the first time she has got me in a spot and yet I continue to carry her along. I should just wash my hands of her. She is neither my sister nor my mother that I should be running around trying to get her a living. Seriously, Manto sahib, I no longer know what to do.'

We were both sitting in the Iranian teahouse, sipping tea. Dhondoo poured from his cup into the saucer and began slurping up the special mixture he always blended with coffee. 'The fact is that I feel sorry for this *sali* Siraj.'

'Why?'

'God knows why. I wish I did.' He finished his tea and put the cup back on the saucer, upside down. 'Did you know she is still a virgin?'

'No, I didn't, Dhondoo.'

Dhondoo felt the scepticism in my voice and he didn't like it. 'I am not lying to you, Manto sahib. She is a hundred per cent virgin. You want to bet on that?'

'How's that possible?' I asked.

'Why not? A girl like Siraj. I tell you she could stay in this profession the rest of her life and still be a virgin. The thing is she simply does not let anyone so much as touch her. I know her whole bloody history. I know that she comes from Punjab. She used to be on Lymington Road in the private house run by that memsahib, but was thrown out because of her endless bickerings with the "passengers". I am surprised she lasted three months there, but that was because madam had about twenty girls at the time. But Manto sahib, how long can people feed you? One day madam pushed her out of the house with nothing on her except the clothes she was wearing. Then she moved to that other madam on Faras Road. She did not change her ways and one day she actually bit a passenger.

'She lasted no more than a couple of months there. I don't know what is wrong with her. She is full of life and nobody can cool it. From Faras Road she found her way into a hotel in Khetwari and created the usual trouble. One day the manager gave her her marching orders. What can I say, Manto sahib, the *sali* doesn't seem to be interested in anything — clothes, food, ornaments, you name it. Doesn't bathe for months until lice start crawling over her clothes. If someone gives her hash, she smokes a couple of joints happily. Sometimes I see her standing outside a hotel, listening to music.'

'Why don't you send her back? I mean it's obvious she's not interested in the business. I'll pay her fare if you like,' I suggested.

Dhondoo didn't like it. 'Manto sahib, it's not a question of paying the *sali*'s fare. I can do that. Won't kill me.'

'Then why don't you send her back?'

He lit a cigarette which he had tucked above his ear, drew on it deeply, exhaled the smoke through his nose and said: 'I don't want her to go.'

'Do you love her?' I asked.

'What are you talking about, Manto sahib!' He touched both his ears. 'I swear by the Quran that such a vile thought has never entered my head. It is just . . . just that I like her a bit.'

'Why?'

'Because she's not like the others who are only interested in money — the whole damn lot of them. This one is different. When I make a deal on her behalf, she goes most willingly. I put her in a taxi with the passenger and off they go.

'Manto sahib, passengers come for a good time. They spend money. They want to see what they are getting and like to feel it with their hands. And that's when the trouble starts. She doesn't let anyone even touch her. Starts hitting them. If it's a gentleman, he slinks away quietly. If it's the other kind, then there's hell to pay. I have to return the money and go down on my hands and knees. I swear on the Quran. And why do I do it? Only for Siraj's sake. Manto sahib, I swear on your head that because of this *sali*, my business has been reduced by half.'

One day I decided to see Siraj without Dhondoo's good offices. I was curious. She lived in one of the filthiest slums of Bombay. The streets were almost impassable because of garbage heaps. The city had constructed a lot of tin huts for the poor. She lived in one of them.

Outside her door a goat was tethered. It bleated when I approached. An old woman hobbled out, bent over her stick. I was about to leave when, through a hole in the coarse length of tattered cloth which hung over the door and served as a curtain, I saw large eyes in an oblong face.

She had recognized me. She must have been doing something, but she came out. 'What are you doing here?' she asked.

'I wanted to meet you.'

'Come in.'

'No, I want you to come with me.'

The old woman said: 'That'll cost you ten rupees.'

I pulled out my wallet and gave her the money. 'Come,' I said to Siraj.

She looked at me with those big window-like eyes of hers.

It once again occurred to me that she was pretty, but in a withdrawn, frozen kind of way, like a mummified but perfectly preserved queen.

I took her to a hotel. There she sat in front of me in her not-quite-clean clothes, staring at the world through eyes which were so big that her entire personality had become secondary to them.

I gave Siraj forty rupees.

She was quiet and to make a pass at her, I had to drink something quickly. After four large whiskies, I put my hands on her like passengers are expected to, but she showed me no resistance. Then I did something quite lewd and was sure she would go up like a keg of gunpowder but, surprisingly, she did not react at all. She just looked at me with her big eyes. 'Get me a joint,' she said.

'Take a drink,' I suggested.

'No, I want a joint.'

I sent for one. It was easy to get. She began to drag on it like experienced hash smokers. Her eyes had somehow lost their overpowering presence. Her face looked like a ravaged city. Every line, every feature suggested devastation. But what was this devastation? Had she been ravaged before even becoming whole? Had her world been destroyed long before the foundations could be raised?

Whether she was a virgin or not, I didn't care. But I wanted to talk to her, and she did not seem interested. I wanted her to fight with me, but she was simply indifferent.

In the end, I took her home.

When Dhondoo came to learn of my secret foray, he was upset. His feelings, both as a friend and a man of business, had been hurt. He never gave me an opportunity to explain. All he said was: 'Manto sahib, this I did not expect of you.' And he walked away.

I didn't see him the next day. I thought he was ill, but he did not appear the day after either. One week passed. Twice a day I used to go to work past Dhondoo's headquarters and whenever I saw the lamp-post I thought of him.

I even went looking for Siraj one day, only to be greeted by the old woman there. When I asked her about Siraj, she smiled the million-year-old smile of the procuress and said: 'That one's gone, but I can always get you another.'

The question was where was she. Had she run away with Dhondoo? But that was quite impossible. They were not in love and Dhondoo was not that sort of person. He had a wife and children whom he loved. But the question was where had they disappeared to?

I thought that maybe Dhondoo had finally decided that Siraj should go home, a decision he had always been ambivalent about. One month passed.

Then one evening, as I was passing by the Iranian teahouse, I saw him leaning against his lamp-post. When he saw me, he smiled.

We went into the teahouse. I did not ask him anything. He sent for his special tea, mixed with coffee, and ordered plain tea for me. He turned around in his chair and it seemed as if he was going to make some dramatic disclosure, but all he said was: 'And how are things, Manto sahib?'

'Life goes on, Dhondoo,' I replied.

'You are right, life goes on,' he smiled. 'It's a strange world, isn't it?'

'You can say that again.'

We kept drinking tea. Dhondoo poured his into the saucer, took a sip and said: 'Manto sahib, she told me the whole story. She said to me that that friend of mine, meaning you, was crazy.'

I laughed. 'Why?'

'She told me that you took her to a hotel, gave her a lot of money and didn't do what she thought you would do.'

'That was the way it was, Dhondoo,' I said.

He laughed. 'I know. I'm sorry if I showed annoyance that day. In any case, that whole business is now over.'

'What business?'

'That Siraj business, what else?'

'What happened?'

'You remember the day you took her out? Well, she came to me later and said that she had forty rupees on her and would I take her to Lahore. I said to her: "*Sali*, what has come over you?" She said: "Come on Dhondoo, for my sake, take me." And Manto sahib, you know I could never say no to her. I liked her. So I said: "OK, if that's what you want."

'We bought train tickets and arrived in Lahore. She knew what hotel we were going to stay in.

'The next day she says to me: "Dhondoo, get me a *burqa*." I went out and got her one. And then our rounds began. She would leave in the morning and spend the entire day on the streets of Lahore in a *tonga*, with me keeping company. She wouldn't tell me what she was looking for.

'I said to myself: "Dhondoo, have you gone bananas? Why did you have to come with this crazy girl all the way from Bombay?"

'Then, Manto sahib, one day, she asked me to stop the *tonga* in the middle of the street. "Do you see that man there? Can you bring him to me? I am going to the hotel. Now."

'I was confused, but I stepped down from the *tonga* and began to follow the man she had pointed out. Well, by the grace of God, I am a good judge of men. I began to talk to him and it did not take me long to find out that he was game for a good time.

'I said to him: "I have a very special brand of goods from Bombay." He wanted me to take him with me right away, but I said: "Not that fast, friend, show me the colour of your money." He brandished a thick wad of bank notes in my face. What I couldn't understand was why, of all the men in Lahore, Siraj had picked this one out. In any case, I said to myself: "Dhondoo, everything goes." We took a *tonga* to the hotel.

'I went in and told Siraj I had the man waiting outside. She said: "Bring him in but don't go away." When I brought him in and he saw her, he wanted to run away, but Siraj grabbed hold of him.'

'She grabbed hold of him?'

'That's right. She grabbed hold of the *sala* and said to him: "Where are you going? Why did you make me run away from home? You knew I loved you. And remember you had said to me that you loved me too. But when I left my house and my parents and my brothers and my sisters and came with you from Amritsar to Lahore and stayed in this very hotel, you abandoned me the same night. You left while I was asleep. Why did you bring me here? Why did you make me run away from home? You know, I was prepared for everything and you let me down. But I have come back and found you. I still love you. Nothing has changed."

'And Manto sahib, she threw her arms around him. That *sala* began to cry. He was asking her to forgive him. He was saying he had done her wrong. He had got cold feet. He was saying he would never leave her again. He kept repeating he would never leave her again. God knows what rot he was talking.

'Then Siraj asked me to leave the room. I lay on a bare cot outside and went to sleep at some point. When she woke me up, it was morning. "Dhondoo," she said, "let's go." "Where?" I asked. She said: "Let's go back to Bombay." I said: "Where is that *sala*?" "He is sleeping, I have covered his face with my *burqa*," she replied.

Dhondoo ordered himself another cup of tea mixed with coffee. I looked up and saw Siraj enter the hotel. Her oval face was glowing, but her two big eyes looked like fallen train signals.

The Room with the Bright Light

He stood quietly by a lamp-post off the Qaiser Gardens, thinking how desolate everything looked. A few *tongas* waited for customers who were nowhere in evidence.

A few years ago, this used to be such a gay place, full of bright, happy, carefree men and women, but everything seemed to have gone to seed. The area was now full of louts and vagabonds with nowhere to go. The bazaar still had its crowds, but it had lost its colour. The shops and buildings looked derelict and unwashed, staring at each other like empty-eyed widows.

He stood there wondering what had turned the once-fashionable Qaiser Gardens into a slum. Where had all the life and excitement gone? It reminded him of a woman who had been scrubbed clean of all her make-up.

He remembered that many years ago when he had moved to Bombay from Calcutta to take up a job, he had tried vainly for weeks to find a room in this area. There was nothing going.

How times had changed. Judging by the kind of people in the streets, just anybody could rent a place here now — weavers, cobblers, grocers.

He looked around again. What used to be film company offices were now bed-sitters with cooking stoves, and where the elegant people of the city used to gather in the evenings had been turned into washermen's backyards.

It was nothing short of a revolution, but a revolution which had brought decay. In between, he had left the city, but knew through newspaper reports and friends who had stayed back what had happened to Qaiser Gardens in his absence.

There had been riots, accompanied by massacres and rapes. The violence Qaiser Gardens had witnessed had left its ugly mark on everything. The once splendid commercial buildings and residential houses looked sordid and unclean.

He was told that during the riots women had been stripped naked and their breasts chopped off. Was it then surprising that everything looked naked and ravaged?

He was here this evening to meet a friend who had promised to find him a place to live.

Qaiser Gardens used to have some of the city's best restaurants and hotels. And if one was that way inclined, the best girls in Bombay could be obtained through the good offices of the city's high class pimps who used to hang out here.

He recalled the good times he had here in those days. He thought nostalgically of the women, the drinking, the elegant hotel rooms! Because of the war, it was almost impossible to obtain Scotch whisky, but he had never had to spend a dry evening. Any amount of expensive Scotch was yours for the asking, as long as you were able to pay for it.

He looked at his watch. It was going on five. The shadows of the February evening had begun to lengthen. He cursed his friend who had kept him waiting. He was about to slip into a roadside place for a cup of tea when a shabbily dressed man came up to him.

'Do you want something?' he asked the stranger.

'Yes,' he replied in a conspiratorial voice.

He took him for a refugee who had fallen on bad times and wanted some money. 'What do you want?' he asked.

'I don't want anything.' He paused, then drew closer and said: 'Do you need something?'

'What?'

'A girl, for instance?'

'Where is she?'

His tone was none too encouraging for the stranger, who began to walk away. 'It seems you are not really interested.'

He stopped him. 'How do you know? What you can provide is something men are always in need of, even on the gallows. So look, my friend, if it is not too far, I am prepared to come with you. You see I was waiting for someone who hasn't turned up.'

The man whispered: 'It is close, very close, I assure you.'

'Where?'

'That building across from us.'

'You mean that one?' he asked.

'Yes.'

'Should I come with you?'

'Yes, but please walk behind me.' They crossed the road. It was a run-down building with the plaster peeling off the walls and rubbish heaps littering the entrance.

They went through a courtyard and then through a dark corridor. It seemed that construction had been abandoned at some point before completion. The bricks in the walls were unplastered and there were piles of lime mixed with cement on the floor.

The man began to ascend a flight of dilapidated stairs. 'Please wait here. I'll be back in a minute,' he said.

He looked up and saw a bright light at the end of the landing.

He waited for a couple of minutes and then began to climb the stairs. When he reached the landing, he heard the man who had brought him screaming: 'Are you going to get up or not?'

A woman's voice answered: 'Just let me sleep.'

The man screamed again: 'You heard me, are you getting up or not? Or you know what I'll do to you.'

The woman's voice again: 'You can kill me but I won't get up. For God's sake have mercy on me.'

The man changed his tone: 'Darling, don't be obstinate. How are we going to make a living if you don't get up?'

'Living be damned. I'll starve to death, but for God's sake, don't drag me out of bed. I'm sleepy,' answered the woman.

The man began to roar with anger: 'So you're not going to leave your bed, you bitch, you filthy bitch ... !'

The woman shouted back: 'I won't, I won't, I won't!'

The man changed his tone again: 'Don't shout like that. The whole world can hear you. Come on now, get up. We could make thirty, even forty rupees.'

The woman began to whimper: 'I beg of you, don't make me go. You know how many days and nights I have gone without sleep. Have pity on me, please.'

'It won't be long,' the man said, 'just a couple of hours and then you can sleep as long as you like. Look, don't make me use other methods to persuade you.'

There was a brief silence. He crossed the landing on tip-toe and peeped into the room where the very bright light was coming from. It was not much of a room. There were a few empty cooking pots on the floor and a woman stretched out in the middle with the man he had come with crouching over her. He was pressing her legs and saying: 'Be a good girl now. I promise you, we'll be back in two hours and then you can sleep to your heart's content.'

He saw the woman suddenly get up like a firecracker which has been shown a match. 'All right,' she said, 'I'll come.'

He was suddenly afraid and ran down the stairs. He wanted to put as much distance between this place and himself as he could, between himself and this city.

He thought of the woman who wanted to sleep. Who was she? Why was she being treated with such inhumanity?

And who was that man? Why was the room so unremittingly bright? Did they both live there? Why did they live there?

His eyes were still partly blinded by the dazzling light bulb in that terrible room upstairs. He couldn't see very well. Couldn't they have hung a softer light in the room? Why was it so nakedly, pitilessly bright?

There was a noise in the dark and a movement. All he could see were two silhouettes, one of them obviously that of the man whom he had followed to this awful place.

'Take a look,' he said.

'I have,' he replied.

'Is she all right?'

'She is all right.'

'That will be forty rupees.'

'All right.'

'Can I have the money?'

He could no longer think clearly. He put his hand in his pocket, pulled out a fistful of bank notes and handed them over. 'Count them,' he said.

'There's fifty there.'

'Keep it.'

'Thank you.'

He had an urge to pick up a big stone and bash in his head.

'Please take her, but be nice to her and bring her back in a couple of hours.'

'OK.'

He walked out of the building with the woman, found a *tonga* waiting outside. He jumped quickly in the front. The woman took the back seat.

The *tonga* began to move. He asked him to stop in front of a ramshackle, customerless hotel. They went in. He took his first look at the woman. Her eyes were red and swollen. She looked so tired that he was afraid she would fall to the floor in a heap.

'Raise your head,' he said to her.

'What?' she was startled.

'Nothing, all I said was raise your head.'

She looked up. Her eyes were like empty holes topped up with ground chilli.

'What is your name?' he asked.

'Never mind.' Her tone was like acid.

'Where are you from?'

'What does it matter?'

'Why are you so unfriendly?'

The woman was now wide awake. She stared at him with her blood-red eyes and said: 'You finish your business because I have to go.'

'Where?'

'Where you picked me up from,' she answered indifferently.

'You are free to go.'

'Why don't you finish your business? Why are you trying to ridicule me?'

'I'm not trying to ridicule you. I feel sorry for you,' he said in a sympathetic voice.

'I want no sympathizers. You do whatever you brought me here for and then let me go,' she almost screamed.

He tried to put his hand on her shoulder, but she shook it off rudely.

'Leave me alone. I haven't slept for days. I've been awake ever since I came to that place.'

'You can sleep here.'

'I didn't come here to sleep. This isn't my home.'

'Is that room your home?'

This seemed to have infuriated her even more.

'Cut out the rubbish. I have no home. You do your job or take me back. You can have your money returned by that . . .'

'All right, I'll take you back,' he said.

The next day he told the story of his encounter to his

friend who hadn't turned up for the appointment. He was quite moved. 'Was she young?' he asked.

'I don't know,' he replied. 'The fact is that I didn't really look at her. I only had this savage desire to kill that man who took me to her.'

They parted because his friend had to go somewhere. He felt morbidly depressed.

He walked towards Qaiser Gardens, his eyes scanning the area, looking for that man, but he was nowhere to be seen. It was already evening. Across the road, he could see the building. Involuntarily, he began to walk towards it.

He went through the courtyard and found himself at the bottom of the dilapidated stairs. He looked up. There was a bright light in the room at the top of the landing. He began to go up, one step at a time. It was very quiet. No voices, nothing.

The door was open. He peeped in. The first thing which hit him was the blinding light from the naked bulb. He turned away his face abruptly to get the dazzle away from his eyes.

Shading them with his hand, he looked through the open door again. A woman was asleep on the floor, her face covered with a thin sheet, her bosom gently rising and falling as she breathed rhythmically. He half stepped into the room and nearly screamed.

Next to the woman, on the bare floor, lay a man, his head bashed into a pulp with a bloodied brick.

He rushed out, slipped and crashed down the stairs. But he did not stop to examine his injuries. Like a madman, he ran out of the courtyard and into the dark street.

A Man of God

Chaudhry Maujoo sat on a string cot under a leafy pipal tree, smoking his hookah. The afternoon was hot, but a gentle breeze blew across the fields, wafting the blue smoke away.

He had been ploughing his field since early morning, but was quite tired now. The sun was harsh, but it did not seem to bother him. He was enjoying his well-earned rest.

He sat there waiting for his only daughter Jeena to bring him his midday meal — baked bread and buttermilk. She was always on time, though there was nobody to help her with the housework. He had divorced her mother in a fit of temper about two years ago after a bitter domestic fight.

Jeena was a very obedient daughter who took good care of her father. She was never idle. When household chores were done, she would occupy herself with her spinning wheel. Only occasionally would she gossip with her friends.

Chaudhry Maujoo did not have much land, but it was enough to take care of his modest needs. The village was small and the nearest railway station was miles away. A mud road linked it to another village to which Chaudhry Maujoo rode twice a month to buy provisions.

He used to be a happy man, but since his divorce it had often troubled him that he had no other children. However, being a very religious man, he had managed to console himself with the thought that it was God's will.

His faith was deep, but he knew very little about religion,

except that there was no God but God and He must be worshipped, and Mohammad was His Prophet and The Quran was God's word revealed to Mohammad. That was all.

He had never fasted or prayed. In fact the village was so small that it did not even have a mosque. The people prayed at home and were generally God-fearing. Every household had a copy of the Quran but nobody knew how to read. It was kept wrapped up on the top shelf, to be used only when someone was required to take an oath.

A *maulvi* would be invited to the village to solemnize marriages. Funeral prayers were offered by the villagers themselves — not in Arabic, but in their own language, Punjabi.

Chaudhry Maujoo was much in demand on such occasions. He had developed a style of his own for funeral orations.

For instance, the year before when his friend Dinoo had lost his son, Chaudhry Maujoo had addressed the villagers after the body had been lowered into the grave.

'What a strong handsome young man he was! When he spat, it landed at a distance of twenty yards and he had such strength in his abdomen that he could urinate farther than any other young man in the village. He never lost an arm-wrestling competition. He could fight free of a hold as easily as you unbutton a shirt.

'Dinoo my friend, for you judgment day is already here. I doubt if you will survive it. I think you should die, because how are you going to live through this great shock! Oh what a handsome young man your son was. I know for a fact that Neeti, the goldsmith's daughter, cast many spells on him to win his love but he spurned her. He was not tempted by her youth and beauty. May God grant him a houri in paradise and may he remain as untempted by her as he was by Neeti the goldsmith's daughter. God bless his soul.'

This brief address was so effectively delivered that everyone broke down, including Chaudhry Maujoo himself.

When Maujoo decided to divorce his wife, he did not
bother to send for a *maulvi*. He had heard from his elders
that all it required was for the man to say thrice: I divorce
you. And that was exactly what he had done. He had felt
sorry the next day and even a bit ashamed of himself. It was
no more serious than everyday quarrels between husband
and wife and should not have ended in divorce.

It was not that he wasn't fond of Phatan, his wife. He
liked her, and though she was no longer young, her body
was still well-preserved. What was more, she was the
mother of his daughter. But he had made no effort to get
her back and life had gone on.

Jeena was beautiful like her mother was in her youth and
in two years she had grown from a little girl into a young
and luscious woman. He often worried about her marriage
and on such occasions he particularly missed his wife.

He was still reclining on his string cot, enjoying his
smoke, when he heard a voice: 'May the blessings and
peace of God be upon you.'

He turned round and found an old man with a flowing
beard and shoulder-length hair, all dressed in white, standing there. Maujoo greeted him, wondering where he had
materialized from.

The man was tall and his eyes were the most striking
feature of his face — large and tinged with black Indian eye
shadow. He wore a big white turban on his head and a
yellow silk scarf was thrown over one of his shoulders. He
held a silver-headed staff in his hand. His shoes were made
of soft leather.

Chaudhry Maujoo was immediately impressed. In fact
he felt a deep respect, bordering on awe, for this imposing
elderly figure. He rose from his cot and said: 'Where did
you come from and when?'

The man smiled: 'We men of God come from nowhere

and have no home to go to. No particular moment is
ordained for our arrival and none for our departure. It is the
Lord who directs us to move in fulfilment of His will and it
is the Lord who orders us to break our journey at a particular point.'

Chaudhry Maujoo was deeply affected by these words.
He took the holy man's hand, kissed it with great reverence
and put it to his eyes. 'My humble house is yours,' he said.

The holy man smiled and sat down on the cot. He held
his silver-tipped staff in both hands, and resting his head
against it said: 'Who can say what particular deed of yours
found approval in the eyes of the Lord that he directed this
sinner to come to you?'

Chaudhry Maujoo asked: 'Maulvi sahib, have you come
to me on orders from the Lord?'

The holy man raised his head and said in an angry tone:
'And do you think we came at your orders? Do we obey you
or that supreme being whom we have humbly worshipped
for forty years and can at last count ourselves among those
He has chosen to favour?'

Chaudhry Maujoo was terrified. In his simple, rustic
manner he whimpered: 'Maulvi sahib, we illiterate people
know nothing about these matters. We do not even know
how to say our prayers. Were it not for men of God like you,
we would never find forgiveness in His eyes.'

'And that's why we are here,' the holy man said, his eyes
half-shut.

Chaudhry Maujoo sat down on the ground and began to
press his visitor's legs. Presently, Jeena appeared with his
food. When she saw the stranger, she covered her face.

'Who is that, Chaudhry Maujoo?'

'My daughter Jeena, Maulvi sahib.'

Maulvi sahib glanced at Jeena through slanted eyes:
'Ask her why she is hiding her face from holy mendicants
like us?'

'Jeena,' he said to his daughter, 'Maulvi sahib is God's

special emissary. Uncover your face.'

Jeena did what she was told. Maulvi sahib sized her up and said: 'Your daughter is beautiful, Chaudhry Maujoo.'

Jeena blushed. 'She takes after her mother,' Maujoo said.

'Where is her mother?' Maulvi sahib asked, surveying Jeena's young and virginal body.

Chaudhry Maujoo hesitated, not knowing how to answer that.

'Where is her mother?' Maulvi sahib asked again.

'She is dead,' Maujoo replied hurriedly.

Maulvi sahib looked at Jeena, carefully noting her startled reaction. Then he thundered: 'You are lying.'

Maujoo fell at his feet and said in a guilty voice: 'Yes, I told you a lie. Please forgive me. I am a liar. The truth is that I divorced her, Maulvi sahib.'

'You are a great sinner. What was the fault of that poor woman?'

'I don't know, Maulvi sahib. It was really nothing, but it ended up in my divorcing her. I am indeed a very sinful man. I realized my error the very next day, but by then it was too late. She had already returned to her parents.'

Maulvi sahib touched Maujoo's shoulder with his silver-tipped staff and said: 'God is great and He is merciful and kind. All wrongs can be righted if He wishes. And if that is His command, perhaps this servant of His will be empowered to lead you to your salvation and find you forgiveness.'

A grateful and totally humiliated Chaudhry Maujoo threw himself at Maulvi sahib's feet and began to weep. Maulvi sahib looked at Jeena and found tears rolling down her cheeks as well.

'Come here, girl,' he ordered.

There was such authority in his voice that she found it impossible not to obey. She placed the food aside and walked up to him. Maulvi sahib grabbed her arm and said: 'Sit down.'

She was about to sit on the ground, but Maulvi sahib pulled her to him. 'Sit next to me here,' he commanded.

Jeena sat down. Maulvi sahib put his arm around her waist and pressing her close, asked: 'And what have you brought for us?'

Jeena wanted to move away, but Maulvi sahib's hold was vice-like. 'I have some baked bread and buttermilk and some greens,' she said in a low voice.

Maulvi sahib squeezed her slim waist once again and said: 'Then go get it and feed us.'

As Jeena rose, Maulvi sahib struck Maujoo gently on the shoulder with his staff and said: 'Maujoo, help us wash our hands.'

Maujoo went to the well which was nearby and came back with a bucket of fresh water. He helped Maulvi sahib wash his hands like a true disciple. Jeena put the food in front of him.

Maulvi sahib ate everything. Then he ordered Jeena to pour water on his hands. She obeyed, such was the authority of his manner.

Maulvi sahib belched loudly, thanked God even more loudly, ran his wet hand over his beard and lay down on the cot. With one eye he watched Jeena, and with the other her father. She picked up the utensils she had brought the food in and left. Maulvi sahib said to maujoo: 'Chaudhry, we are going to take a nap.'

Chaudhry Maujoo pressed his legs and feet for some time and when he was sure he had fallen asleep, he stepped aside and warmed up his hookah. He was very happy. He felt as if a great weight had been lifted off his chest. In his heart, he thanked God in his simple words for having sent to him, in the form of Maulvi sahib, one of His angels of mercy.

He sat there for some time, watching Maulvi sahib resting, then he returned to his field and got down to work. He hadn't even noticed his hunger. In fact he was thrilled that the honour of feeding Maulvi sahib with food meant for him had fallen to his lot.

When he returned in the evening, he was gravely disappointed to see Maulvi sahib gone. He cursed himself. By walking off, he had offended that man of God. Perhaps he had put a curse on him before leaving. He trembled with fear and tears welled up in his eyes.

He looked for Maulvi sahib around the village but did not find him. The evening deepened into night, but there was no trace of Maulvi sahib. He was walking back to his house, his head down, feeling the weight of the world on his shoulders, when he came upon two boys from the village. They looked scared. First they wouldn't tell him what was wrong, but when he insisted they told him their story.

Some time earlier, they had brewed strong country liquor, put it in an earthen pitcher and buried it under a tree. That evening they had gone to the spot, unearthed their forbidden treasure and were about to imbibe it when an old man, whose face radiated a strange light, had suddenly appeared and asked them what they were doing.

He had admonished them for the evil deed they were about to commit. He had asked them how they could even think of drinking something which God Himself had forbidden men to touch. They had been so terrified that they had run away, leaving the earthen pitcher behind.

Chaudhry Maujoo told them that the old man with the radiant face was a holy man of God and since he had been offended, he was likely to put a curse on the entire village.

'May God save us my sons, may God save us my sons,' he murmured and began to walk back to his house. Jeena was home, but he did not speak to her. He was convinced that the village would not escape Maulvi sahib's wrath.

Jeena had prepared extra food for Maulvi sahib. 'Where is Maulvi sahib, father?' she asked. 'Gone ... he is gone. How could a man of God abide along with sinners like us?' he told her in a grief-stricken voice.

Jeena was sorry too because Maulvi sahib had promised he would find a way to have her mother come back. And now that he was gone, who was going to reunite her with her mother? Jeena sat down on a low stool. The food kept getting cold.

There was a sound of approaching feet at the door. Both father and daughter sprang up. Suddenly, Maulvi sahib entered. In the dim light of the earthen lamp, Jeena noticed that he was staggering. In his hands he held a small pitcher.

Maujoo helped him to a cot. Handing over the pitcher to him, Maulvi sahib said: 'God put us through a severe test today. We chanced upon two youngsters from your village who were about to commit the grave sin of drinking liquor. When we admonished them, they ran away. We were deeply grieved. So young, and in such deep mortal error. But we felt that their youth was to blame for what they were about to do. So we prayed in the heavenly court of the Lord that they be forgiven. And do you know what reply we received?'

'No,' Chaudhry Maujoo said, greatly moved.

'The reply was: are you prepared to face the consequences of their sin? And we said: yes, Almighty God. And then we heard a voice: you are commanded to drink this entire pitcher of liquor. We forgive the boys.'

Maujoo's hair stood on end. 'Did you then drink it?'

Maulvi sahib's tongue became even thicker. 'Yes, we drank to save the souls of those two young sinners and to gain merit in the eyes of God, who alone is to be honoured. There is still some left and that too we have been commanded to drink. Now put it away carefully and make sure that not a drop is wasted.'

Maujoo picked up the pitcher, secured its top with a clean length of cloth and took it into one of the small dark rooms of his modest house. When he returned, Maulvi sahib was sprawled on the cot and Jeena was massaging head. He was telling her: 'He who helps others wins the

Lord's favour. He is pleased with you at this moment ...
and we are pleased with you too.'

Then Maulvi sahib made her sit next to him and planted
a generous kiss on her forehead. She tried to get up, but was
unable to wrest herself free. Maulvi sahib then embraced
her and said to Maujoo: 'Chaudhry, I have awakened your
daughter's sleeping destiny.'

Maujoo was so overwhelmed that he couldn't even
express his gratitude properly. All he managed to say was:
'It is all a result of your prayers and your kindness.'

Maulvi sahib squeezed Jeena against his chest once
again and said: 'Truly, God has touched you with His grace.
Jeena, tomorrow we will teach you a holy prayer and if you
recite it regularly, you will forever find acceptance in the
eyes of the Lord.'

Maulvi sahib rose later the next day. Maujoo had not
gone to the fields, afraid he might be needed. Dutifully, he
waited and when Maulvi sahib was ready, he helped him
wash his face and hands and, in accordance with his wishes,
brought out the earthen pitcher.

Maulvi sahib mumbled a prayer, then he untied the
cloth which covered its top and blew into it three times. He
drank three large cups, mumbled another prayer, looked
up at the sky and declaimed: 'God, You will not find us
wanting in the test You have put us through.'

Then he addressed Maujoo: 'Chaudhry, we have just
received divine orders that you should proceed to your
wife's village and bring her back. The signal we were seek-
ing has come through.'

Maujoo was thrilled. He saddled his horse and promised
to be back by the next day. He instructed Jeena to leave
no stone unturned to keep Maulvi sahib happy and
comfortable.

After her father had left, Jeena got busy with housework.
Maulvi sahib kept drinking steadily. Then he produced a
thick rosary from his pocket and began to run it through his

fingers. When Jeena was finished, he ordered her to perform her ablutions.

Jeena replied innocently: 'Maulvi sahib, I don't know how to.'

Maulvi sahib reprimanded her gently on her lack of knowledge of essential religious practices. Then he began to teach her how to do her ablutions. This intricate exercise was performed with the help of close physical contact.

After the ablutions, Maulvi sahib asked for a prayer mat. There was none in the house. Maulvi sahib was not pleased. He told her to get him a clean bedsheet. He spread it on the floor of the inside room, summoned Jeena in and instructed her to bring the pitcher and cup with her.

Maulvi sahib poured out a large quantity and drank half of it. Then he started to run his rosary through his fingers, while Jeena watched in silence.

For a long time, Maulvi sahib was busy with his rosary. His eyes were closed. Then he blew into the cup three times and ordered Jeena to drink it.

Jeena took it with trembling hands. Maulvi sahib said in a thundering voice: 'We order you to drink it. All your pain and suffering will come to an end.'

Jeena lifted the cup to her lips and drank it down in one go. Maulvi sahib smiled. 'We are going to resume our special prayers, but when we raise our index finger, pour out half a cup from the pitcher and drink it.'

He did not allow her to react and went into a deep reverie. There was an awful taste in Jeena's mouth and a fire blazing in her chest. She wanted to get up and drink buckets of cold water, but she did not dare. Suddenly, Maulvi sahib's index finger rose. Hypnotized, she poured herself the ordained quantity and drank it in one gulp.

Maulvi sahib kept praying. She could hear the rosary beads rubbing against each other. Her head was spinning and she felt very sleepy. She had a vague, almost unconscious feeling that she was in the lap of a young, clean-shaven man who was telling her that he was taking her on a trip through paradise.

When she came to, she was lying on the floor inside the room. Blurry-eyed, she looked around. Why was she lying here and since when? Everything was in a mist. She wanted to go back to sleep, but she got up. Where was Maulvi sahib? And where had that paradise vanished to?

She walked into the open courtyard and was surprised to see that it was almost evening. Maulvi sahib was performing ablutions. He heard her and turned with a smile on his face. She went back to the room, sat down on the floor and began to think about her mother who was going to come home. There was only one night left. She was very hungry but she didn't want to cook. Her mind was full of strange and unanswered questions.

Suddenly, Maulvi sahib appeared at the door. 'We have to offer special prayers for your father. We will pray in a graveyard all night and return in the morning. We will be praying for you too.'

He appeared next morning. His eyes were very red and he stammered a little when he spoke. He wasn't steady on his feet either. He walked into the courtyard and hugged and kissed Jeena with great warmth. Jeena sat on a low stool in a corner trying to untangle the strange, half-remembered events of the last twenty-four hours. She wanted her father to return ... and her mother who had been gone for two years. And then there was that paradise ... what sort of paradise was it she had been taken to ... and the Maulvi sahib ... was it he who had taken her? It couldn't be because she remembered a young man who had no beard.

Maulvi sahib addressed her: 'Jeena, your father has not returned yet.'

She said nothing.

He spoke again: 'All night long he has been in our prayers. He should have returned by now ... with your mother.'

All Jeena could say was: 'I don't know. He should be on his way ... and mother too. I really don't know.'

The front door opened. Jeena rose. It was her mother. The two fell into each other's arms, weeping profusely. Maujoo followed his wife. With great respect, he greeted Maulvi sahib and then said to his wife: 'Phatan, you haven't greeted Maulvi sahib.'

Phatan disengaged herself from her daughter, wiped her eyes and greeted Maulvi sahib, who examined her through bloodshot eyes. 'We have been praying all night for you and have just returned. God has answered our prayers. All will be well.'

Chaudhry Maujoo sat down on the ground and began to press Maulvi sahib's feet. With a lump in his throat, he said to his wife: 'Phatan, come here and express your gratitude to Maulvi sahib. I don't know how to.'

Phatan came forward: 'We are poor and humble folk. There is nothing we can do for you, holy man of God.'

Maulvi sahib looked at her penetratingly. 'Maujoo Chaudhry, you were right. Your wife is beautiful and even at this age, she looks young. She is another Jeena, even better. We will set everything right, Phatan. God has decided to be kind and merciful to you.'

Chaudhry Maujoo kept pressing Maulvi sahib's feet, while Jeena got busy with cooking.

After a while, Maulvi sahib rose, patted Phatan's head affectionately and said to Maujoo: 'It is the Almighty's law that when a man divorces his wife and then wants to bring her back, he may not do so unless the woman first marries another man and is divorced by him to be reunited with her first husband.'

Maujoo said in a low voice: 'That I've heard, Maulvi sahib.'

Maulvi sahib asked him to rise, put his hand on his shoulder and said: 'Last night, we begged of the Almighty to spare you the punishment due to you because of your error. And the voice from beyond said: "How long are we going to accept your intercession on behalf of others? Ask something for yourself and it shall be granted." He begged again: "King of the universe, sovereign of all the lands and seas, we ask nothing for ourselves. You have given us enough. Maujoo Chaudhry is in love with his wife." And the voice said: "We are going to put his love and your faith to the test. You are to wed her for one day and divorce her the next and return her to Maujoo. That's all we can grant you, because for forty long years you have worshipped us faithfully."'

Maujoo was ecstatic. 'I accept, Maulvi sahib ... I accept.' The he looked at Phatan, his eyes shining with inner happiness. 'Right, Phatan?' He didn't wait for her answer. 'We both accept.'

Maulvi sahib closed his eyes, recited a prayer, blew it in their faces and raised his eyes heavenwards: 'God of all the skies, grant us the strength not to fail the test You are putting us through.'

Then he said to Maujoo: 'We are leaving now, but we want you and Jeena to go away somewhere for the night. We shall return later.'

When he came back in the evening, Jeena and Maujoo were ready to leave. Maulvi sahib was reciting something under his breath. He didn't speak to them, but made a sign that they were to leave. They left.

Maulvi sahib bolted the door and said to Phatan: 'For one night you are our wife. Go inside, get the bedding and spread it on this cot. We wish to take a nap.'

Phatan went inside, brought out the bedding and spread it neatly on the string cot. Maulvi sahib asked her to wait for him. He went inside.

An earthen lamp cast a shadowy light around the little room. The pitcher stood in a corner. Maulvi sahib shook it to see if there was anything left in it. There was. He raised the pitcher to his lips and took a few quick swigs. He wiped his mouth with his yellow silk scarf and went out.

Phatan sat on the cot. Maulvi sahib carried a cup in his hand. He blew some holy words on it thrice and offered it to Phatan: 'Drink it down.'

She drank and was almost immediately sick, but Maulvi sahib patted her on the back vigorously and said: 'You will be all right.' Then he lay down.

Next morning, when Jeena and Maujoo returned, they found Phatan sleeping on the cot in the courtyard. Maulvi sahib was not around. Maujoo thought he had gone for a walk in the fields. He woke up his wife, who opened her eyes and mumbled: 'Paradise ... paradise.' When she saw Maujoo, she sat up.

'Where is Maulvi sahib?' he asked.

Phatan was still a little groggy. 'Maulvi sahib, which Maulvi sahib ... I don't know where he is ... he is not here.'

'No,' Maujoo exclaimed, 'I'll go and look for him.'

He was at the door when he heard Phatan scream. She was fumbling with something she had found under the pillow.

'What is it?' she asked.

'Looks like hair,' Maujoo said.

Phatan threw away the black bunch on the floor. Maujoo picked it up, examined it and said: 'Looks like human hair.'

'Maulvi sahib's beard and shoulder-length hair,' Jeena exclaimed.

Maujoo was confused. 'And where is Maulvi sahib?' he asked. Then his simple and believing heart provided him with the answer. 'Jeena, Phatan — you don't understand. He was a man of God who could perform miracles. He brought us what our hearts desired and he has left us something of his person to remember him by.'

He kissed the false beard and hairpiece, touched his eyes with them reverently and handed them to Jeena. 'Go and wrap them up in a clean piece of cloth and place them on top of the big wooden chest. The grace of God shall never abandon the house.'

Jeena went in. Maujoo sat down next to Phatan and said: 'I am going to learn how to pray and I will remember that saint in my prayers every day.'

Phatan remained silent.

Mummy

Her name was Mrs Stella Jackson, but everyone called her mummy. A short, active woman in her middle years, her husband had been killed in the last great war. His pension still came every month.

I had no idea how long she had lived in Poona. The fact was that she was such a fascinating character that after meeting her once, such questions somehow became irrelevant. She herself was all that mattered. To say that she was an integral part of Poona may sound like an exaggeration, but as far as I am concerned, all my memories of that city are inextricably linked with her.

I am a very lazy person by nature, which is not to say that I do not dream about great travels. If you hear me talking, you would think I was about to set out to conquer the Kinchinchunga peak in the Himalayas. It is another matter that once I get there, I might decide not to move at all.

I can't really remember how many years I had been in Bombay when I decided one day to take my wife to Poona. Let me work it out. Our first child had been dead four years and it was another four years since I had moved to Bombay. So, actually, I had been living there for eight years, but not once had I taken the trouble to visit the famous Victoria Gardens or the museum. It was therefore quite unusual for me to get up one morning and take off for Poona. I had recently had a tiff at the film studio where I was employed as a writer. I wanted to get away — a change of scene, if you like. For one thing, Poona was not far and there were a number of my old movie friends living there.

We took a train, arrived, scampered out of the station and realized that the Parbhat Nagar suburb where we planned to stay with friends was quite far. We got into a *tonga* which turned out to be the slowest thing I had ever been in. I hate slowness, be it in men or animals. However, there was no alternative.

We were in no particular hurry to get to Parbhat Nagar, but I was getting impatient with the absurd conveyance we were in. I had never seen anything more ridiculous since Aligarth, which is notorious for its horse-drawn *ikkas*. The horse moves forward and the passengers slip backwards. Once or twice, I suggested to my wife that perhaps we should walk the rest of the way, or get hold of a better specimen of *tonga*, but she quite logically observed that there was nothing to choose from between one tonga and the next and, besides, the sun would be unbearable. Wives.

Another equally ridiculous-looking tonga was coming from the opposite direction. Suddenly, I heard someone shout, 'Hey Manto, you big horsie.' It was Chadda, my old friend, huddled in the back with a worn-out woman. My first reaction was regret. What had gone wrong with his aesthetic sense that he was now running around with a woman old enough to be his mother? I couldn't guess her age, but I noticed that despite her heavy make-up, the wrinkles on her face were visible. It was so grossly painted that it hurt the eye.

I had not seen Chadda for ages. He was one of my best friends and had he not been with the sort of woman he was with, I would have greeted him with something equally mindless. In any case, both of us got down.

He said to the woman, 'Mummy, just a minute.' He pumped my hand vigorously, then tried to do the same to my extremely formal wife. 'Bhabi, you have performed the impossible, I mean, getting this bundle of lazy bones all the way from Bombay to Poona.'

'Where are you headed for?' I asked.

'On important business. Now, listen, don't waste time. You are going straight to my place.' He began to issue instructions to the *tongawala*, adding, 'Don't charge the fare. It'll be settled.'

Then he turned to me. 'There is a servant around. See you later.' Without waiting for an answer, he jumped into his *tonga* where the woman whom he had called mummy sat waiting for him. The embarrassment I had felt earlier was gone.

His house was not far from where we had met. It looked like an old *dak* bungalow. 'This is it,' the *tongawala* said. 'I mean Chadda sahib's house.' I could see from my wife's expression that she was not overly enthusiastic about the prospects. As a matter of fact, she had not been overly enthusiastic about coming to Poona. She was afraid that once there, I would team up with my drinking friends, and since I was supposed to be having a change of scene, most of my time would be spent in what was to her highly objectionable company. I got down and asked my wife to follow me, which she did after some hesitation, as it was clear to her that my mind was made up.

It was the kind of house the army likes to requisition for a few weeks and then abandon. The walls were badly in need of paint and the rooms could only have belonged to a careless bachelor, an actor most likely, paid every two or three months — and that, too, in instalments.

I was conscious that this was no place for wives, but there was nothing to do but wait for Chadda, and then move to Parbhat Nagar, where this old friend of mine lived with his wife in more reasonable surroundings.

The servant in a way suited the place. When we arrived we found all the doors open and nobody in sight. When he finally materialized he took no notice of us, as if we had lived there for years. He came into the room and sailed past us without saying a word. I thought he was an out-of-work actor sharing the house with Chadda. However, when he came again and I asked him where the servant was to be found, he informed me gravely that he himself was the holder of that office.

We were both thirsty. When I asked him to get us a drink of water, he began looking for a glass. Finally, he produced a chipped glass mug from the bottom drawer of a cupboard and murmured, 'Only last night, sahib sent for half a dozen glasses. Now what on earth could have happened to them!'

My wife said she did not want a drink after all. He put the mug back exactly where he had unearthed it — in the bottom drawer of the cupboard — as if without this elaborate ritual, the entire household would come tumbling down. Then he left the room.

While my wife took one of the armchairs, I made myself comfortable on the bed, which was probably Chadda's. We did not say anything to each other. After some time, Chadda arrived. He was alone. He seemed to be quite indifferent to the fact that we were his guests.

'What's what old boy,' he said. 'Let's run up to the studio for a few minutes. With you in tow, I'm sure I can pick up an advance, because this evening ...' Then he looked at my wife. 'Bhabi, I hope you haven't made a mullah out of him.' He laughed. 'To hell with all the mullahs of the world. Come on, Manto, get moving. I am sure bhabi won't mind.'

My wife said nothing, although it wasn't difficult to guess what she was thinking. The studio was not far. After a noisy meeting with Mr Mehta the accountant, Chadda succeeded in making him cough up an advance of two hundred rupees. When we returned to the house, we found my wife sleeping in the armchair. We did not disturb her and moved into the next room where I noticed everything was either broken or in an advanced state of disrepair. At least it gave the place a uniformity of sorts.

There was dust on everything, an essential touch to the Bohemian character of Chadda's lodgings. From somewhere, he found the elusive servant, handed him a hundred rupees and said, 'Prince of Cathay, get us two bottles of third-class rum, I mean, 3-X rum and six new glasses.'

I later discovered that the servant was not only the Prince of Cathay, but the prince of practically every major country and civilization in the world. It all depended on Chadda's mood of the moment.

The Prince of Cathay left, fondling the money he had been given. Lowering himself on the bed, which had a broken spring mattress, Chadda ran his tongue over his lips in anticipation of the rum he had ordered and said, 'What's what. So you did hit Poona after all.' Then he added in a worried voice, 'But what about bhabi? I'm sure she's bloody upset.'

Chadda did not have a wife, but he was always worried about the wives of his friends. He used to say that he had remained single because he felt insecure when dealing with wives. 'When it's suggested to me that I should get married, my first reaction is always positive. Then I start thinking and in a few minutes come to the conclusion that I don't really deserve a wife. And that's how the project gets thrown into cold storage every time,' was one of his favourite explanations.

The rum arrived, and with it, the glasses. Chadda had sent for six, but the Prince of Cathay had dropped three on the way. Chadda was unconcerned. 'Praise be to the Lord that at least the bottles are unharmed,' he observed philosophically.

Then he opened the bottle hurriedly, poured the rum into virgin glasses and toasted me: 'To your arrival in Poona.' We downed our drinks in long swigs. Chadda poured more, then tiptoed into the other room to see if my wife was still asleep. She was. 'This is no good,' he announced. 'Let me make some noise so that she wakes up ... but before that let me organise some tea for her. Prince of Jamaica,' he shouted.

The Prince of Jamaica materialized at once. 'Go to mummy's place and ask her to kindly prepare some first-class tea and have it sent over. Immediately.'

Chadda drank up, then poured himself a more civilized measure and said, 'For the time being, I am watching my drinking. The first four drinks make me very sentimental and we still have to go to Parbhat Nagar to dump bhabi.'

The tea came, set on a nice tray. Chadda lifted the lid of the teapot, smelled the brew and declared, 'Mummy is a jewel.' Then he sent for the Prince of Ethiopia and began screaming at him. When he was sure that the racket had awakened my wife, he picked up the tray daintily and told me to follow him. He put it down with an exaggerated flourish on a table and announced, 'Tea is served, madam.'

My wife did not appear too amused by Chadda's antics, but she drank two cups and said, not so ill-humouredly, 'I suppose the two of you have already had yours.'

'I must plead guilty to that charge, but we did it in the secure knowledge that we'd find forgiveness,' Chadda said.

My wife smiled, encouraging Chadda to continue: 'Actually, both of us are pigs of the purest breed who are permitted to eat every forbidden fruit on earth. It is therefore time that we took steps to move you to a holier place than this.'

My wife was not amused. She did not care for Chadda. The fact is that she did not care much for any of my friends, especially him because she thought he was always transgressing the limits of what she considered correct behaviour. I don't think it had ever occurred to Chadda how people reacted to him. He considered it a waste of time, like playing indoor games. He beamed at my wife and shouted, 'Prince of Kababistan, get us a Rolls-Royce *tonga*.'

The Rolls-Royce *tonga* came and we left for Parbhat Nagar. My friend Harish Kumar was not at home, but his wife was, which we found helpful. Chadda said, 'As melons influence melons, in the same way, wives influence wives. We are off to the studio now, but we will soon return to verify the results.'

Chadda's strategy was always simple. Create so much confusion that enemy forces get no opportunity to plan theirs. He pushed me towards the door, giving my wife no time to object. 'Operation successfully accomplished. What now? Yes, mummy great mummy,' Chadda declared.

I wanted to ask him who this mummy of his was, daughter of what Tutankhamun, but he began to speak about totally unconnected matters, leaving my question to wither on the vine.

The *tonga* took us back to the house which was called Saeeda cottage. Chadda had christened it Kabida Cottage, the abode of the melancholy, as it was his theory that all its residents were in a state of advanced melancholia. Like many of his other theories, this one too was not quite consistent with the facts.

Chadda was not the only resident of Saeeda Cottage. There were others, all actors, and all working for the same film company which paid salaries every third month — in the form of advance. Almost all the inmates of the establishment were assistant directors. There were chief assistant directors, their deputies and assistants who, in turn, had their own assistants. It seemed to me that everyone was everyone's assistant and on the lookout for a financier to help him set up his own film company.

Because of the war, food rationing was in effect, but none of the Saeeda Cottage residents had a ration card. When they had money, they used to buy from the black market at exorbitant prices. They always went to the movies and, during the season, to the races. Some even tried their luck at the stock exchange, but no one had so far made a killing.

Since space was limited, even the garage was used for residential purposes. It was occupied by a family. The husband was not an assistant director, but the film company chauffeur, who kept odd hours. His wife, a good-looking young woman, was named Shireen. She had a little boy who had been collectively adopted by the residents of Saeeda Cottage.

The more liveable rooms in the cottage were occupied by Chadda and two of his friends, both actors, who had yet to make the big time. One was called Saeed, but his professional name was Ranjeet Kumar, a quiet, nice-looking man. Chadda often referred to him as the tortoise because he did everything very, very slowly.

I do not now remember the real name of the other actor, but everybody called him Gharib Nawaz. He came from a well-to-do family of the princely state of Hyderabad. He had come to Poona to get into the movies. He was paid two hundred and fifty rupees a month, but since his being hired a year earlier, had been paid only once — an advance against salary. The money had gone to rescue Chadda from the clutches of a very angry Pathan moneylender. There was hardly anyone in Saeeda Cottage who did not owe money to Gharib Nawaz.

Despite Chadda's theory, none of them was particularly melancholy. In fact they lived fairly happily, and even when they talked of their strained circumstances, it was in an off-hand, cheerful manner.

When Chadda and I returned, we ran into Gharib Nawaz outside the front gate. Chadda pulled out some money from his pocket and gave it to him — without counting — and said, 'Four bottles of Scotch. If I've given you less, then I know you'll make up for it. If I've given you more, I know I'll get it back. Thank you.'

Gharib Nawaz smiled. 'This is Mr one-two,' he said to him, meaning me. 'Detailed discussions are not possible at this stage because he has had a few rums. But wait until the evening when the Scotch begins to flow.'

We went inside. Chadda yawned, picked up the half-empty bottle of rum, took stock of its contents and shouted for the Prince of the Cossacks. There was no answer. 'I think he is drunk,' he observed, pouring himself another drink.

Chadda's room was like an old junk shop. However, it had a window or two, through one of which I now saw Venkutrey the music director, another old friend of mine, peeping in. It was difficult to tell by looking at him what race he belonged to — whether he was Mongol, Negroid, Aryan or something completely unknown to anthropology.

While one particular feature might, for a moment, suggest certain origins, it was immediately cancelled out by another feature, pointing at entirely different possibilities. However, he was from Maharashtra. His nose, unlike that of his famous forebear, the warrior Sivaji, was flat, which he always assured people was a great help in reproducing certain notes.

'Manto *seth*,' he screamed when he saw me.

'The hell with *seths*,' Chadda said. 'Don't stand there. Come in.' Venkutrey appeared, put a bottle of rum on the table and said he was at mummy's when he was told that one of Chadda's friends was in town. 'I was wondering who that could be. Didn't know it was *sala* Manto the old sinner.'

Chadda slapped his head. 'Shut your trap. You've produced a bottle of rum, that's enough.' Venkutrey picked up my empty glass and poured himself a large measure. 'Manto, this *sala* Chadda was telling me this morning: Venkutrey, I want to get drunk tonight. Get some booze. Now I was broke and I was wondering where I was going to get the money ...'

'You are an imbecile,' Chadda said.

'Is that so; then where do you think I managed to get this big bucket of rum from? It wasn't a gift from your father, I can tell you that.' He finished his glass. 'What did mummy say?' Chadda asked. 'Was Polly there, and Thelma ... and that platinum blonde?'

Chadda didn't wait for his answer. 'Manto, what a bundle of goods that one is! I had always heard of platinum blondes, but by God I had never set eyes on one, that is, until yesterday. She's lovely. Her hair is like threads of fine silver. She is great, Manto. I tell you she's great. Mummy zindabad. Mummy zindabad.' Then he said to Venkutrey, 'You bloody man, say mummy zindabad.'

Chadda grabbed my arm. 'Manto, I think I am getting very sentimental. You know in tradition the beloved is supposed to have black hair like a rain cloud, but what we have here is an entirely different bill of fare. Her hair is like finely spun silver ... or maybe not ... now I don't know what platinum looks like. I have never seen the bloody thing in my life. How can I describe the colour! Just try to imagine blue steel and silver mixed together.'

'And a shot of 3-X rum,' Venkutrey suggested, knocking back his.

'Shut up,' Chadda told him. 'Manto, I am really going bananas over this girl. Oh, the colour of her hair. What are those things fish have on their bellies, or it is all over? The pomfret fish. What are those things called? Damn fish, I think snakes have them too, those tiny shimmering things. Scales, that's right, they're called scales. In Urdu they're called *khaprey*, which is a ridiculous name for something so beautiful. We have a word for them in Punjabi. I know it. Yes ... *chanay*. What a lovely word. It sounds right. It sounds just right. That's what her hair is like ... small, brilliant, slithering snakes.'

He got up. 'To hell with small, brilliant, slithering snakes. I'm going out of my mind. I'm getting sentimental.'

'What was that?' Venkutrey asked absent-mindedly.

'Beyond your feeble powers of comprehension, my friend,' Chadda replied.

Venkutrey mixed himself another drink. 'Manto, this *sala* Chadda thinks I don't understand English. You know I'm a matriculate. My father loved me. He sent me to ...'

'Your father was mad. He made you the greatest musician in the world. He twisted your nose and made it flat so that you could sing flat notes. Manto, whenever he has had a couple of drinks, he starts talking about his father. Yes, he's a matriculate, but should I then tear up my BA degree?'

I drank. 'Manto,' Chadda said, 'if I fail to conquer this platinum blonde, I promise you Mr Chadda will renounce the world, go to the highest peak in the Himalayas and contemplate his navel.'

He said he was throwing a big party that night: 'Had you not hit town, that rascal Mehta would never have given me the advance. Well, tonight is the night.' He began to sing in his highly unmusical voice. Before Venkutrey could protest at this most foul murder of music, the door opened to reveal Gharib Nawaz and Ranjeet Kumar, each holding two bottles of Scotch. We poured them some rum.

It turned out that the name of this jewel was Phyllis. She worked in a hairdressing salon and was generally to be seen with a young fellow, who, everybody assured me, looked like a sissy. The entire male population of Saeeda Cottage was infatuated with her.

Gharib Nawaz had declared that morning that he might rush back to Hyderabad, sell some property, return with the proceeds and sweep her off her feet. Chadda's only plus was his good looks. Venkutrey was of the view that she would fall into his lap the moment she heard him sing. Ranjeet Kumar was in favour of a more direct approach. However, in the end, it was clear that success would depend on whom mummy favoured.

Chadda looked at his watch. 'Let the bloody platinum blonde go to the blazes. We have to be in Parbhat Nagar, because I am sure by now Mrs Manto is angry. Now, if I get a sentimental fit in her presence, you'll have to look after me.' He finished his drink and called for the Prince of

Egypt, the land of mummies.

The prince appeared, rubbing his eyes as if he had just been disinterred from the earth after hundreds of years. Chadda sprinkled his face with some rum and told him to conjure up two royal Egyptian chariots.

The chariots came and soon we were on our way to Parbhat Nagar. My friend Harish Kumar was home and my wife seemed to be in a good mood. Chadda winked at him as we entered to indicate that something was on the cards for the evening.

Harish asked my wife if she'd like to come to the studio to watch him shoot a couple of scenes. She wanted to know if a musical sequence was being filmed. When told that it would be the next day, she seemed to lose interest. 'Why not tomorrow then?' Harish's wife suggested. The poor woman was sick of taking guests to the studios. She told my wife, 'You look tired. I think you should take some rest.'

Harish said it was a good idea. 'Manto, you'd better come with me to see the studio chief. He has expressed an interest in your writing a film for him.' My wife was pleased. Chadda provided the final touch to the drama. He said he was leaving as he had something important to do. We said our goodbyes. When we met later on the road, Chadda shouted lustily, 'Raja Harish Chander zindabad.'

Harish did not come with us. He had to meet his girl-friend.

From the outside, mummy's house looked like Saeeda Cottage, but there the resemblance ended. I had expected to find myself in a sort of brothel, but it was a perfectly normal, middle-class, Christian household. It looked a bit younger than mummy, perhaps because it was simple and wore no make-up. When she walked in, I felt that while everything around her had remained the same age as the day it was bought, she had moved on and grown old. She was wearing the same bright make-up.

Chadda introduced her briefly: 'This is mummy the

great.' She smiled, then admonished him gently. 'You sent for tea in such an unholy hurry that I am sure Mrs Manto could not have found it drinkable. It was all your friend Chadda's fault,' she told me.

I said the tea was great. Then she said to Chadda, 'I fixed dinner, otherwise you always get impatient at the last moment.' Chadda threw his arms around her. 'You are a jewel, mummy. Of course we are going to eat that dinner.'

Mummy wanted to know where my wife was. When we told her that she was with friends in Parbhat Nagar, she said, 'That's awful, why didn't you bring her?'

'Because of the party tonight,' Chadda replied.

'What party? I decided to call it off the moment I saw Mrs Manto.'

'What have you done, mummy?' Chadda exclaimed. 'And to think that we planned this entire charade just for that!'

Then on an impulse he jumped up. 'But you only thought of calling the party off. You didn't actually call it off. As such, hereby I call off your decision to call off the party. Cross your heart.' He drew a cross across mummy's heart and shouted, 'Hip hip hurray!'

The fact was that mummy had called off the party. I could also see that she didn't want to disappoint Chadda. She touched him on the cheek affectionately and said, 'Let me see what I can do.'

She left. Chadda's spirits rose. 'General Venkutrey, report to headquarters and arrange immediate transportation of all heavy guns to the battlefront.'

Venkutrey saluted smartly and left for Saeeda Cottage. He was back in ten minutes with the heavy guns — the four bottles of Scotch — with the servant bringing up the rear. 'Come in, come in, my Caucasian prince. The girl with hair the colour of snake scales is coming tonight. You too can try your luck.'

I was thinking about mummy. Chadda, Gharib Nawaz

and Ranjeet Kumar were like little children waiting for their mother who had gone out to buy them tóys. Chadda was more confident because he was the favourite child and he knew that he would get the best toy. The others were not altogether without hope. Every situation has its own music. The one in mummy's home had no harsh notes. Drinking did not feel like something which should not be done. It was like imbibing milk.

Her make-up still bothered me, however. Why did she have to paint her face like that? It was an insult to the love she showered with such generosity on Chadda, Gharib Nawaz and Venkutrey ... and who knew how many more.

I asked Chadda, 'Why does your mummy look so flashy?'

'Because the world likes flashy things. There are not many idiots around like you and me who wish colours to be sober and understated, music to be soft, who don't want to see youth clad in the garments of childhood and age in the mantle of youth. We who call ourselves artists are actually second-class asses, because there is nothing first class on this earth. It is either third or second class, except ... except Phyllis. She alone is first class.'

Venkutrey poured his drink over Chadda's head. 'Snakes, scales ... you have gone mad.'

Chadda lapped it up. 'This has cooled me down.'

Venkutrey poured his drink over Chadda's head. 'Snakes, his long, rambling story about how much his father loved him, but Chadda was having none of that.

'To hell with your entire family,' he said. 'I want to talk about Phyllis.' He looked at Gharib Nawaz and Ranjeet Kumar, who were huddled together in a corner whispering in each other's ears. 'You leaders of the great gunpowder plot, your conspiracies will never succeed. Victory in battle will kiss Chadda's feet. Isn't that so, my Prince of Wales?'

The Prince of Wales seemed more worried about the bottle of rum, which was getting emptier by the minute.

Chadda laughed and poured him a hefty measure.

The lights had been switched on, and outside the evening had fallen. Then we heard mummy on the veranda. Chadda shouted a slogan and ran out. Ranjeet Kumar and Gharib Nawaz exchanged glances, waiting for the door to open.

Mummy came in, followed by four or five Anglo-Indian girls. There were Polly, Dolly, Kitty, Elma, Thelma and a young man who answered to the description that had been provided to me of Phyllis's friend.

Phyllis was the last to appear. Chadda had his arm around her. He had already declared victory. Gharib Nawaz and Ranjeet Kumar looked positively unhappy at this unsporting behaviour.

All hell broke loose. Suddenly everyone was jabbering away in English, trying to impress the girls. Venkutrey failed his matriculation several times in a row. Soon he went into a corner with Thelma, offering free instruction in Indian classical dance.

Chadda was surrounded by a bevy of giggling girls. He was reciting dirty limericks which he knew by the hundred. Mummy was busy with her arrangements. Ranjeet Kumar sat alone, smoking cigarette after cigarette. Gharib Nawaz was asking mummy if she needed any money.

The Scotch was brought in ceremoniously. Phyllis was offered a drink, but she shook her head. She said she did not like whisky. Even Chadda was refused. Finally, mummy prepared a light drink, put the glass to her lips and said, 'Now be a brave girl and gulp it down.'

Chadda was so thrilled that he recited another twenty limericks. I was thinking. Man must have got bored with nakedness when he decided to don clothes, which is why sometimes he gets bored with them and reverts to his original state. The reaction to good manners is certainly bad manners.

I watched mummy. She was surrounded by the girls and

was giggling with the rest of them at Chadda's antics. She was wearing the same vulgar, tasteless make-up under which her wrinkles could be seen in high relief. She looked happy. I wondered why people thought escape to be a bad thing. Here was an act of escape. The exterior was unattractive, but the soul was beautiful. Did she need all those unguents, lotions and colouring liquids?

Polly was telling Ranjeet Kumar about her new dress which she had picked up as a bargain and had done something to at home. And now it was perfectly lovely. Ranjeet Kumar was offering to buy her two new ones, although he was unlikely to get an advance in the near future. Dolly was trying to talk Gharib Nawaz into lending her some more money. He knew perfectly well that he would never see it again, but was still trying to convince himself to the contrary.

Thelma was being tutored in the intricacies of Indian classical dance by Venkutrey, who knew that she would never make a dancer. She knew that too, but she was still listening to him with great concentration. Elma and Kitty were drinking steadily.

In this tableau it was difficult to be sure about the rights and wrongs. Was mummy's flashiness right or a part of the situation? Who could say? In her heart there was love for everyone. Perhaps she had coloured her face, I said to myself, so that the world should not see what she was really like. Maybe she did not have the emotional strength to play mother to the whole world. She had just chosen a few.

Mummy did not know that during her absence in the kitchen, Chadda had persuaded Phyllis to take a massive drink, not on the sly, but in front of the others. Phyllis was slightly high, but only slightly. Her hair was like polished steel, waving gently from side to side like her young sinuous body.

It was midnight. Venkutrey was no longer trying to make a classical dancer out of Thelma. Now he was telling her about his father, who loved him to the point of distraction. Gharib Nawaz had forgotten that he had already lent some more money to Dolly. Ranjeet Kumar had disappeared with Polly. Elma and Kitty were sleepy.

Around the table sat Phyllis, her friend and mummy. Chadda was no longer sentimental. He sat next to Phyllis and it was evident he was determined to take her tonight.

At some point, Phyllis's friend got up, laid himself down on the sofa and went to sleep. Gharib Nawaz and Dolly left the room. Elma and Kitty said their goodnights and went home. Venkutrey, after praising his wife's beauty one more time, cast a longing look at Phyllis, put his arm around Thelma and took her out into the garden.

Suddenly, a loud argument developed between mummy and Chadda. He was drunk, angry and foul-mouthed. He had never spoken to her like that. Phyllis had given up her feeble efforts to make peace between the two. Chadda wanted to take her to Saeeda Cottage and mummy had told him that she would not permit that. He was screaming at her now: 'You old pimp, you have gone mad. Phyllis is mine. Ask her.'

'Chadda, my son, why don't you understand? She is young, she is very young,' mummy said to him, but Chadda was beyond reason. For the first time it occurred to me how young Phyllis was, hardly fifteen. Her face was like a raindrop surrounded by silver clouds.

Chadda pulled Phyllis towards him, squeezed her against his chest in a passionate B-grade movie embrace. 'Chadda, leave her alone. For God's sake let her go,' mummy screamed, but he paid no attention to her.

Then it happened. She slapped him across the face. 'Get out, get out!' she shouted.

Chadda pushed Phyllis aside, gave mummy a furious look and walked out. I followed him.

When I arrived at Saeeda Cottage, he was lying on his bed, face down, fully clothed. We did not speak. I went to my room and slept.

I got up late next morning. Chadda was not in his room. I washed and as I was coming out of the bathroom, I heard his voice outside: 'She is unique. By God, she is great. You should pray that when you reach her age you should become like her.'

I did not want to hang around much longer. I waited for him to come back to the house, but after about half an hour, I left for Parbhat Nagar.

Harish hadn't returned home. I told his wife that we had had a late night, so he had decided to sleep at Saeeda Cottage. We took our leave and on the way I told my wife about the night's incident. Her theory was that Phyllis was either related to mummy or the old woman wanted to save her for some better client. I kept quiet.

After several weeks I had a letter from Chadda. All it said was, 'I behaved like a beast that evening. Damn me.'

I went to Poona a few months later on business. When I called at Saeeda Cottage, Chadda was out. Gharib Nawaz was playing with Shireen's son. We shook hands. I learnt from him that Chadda hadn't spoken to mummy after that night, nor had she visited Saeeda Cottage.

She had sent Phyllis back to her parents. It turned out that she had run away from home with that young fellow. Ranjeet Kumar — who had just walked in — was confident that had Phyllis stayed on, he would have scored. Gharib Nawaz had no such illusions, but he was sorry she was gone.

They said Chadda had not been well for some time, but refused to see a doctor. As we were talking, Venkutrey rushed in. He looked very nervous. He had met Chadda on the street, found him feeling groggy and put him in a *tonga* to get him home, but he had fainted on the way. We ran out. Chadda lay in the tonga looking very ill. We brought him in. He was unconscious.

I told Gharib Nawaz to get a doctor. He consulted

Venkutrey and left. They returned a little later with mummy. 'What has happened to my son?' she asked. 'What kind of friends are you? Why didn't you send me word?' she said.

She immediately took charge. Get hold of some ice and rub his forehead. Massage his feet. Fan his face, Then she went out to get a doctor. Everyone looked relieved, as if the entire responsibility of bringing Chadda back to health was now mummy's.

Chadda had begun to regain consciousness when mummy returned with the doctor. The doctor examined him, then took mummy aside. She told us there was no cause for worry. Chadda was still a bit disoriented. He saw mummy. He took her hand in his and said, 'Mummy, you are great.'

She ran her hand gently over Chadda's burning face. 'My son, my poor son,' she said.

Tears came to Chadda's eyes. 'Don't say that. Your son is a scoundrel of the first order. Go get your husband's old service revolver and shoot him.'

'Don't talk rubbish,' she said. She rose. 'Boys, Chadda is very ill. I'm going to take him to the hospital.'

Gharib Nawaz sent for a taxi. Chadda could not understand why he was being taken to hospital, but mummy told him that he would be more comfortable there than at home. 'It's nothing,' she said.

He was laid up for many days, with mummy spending most of her time with him. However, he did not seem to be getting better. His skin had become sallow and he was losing strength. The doctors were of the view that he should be taken to Bombay, but mummy said, 'No, I'm going to take him home and he's going to get well.'

I had to leave Poona, but I phoned from Bombay every other day. I had started to lose hope, but slowly, very slowly, Chadda began to come round. I had to go to Lahore for a few weeks. When I returned to Bombay there was a letter from Chadda. 'The great mummy has reclaimed her unworthy son from the dead,' he had written. There was so much love in that line. When I told my wife, she observed icily, 'Such women are generally good at these things.'

I wrote to Chadda a few times, but he didn't answer. Later, somebody told me that mummy had sent him to the hills to stay with friends. He was soon better — and bored — and returned to Poona. I was there that day.

He looked weak, but nothing else had changed. He talked about his illness as if he had had a minor bicycle accident. Saeeda Cottage had seen a few changes in his absence. A Bengali music director called Sen had moved in. He shared his room with Ram Singh, a young boy from Lahore, who had come to Bombay, like so many others, to get into films.

Ranjeet Kumar had been picked up to play the lead in a movie. He had been promised the direction of the next one, provided the one under production did well. Chadda had finally managed to raise an advance of one thousand five hundred rupees from the studio. Gharib Nawaz had just come back from Hyderabad and the general finances of Saeeda Cottage were in good shape as a result of that. Shireen's boy had new clothes and new toys.

My friend Harish was currently trying to seduce his new leading lady, who was from Punjab. He was, however, afraid of her husband, who had a formidable moustache and looked like a wrestler. Chadda's advice to Harish had been sound: 'Don't worry about him at all. He may be a wrestler, but in the field of love he is bound to fall flat on his face. All you need to learn are a few heavyweight Punjabi swear-words from me. I'll settle for one hundred rupees per lesson. You'll need them in awkward situations.'

Harish had struck a deal, and at the rate of a bottle of rum per choice Punjabi swearword, had learnt half a dozen of them. However, there had been no occasion to test his new powers. His affair was doing well without them.

Mummy's parties had been reconvened and the old crowd — Polly, Dolly, Elma, Thelma etc. — was back. Venkutrey had still not given up his efforts to induct Thelma into the mysteries of Indian classical dance. Gharib Nawaz was still lending money and Ranjeet Kumar, who was about to hit the big screen, was using his new position to ingratiate himself with the girls. Chadda's dirty limericks were still flowing.

There was only one thing missing — the girl with the platinum blonde hair, the colour of snake scales and blue steel and silver. Chadda never mentioned her. Occasionally, one would see him looking at mummy, then lowering his eyes, recalling the events of that night. Off and on, after his fourth drink, he would say, 'Chadda, you are a damned brute.'

Mummy was still the old mummy — Polly's mummy, Dolly's mummy, Chadda's mummy, Ranjeet Kumar's mummy — still the wonderful manageress of her unique establishment. Her make-up was still flashy, and her clothes even flashier. Her wrinkles still showed, but for me they had come to assume a sacred dimension.

It was mummy who had come to the rescue of Venkutrey's wife when she had had a miscarriage. She had taken charge of Thelma when she had caught a dangerous infection from a dance director who had promised to put her in the movies. Recently, Kitty had won five hundred rupees in a crossword puzzle competition and mummy had persuaded her to give some of it to Gharib Nawaz, who was a bit short. 'Give it to him now and you can keep taking it back,' she had advised her.

There was only one man she didn't like: the music director Sen. She had told Chadda repeatedly, 'Don't bring him to my house. There is something about him that makes me uneasy. He doesn't fit.'

I returned to Bombay, carrying with me the warmth of

mummy's parties. Her world was simple and beautiful and reassuring. Yes, there was drinking and sex and a general lack of seriousness, but one felt no emotional unease. It was like the protruding belly of a pregnant woman; a bit odd, but perfectly innocent and immediately comprehensible.

One day I read in the papers that the music director Sen had been found murdered in Saeeda Cottage. The suspect was said to be a young man named Ram Singh.

Chadda wrote me an account of the incident later.

'I was sound asleep that night. Suddenly, I felt someone slump into my bed. It was Sen. He was covered in blood. Then Ram Singh rushed into the room holding a knife. By this time, everyone was up. Ranjeet Kumar and Gharib Nawaz ran in and disarmed Ram Singh. Sen's breathing grew uneven and then stopped. "Is he dead?" Ram Singh asked. I shook my head. "Please let go of me. I won't run away," he said calmly.

'We didn't know what to do, so we immediately sent for mummy. She took stock of the situation in her unruffled manner and escorted Ram Singh to the police, where he made a statement confessing to the killing. The next few weeks were awful. Police, courts, lawyers, the works. There was a trial and the court acquitted Ram Singh.

'He had made the same statement under oath that he had made to the police. Mummy had said to him, "Son, speak the truth. Tell them what happened." Ram Singh had spoken the truth. He had told the court that Sen had promised to get him to sing for films, provided he would sleep with him. He had let himself be persuaded, but was always troubled by what he was doing. One day he had told Sen that if he tried to force him to perform the unnatural act again, he would kill him. And that was exactly what had happened that night. Sen had tried to force him and Ram Singh had stabbed him repeatedly with a kitchen knife.'

Chadda had written, 'In this age of untruth, the triumph of truth is astonishing.'

A party had been organized to celebrate Ram Singh's acquittal and after it was over, mummy had suggested that he should return to his parents in Lahore. Gharib Nawaz had bought him a ticket and Shireen had prepared food for him to take on the long journey. Everyone had gone to the station to see him off.

A week or so after this, I was asked by the studio to come to Poona to complete an assignment. Nothing had changed at Saeeda Cottage. It was still the way it always was. When I arrived, a minor party was in progress to celebrate the birth of another son to Shireen. Venkutrey had got hold of two tins of Glaxo baby food from somewhere, not an easy thing at the time. Suggestions were also being invited as to a name for the child.

Everybody was trying to look cheerful, but I couldn't help feeling that there was something the matter with Chadda, Gharib Nawaz and Ranjeet Kumar. A vague sadness hung in the air. Was it the weather which was beginning to turn chilly or was it Sen's murder? I could not decide.

For one week I was shut up in Harish's house because I was in a hurry to complete my assignment. I was a bit surprised that Chadda hadn't come to see me all this time, nor Gharib Nawaz for that matter.

Then one afternoon Chadda burst into the house. 'This rubbish you've been writing, have you been paid something for it yet?' he asked. I told him I had received two thousand rupees only the other day and the money was in my jacket. He took out four hundred rupees and rushed out, pausing just long enough to tell me that there was a party at mummy's house that evening and I was expected.

When I arrived, it was already in full swing. Ranjeet and Venkutrey were dancing with Polly and Thelma. Kitty was dancing with Elma and Chadda was jumping around like a rabbit with mummy in his arms. Everyone was quite drunk. My entrance was greeted with guffaws and slogans.

Mummy, who had always maintained a certain formality with me, took hold of my hand and said, 'Kiss me, dear.'

'That's enough dancing,' Chadda announced above the din. 'I want to do some serious drinking now. Open a new bottle, my Prince of Scotland.' The Prince, who was very drunk, appeared with a bottle and dropped it on the floor. 'It is only a bottle, mummy. What about broken hearts?' Chadda said before she could scold the servant.

A chill fell over the party. A new bottle was duly produced. Chadda poured everyone a huge drink. Then he began to make a speech: 'Ladies and gentlemen, we have among us this evening this man called Manto. He thinks he's a great story writer, but I think that's rubbish. He claims that he can fathom the depths of the human soul. That too is a lot of rubbish. This world is full of rubbish. I met someone yesterday after ten years and he assured me that we had met only the other week. That too is rubbish. That man was from Hyderabad. I pronounce a million curses on the Nizam of Hyderabad who has tons of gold but no mummy.'

Someone shouted Manto zindabad, but Chadda continued with his speech. 'This is a conspiracy hatched by Manto, otherwise my instructions were clear. We should have greeted him with catcalls. I have been betrayed. But let me talk of that evening when I behaved like a beast with mummy because of that girl with hair the colour of snake scales. Who did I think I was? Don Juan?

'Be that as it may, but it could have been done. With one kiss, I could have sucked in all her virginity with these big fat lips of mine. She was very young, very weak . . . what's the word, Manto? . . . yes, very unformed. After a night of love, she would either have carried the guilt with her the rest of her life, or she would have completely forgotten about it the next morning.

'I am glad mummy threw me out that night. Ladies and gentlemen, now I end my speech. I've already talked a lot of rubbish. Actually, I was planning a longer speech, but I can't speak any longer. I'm going to get myself a drink.'

Nobody spoke. It occurred to me that he had been heard in complete silence. Mummy also looked a bit lost. Chadda sat there nursing his drink. He was quiet. His speech seemed to have drained him out. 'What's with you?' I asked.

'I don't know — tonight the whisky is not battering in the buttocks of my brain as it always does,' he answered philosophically.

The clock struck two. Chadda, who in the meanwhile had begun a dance with Kitty, pushed her aside and said to Venkutrey, 'Sing us something, but I warn you, none of your classical mumbo-jumbo.'

Venkutrey sang a couple of songs, set to the melancholy evening *raaga* Malkauns. The atmosphere grew even sadder. Gharib Nawaz was so moved that his eyes became wet. 'These Hyderabadis have weak eye-bladders. You never know when they might start dripping,' Chadda observed.

Gharib Nawaz wiped his eyes and took Elma on to the floor. Venkutrey put a record on. Chadda picked up mummy and began to bounce around.

At four o'clock, Chadda suddenly said, 'That's it.' He picked up a bottle from the table, put it to his mouth and drank what was left of it. 'Let's go, Manto.'

When I tried to say goodbye to mummy, he pulled me away. 'There are going to be no goodbyes tonight.'

When we were outside, I thought I heard Venkutrey crying. I wanted to go back, but Chadda stopped me. 'He too has a faulty eye-bladder.'

Saeeda Cottage was only a few minutes' walk. We did not speak. Before going to bed, I tried to ask Chadda about the strange party, but he said he was sleepy.

When I got up the next morning, I found Gharib Nawaz standing outside the garage wiping his eyes.

'What's the matter?' I asked him.

'Mummy's gone.'

'Where?'

'I don't know.'

Chadda was still in bed, but it seemed he hadn't slept at all. He smiled when I asked him if it was true. 'Yes, she's gone. Had to leave Poona by the morning train.'

'But why?' I asked.

'Because the authorities did not approve of her ways. Her parties were considered objectionable, outside the limits of the law. The police tried to blackmail her. They offered to leave her alone if she would do their dirty work for them. They wanted to use her as a procuress, an agent. She refused. Then they dug up an old case they had registered against her. They had her charged with moral turpitude and running a house of ill repute and they obtained court orders expelling her from Poona.'

'If she was a procuress, a madam, and her presence was bad for society's health, then she should have been done away with altogether. Why, if she was a heap of filth, was she removed from Poona and ordered to be dumped elsewhere?'

He laughed bitterly. 'Manto, with her a purity has vanished from our lives. Do you remember that awful night? She cleansed me of my lust and meanness. I am sorry she's gone, but I shouldn't be sorry. She has only left Poona. She will go elsewhere and meet more young men like me and she will cleanse their souls and make them whole. I hereby bestow my mummy on them.

'Now, let's go and look for Gharib Nawaz. He must have cried himself hoarse. As I told you, these Hyderabadis have weak eye-bladders. You never know when they might start dripping.'

I looked at Chadda. Tears were floating in his eyes like corpses in a river.

The Wild Cactus

The name of the town is unimportant. Let us say it was in the suburbs of the city of Peshawar, not far from the frontier, where that woman lived in a small mud house, half hidden from the dusty, unmetalled, forlorn road by a hedge of wild cactus.

The cactus was quite dry but it had grown with such profusion that it had become like a curtain shielding the house from the gaze of passers-by. It is not clear if it had always been there or whether it was the woman who had planted it.

The house was more like a hut with three small rooms, all kept very spick and span. There wasn't much in it by way of furniture, but what there was, was nice. In the backroom was a big bed, and beside it an alcove where an earthen lamp burned all night. It was all very orderly.

Let me now tell you about the woman who lived there with her young daughter.

There were various stories. Some people said the young girl was not really her daughter, but an orphan whom she had taken in and raised. Others said she was her illegitimate child, while there were some who believed her to be her real daughter. One does not know the truth.

I forgot to tell you the woman's name, not that it matters. It could be Sakina, Mehtab, Gulshan or something else, but let's call her Sardar for the sake of convenience.

She was in her middle years, but must have been beautiful in her time. Her face had now begun to wrinkle, though she still looked years younger than she was.

Her daughter — if she was her daughter — was extremely beautiful. There was nothing about her to suggest that she was a woman of pleasure, which is what she was. Business was brisk. The girl, whom I will call Nawab, was not unhappy with her life. She had grown up in an atmosphere where no concept of marital relations existed.

When Sardar had brought her her first man in the big bed in the backroom, it had seemed to her quite a natural thing to have happened to a girl who had just crossed the threshold of puberty. Since then it had become the pattern of her life and she was happy with it.

And although, according to popular definition, she was a prostitute, she had no knowledge or consciousness of sin. It simply did not exist in her world.

There was a physical sincerity about her. She used to give herself completely, without reservations, to the men who were brought to her. She had come to believe that it was a woman's duty to make love to men, tenderly and without inhibitions.

She knew almost nothing about life as it was lived in the big cities, but through her men she had come to learn something of their city habits, like the brushing of teeth in the morning, drinking a cup of tea in bed and taking a quick bath before dressing up and driving off.

Not all men were alike. Some only wanted to smoke a cigarette in the morning, while others wanted nothing but a hot cup of tea. Some were bad sleepers, others slept soundly and left at the crack of dawn.

Sardar was a woman without a worry in the world. She had faith in the ability of her daughter — or whoever she was — to look after the clients. She generally used to go to bed early herself, happily drugged on opium. It was only in emergencies that she was woken up. Often customers had to be revived after they had had too much to drink. Sardar would say philosophically: 'Give him some pickled mango or make him drink a glass of salt water so that he can vomit. Then send him to sleep.'

Sardar was a careful woman. Customers were required to pay in advance. After collecting the money she would say: 'Now you two go and have a good time.'

While the money always stayed in Sardar's custody, presents, when received, were Nawab's. Many of the clients were rich and gifts of cloth, fruit and sweets were frequent.

Nawab was a happy girl. In the little three-bed mud house, life was smooth and predictable. Not long ago, an army officer had brought her a gramophone and some records which she used to play when alone. She even used to try to sing along, but she had no talent for music, not that she was aware of it. The fact was that she was aware of very little, and not interested in knowing more. She might have been ignorant, but she was happy.

What the world beyond the cactus hedge was like, she had no idea. All she knew was the rough, dusty road and the men who drove up in cars, honked once or twice to announce their arrival and when told by Sardar to park at a more discreet distance, did so, then walked into the house to join Nawab in the big bed.

The regulars numbered not more than five or six, but Sardar had arranged things with such tact that never had two visitors been known to run into each other. Since every customer had his fixed day, no problems were ever encountered.

Sardar was also careful to ensure that Nawab did not become pregnant. It was an ever-present possibility. However, two and a half years had passed without any mishap. The police were unaware of Sardar's establishment and the men were discreet.

One day, a big Dodge drove up to the house. The driver

honked once and Sardar stepped out. It was no one she
knew, nor did the stranger say who he was. He parked the
car and walked in as if he was one of the old regulars.

Sardar was a bit confused, but Nawab greeted the
stranger with a smile and took him into the back room.
When Sardar followed them in, they were sitting on the
bed, next to each other, talking. One look was enough to
assure her that the visitor was rich and, apart from that,
handsome. 'Who showed you the way?' she asked,
nevertheless.

The stranger smiled, then put his arm amorously around
Nawab and said, 'This one here.' Nawab sprung up flirtatiously and said, 'Why, I never saw you in my life!' 'But I
have,' the stranger answered, grinning.

Surprised, Nawab asked, 'When and where?' The
stranger took her hand in his and said, 'You won't understand; ask your mother.' 'Have I met this man before?'
Nawab asked Sardar like a child. By now Sardar had come
to the conclusion that the tip had come from one of her
regulars. 'Don't worry about it. I'll tell you later,' she said to
Nawab.

Then she left the room, took some opium and lay on her
bed, satisfied. The stranger did not look the kind to make
trouble.

His name was Haibat Khan, the biggest landlord in the
neighbouring district of Hazara. 'I want no men visiting
Nawab in future,' he said to Sardar on his way to his car
after a few hours. 'How's that possible, Khan sahib? Can
you afford to pay for all of them?' Sardar asked, being the
woman of the world she was.

Haibat Khan did not answer her. Instead, he pulled out
a lot of money from his pocket and threw it on the floor. He
also removed a diamond ring from his finger and slipped it
on Nawab. Then he walked out hurriedly, past the cactus
hedge.

Nawab did not even look at the money, but she kept

gazing at the ring with the big resplendent diamond. She heard the car start and move away, leaving clouds of dust in its wake.

When she returned, Sardar had picked up the money and counted it. There were nineteen hundred rupees in bank notes. One more, and it would have been two thousand, she thought, but it didn't worry her. She put the money away, took some opium and went to bed.

Nawab was thrilled. She just couldn't take her eyes off the diamond ring. A few days passed. In between, an old client came to the house, but Sardar sent him packing, saying she anticipated a police raid and had therefore decided to discontinue business.

Sardar's logic was simple. She knew Haibat Khan was rich and money would keep coming in, as before, with the added advantage that there would be only one man to deal with. In the next few days she was able to get rid of all her old clients, one by one.

A week later, Haibat Khan made his second appearance, but he did not speak to Sardar. The two of them went to the back room, leaving Sardar with her opium and her bed.

Haibat Khan was now a regular visitor. He was totally enamoured of Nawab. He liked her artless approach to love-making, untinged by the hard-baked professionalism common to prostitutes. Nor was there anything housewifely about her. She would lie in bed next to him as a child lies next to its mother, playing with her breasts, sticking his little finger in her nose and then quietly going off to sleep.

It was something entirely new in Haibat Khan's experience. Nawab was different, she was interesting and she gave pleasure. His visits became more frequent.

Sardar was happy. She had never had so much money coming in with such regularity. Nawab, however, sometimes felt troubled. Haibat Khan always seemed to be vaguely apprehensive of something. It showed in little things. A slight shiver always seemed to run through his body when a car or bus went speeding past the house. He would jump out of bed and run out, trying to read the numberplate.

One night, a passing bus startled Haibat Khan so much that he suddenly wrested himself free from her arms and sat up. Nawab was a light sleeper and woke up too. He looked terrified. She was frightened. 'What happened?' she screamed.

By now, Haibat Khan had composed himself. 'It was nothing. I think I had a nightmare,' he said. The bus had gone, though it could still be heard in the distance.

Nawab said: 'No, Khan, there is something. Whenever you hear a noise, you get into a state.'

Haibat Khan's vanity was stung. 'Don't talk rubbish,' he said sharply. 'Why should anyone be afraid of cars and buses?'

Nawab began to cry, but Haibat Khan took her in his arms and she stopped sobbing.

He was a handsome man, strong of limb and a passionate lover, who ignited the fires in Nawab's young body every time he touched her. It was really he who had initiated her into the intricacies of love-making. For the first time in her life, she was experiencing the state called love. She used to pine for him when he was gone, and would play her records endlessly.

Many months went by, deepening Nawab's love for Haibat Khan, and also her anxiety. His visits had of late become somewhat erratic. He would come for a few hours, look extremely ill-at-ease and leave suddenly. It was clear he was under some pressure. He never seemed willing or happy to leave, but he always left.

Nawab tried to get to the truth many times, only to be given evasive answers.

One morning his Dodge drove up to the house, stopping at the usual place. Nawab was asleep, but she woke up when she heard him honk the horn. She rushed out and ran into Haibat Khan at the door. He embraced her passionately, picked her up and carried her inside.

 They kept talking to each other for a long time about things lovers talk about. For the first time in her life, Nawab said to him: 'Khan, bring me some gold bangles.'

Haibat Khan kissed her fleshy arms many times and said: 'You will have them tomorrow. For you I can even give my life.'

Nawab squirmed coquettishly: 'Oh no Khan, it is poor me who'll have to give her life.'

Haibat Khan kissed her and said: 'I'll return tomorrow with your gold bangles and I'll put them on you myself.'

Nawab was ecstatic. She wanted to dance with joy. Sardar watched her contentedly, then reached for her opium and went to bed.

Nawab rose the next morning, still in a state of high excitement. This is the day he will bring me my gold bangles, she said to herself, but Haibat Khan never turned up. Perhaps his car has broken down, she consoled herself, but she felt uneasy. That night she couldn't sleep.

She said to her mother: 'The Khan hasn't come. He promised and he hasn't come.' Her heart was full of forebodings.

Has he had an accident? Has he been suddenly taken ill? Has he been waylaid? She heard cars passing and thought of Haibat Khan and how these noises used to terrify him.

One week passed. The house behind the cactus hedge continued to remain without visitors. Off and on, a car would go by, leaving clouds of dust behind. In her mind, passing cars and buses were now associated with Haibat Khan. They had something to do with his absence.

One afternoon, while both women were about to take a nap after lunch, they heard a car stop outside. It honked, but it was not Haibat Khan's car. Who was it then?

Sardar went outside to make sure it was not one of the old customers, in which case, she would send him on his way. It was Haibat Khan. He sat in the driver's seat but it was not his car. With him was a well-dressed, rather beautiful woman.

Haibat Khan stepped out, followed by the woman. Sardar was confused. What was this woman doing with him? Who was she? Why had he brought her here?

They entered the house without taking any notice of her. She followed them inside after a while and found all three of them sitting next to one another on the bed. There was a strange silence about everything. The woman, who was wearing heavy gold ornaments, appeared to be somewhat nervous.

Sardar stood in the door and when Haibat Khan looked up, she greeted him, but he made no acknowledgement. He was in a state of great and visible agitation.

The woman said to Sardar: 'Well, we are here, why don't you get us something to eat.'

'I'll have it ready in no time, whatever you wish,' Sardar replied, suddenly the hostess.

There was something about the woman which suggested authority. 'Go to the kitchen,' she ordered Sardar. 'Get the fire going. Do you have a big cooking pot?'

'Yes.' Sardar shook her head.

'Rinse it well. I'll join you later,' she said. Then she rose from the bed and began examining the gramophone.

Apologetically, Sardar said, 'One cannot buy meat around here.'

'It'll be provided,' the woman said. 'And look, I want a big fire. Now, go and do what you have been told.'

Sardar left. The woman smiled and addressed Nawab: 'Nawab, we have brought you gold bangles.'

She opened her handbag and produced heavy, ornate gold bangles, wrapped in red tissue paper.

Nawab looked at Haibat Khan who sat next to her, very still. 'Who is this woman, Khan?' she asked in a frightened voice.

Playing with the gold bangles, the woman said: 'Who am I? I am Haibat Khan's sister.' Then she looked at Haibat Khan, who seemed to have suddenly shrunk. 'My name is Halakat,' she said, addressing Nawab.

Nawab could not understand what was going on, but she felt terrified.

The woman moved towards Nawab, took her hands and began to slip the gold bangles on them. Then she said to Haibat Khan: 'I want you to leave the room. Let me dress her up nicely and bring her to you.'

Haibat Khan looked mesmerized. He did not move. 'Leave the room. Didn't you hear me?' she told him sharply.

He left the room, looking at Nawab as he walked out.

The kitchen was outside the house. Sardar had got the fire going. He did not speak to her, but walked past the cactus hedge, out on to the road. He looked half-demented.

A bus approached. He had an urge to flag it down, get on board and disappear. But he did no such thing. The bus sped by, coating him with dust. He tried to shout after it, but his voice seemed to have gone.

He wanted to rush back into the house where he had spent so many nights of pleasure, but his feet seemed to be embedded in the ground.

He just stood there, trying to take stock of the situation. The woman who was now in the house, he had known a long time. He used to be a friend of her husband who was dead. He remembered their first encounter many years ago. He had gone to console her after her husband's death and had ended up being her lover. It was very sudden. She had simply commanded him to take her, as if he was a servant being asked to perform a simple task.

Haibat Khan had not been very experienced with women. When Shahina, who had told Nawab her name was Halakat or death, had become his lover, he had felt as if he had accomplished something in his life. She was rich in her own right and now had her husband's money. However, he was not interested in that. She was the first real woman in his life and he had let her seduce him.

For a long time he stood on the road. Finally, he went back to the house. The front door was closed and Sardar was cooking something in the kitchen.

He knocked and it was opened. All he could see was blood on the floor and Shahina leaning against the wall. 'I have dressed up your Nawab for you very nicely,' she said.

'Where is she?' he asked, his throat dry with terror.

'Some of her is on the bed, but most of her is in the kitchen,' she replied.

Haibat Khan began to tremble. He could now see that there was blood on the floor and a long knife. There was someone on the bed, covered with a blood-stained sheet.

Shahina smiled: 'Do you want me to lift the sheet and show you what I have there? It is your Nawab. I have made her up with great care. But perhaps you should eat first. You must be hungry. Sardar is cooking the most delicious meat in the world. I prepared it myself.'

'What have you done?' Haibat Khan screamed.

Shahina smiled again: 'Darling, this is not the first time. My husband, like you, was also faithless. I had to kill him and then throw his severed limbs for wild birds to feast on. Since I love you, instead of you, I have ...'

She did not complete the sentence, but removed the sheet from the heap on the bed. Haibat Khan fainted and fell to the floor.

When he came to, he was in a car. Shahina was driving. They seemed to be in wild country.

By the Roadside

Yes, it was this time of year. The sky had a washed blue look like his eyes. The sun was mild like a joyous dream. The fragrance from the earth had risen to my heart, enveloping my being. And, lying next to him, I had made him an offering of my throbbing soul.

He had said to me: 'You have given me what my life had always lacked. These magic moments that you have allowed me to share have filled a void in my being. My life would have remained an emptiness without your love, something incomplete. I do not know what to say to you and how, but today I have been made whole. I am fulfilled. Perhaps I no longer need you.'

And he had left, never to come back.

I had wept. I had begged him to answer me. 'Why do you no longer need me, when my whole being is on fire with longing and love? The moments you say have filled the emptiness in your soul have created an emptiness in mine.'

He had said: 'These moments we have shared have filled my emptiness. The atoms of your being have made me complete. Our relationship has come to its preordained end.'

These were cruel words, like being stoned alive. I had wept. I had cried, but his mind was made up. I had said to him: 'These atoms of my being that you speak about, these atoms which have made you whole, were a part of my body.

I gave them to you, but is it where our relationship ceases? Can what is left of me ever sever itself from what I have given you? You have become complete, but by leaving me incomplete. Haven't I worshipped you like a god?'

He had said: 'The honey which bees suck from half-opened flowers can never adorn the flowers or sweeten their bitterness. God is to be worshipped, but He is not the worshipper. In the great void, He created being through union with non-being, but then the void ceased to be, because He did not need it. The mother died after giving birth.'

A woman can weep. She cannot argue. Her supreme argument are the tears which spring from her eyes. I had said to him: 'Look at me. I am crying. If you must leave, I cannot hold you back, but wrap these tears in the shroud of your handkerchief and take them away and bury them somewhere, because when I cry again, I would know that you once performed the last rites of love. Do this small thing for me, for my happiness.'

He had said: 'I have made you happy. I have brought you that supreme joy which, until I came, was like a mirage in your life. Can you not live the rest of your life in remembrance of that joy which I conferred on you? You say that my completion has rendered you incomplete, but is incompletion not what life needs if it is to continue? I am a man. Today, you have brought completion to my life. Tomorrow, it will be another woman. I am fashioned out of elements which are destined to experience the same moment of supreme joy many, many times. The emptiness which you filled today will appear again and there will be others to fill it.'

I had kept crying.

I had thought: 'These few moments which I held in my hand so briefly are gone. Why did I let myself be swept away by their magic? Why did I put my restless, throbbing soul into the cage of life? Yes, it was ecstasy beyond words.

Yes, it was like a dream when the two of us held each other. Yes, it was an accident, but he walked away from it, whole and undamaged, leaving me broken. Why does he no longer need me, while the intensity of my desire for him sets my body and soul on fire? I have given my power to him. We were like two clouds in the sky, one heavy with rain, the other a flash of wild lightning, which moved away. What kind of law decrees that this was so? The law of the skies, of the earth, or of their creator?'

Yes, I had thought about these things.

Two souls meet and one acquires the vastness of eternity and moves away. Is it all poetry? When two souls meet, they must converge on that tiny dot which is the embryo of the universe itself. But why is it ordained that of the two, one should be broken on the rack and abandoned? Is it punishment for helping the other to discover that tiny dot which is the embryo of the universe itself?

Yes, it was this time of year. The sky was a wash of blue like his eyes, as it is today. The sun was mild like a joyous dream. And lying next to him, I had made him an offering of my throbbing soul.

He is not here. He is a flash of lightning playing with other clouds in other skies. He left because he had found his completion. He was a snake which bit me and is gone, but what is this strange restlessness in my belly where he had once moved? Is this the beginning of my completion?

No, it cannot be. This is my undoing, my end. But why are the empty spaces in my body filling up? What debris is being used to feed these gaping holes? What are these strange sensations in my veins? Why do I want my entire being to contract and become one with that tiny presence in my belly? In what vast seas will this sinking paper boat, which is my heart, re-emerge?

In the fires of my body I feel milk being boiled. Who is the expected guest? For whom is my heart pumping blood to weave soft eiderdowns? In my mind are a million silken threads of splendid hues being joined together to fashion tiny clothes.

For whom is my complexion turning gold?

It was this time of year. The sky was a wash of blue like his eyes, as it is today. But why has the sky come down to form a blue canopy over my belly? Why do I feel the blue of his eyes running wild in my blood?

Why have my rounding breasts acquired the sanctity of marble domes adorning mosques?

No, there is no sanctity in what is happening. I will demolish these domes. I will put out the fires in my body which are preparing repasts for the uninvited guest. I will tangle up those silken threads of a million hues.

It was this time of year. The sky was a wash of blue like his eyes, as it is today. But why am I trying to recapture the memory of days which no longer bear his footprints? But what is it that I feel in the depths of my belly? Is it a tiny footprint? Do I know it?

I will obliterate it. It is like a cancer, a carbuncle, a terrible affliction.

But why does it feel like a balm which soothes? If it is a balm, what wound is it meant to heal? The wound which he left?

No, this is a wound I have carried with me since the day I was born. A wound which was always in my womb, dormant and unseen.

What is my womb? A useless pot of clay, a child's toy which I will smash into pieces.

But a voice whispers in my ear: this world is a crossroads. Smash not your clay pot in the middle of it. Fingers of accusation will be pointing at you.

This world is a crossroads, but he left me in the middle of two roads, both leading to incompletion. And tears.

A tear has slipped into my oyster to produce a pearl. Whom will it adorn?

Fingers of accusation will be raised when the oyster

opens to reveal its pearl and disgorge it on the crossroads. The fingers will turn into snakes and bite the oyster and the pearl and turn them blue with venom.

The sky was a wash of blue like his eyes, as it is today. Why does it not fall? What pillars are keeping it in place? Will the earthquake which is to come shake the foundations of this immense edifice? Why is the sky like a canopy over my head?

I am drenched in perspiration.

All my pores are open. There is fire blazing everywhere. In my crucible, gold is being melted. Flames are leaping. The gold is seething like molten lava. The blue of his eyes is streaming through my veins. I hear bells ringing. Someone is coming. Board up the doors.

The crucible has been turned over. The molten gold is flowing. The bells are ringing.

It is on its way.

My eyes are heavy with sleep. The blue sky has become soiled. Soon it will come crashing down.

Whose cries are these that I hear? Make them stop. They are like hammer blows on my heart.

Make it stop. Make it stop. Make it stop.

I am a waiting lap. My arms are reaching out to hold it. The milk is boiling on the blazing fires of my body. My rounded breasts have turned into cups. Bring it to me. Lay it gently in my arms.

No, don't snatch it from me. Don't take it away, I beg you in the name of God.

Fingers ... fingers ... let them raise their fingers. I no longer care. The world is a crossroads. Let my clay pot be shattered in the middle of it.

My life will be in ruins. So be it. Give me back my flesh. Don't snatch my soul from me. You do not know how precious it is. It is the supreme fruit of those moments in my life when my body made someone whole. Is this the moment of my completion?

Ask the gaping vacuum in my belly, if you don't belive me. Ask my breasts full of milk. Ask the lullabies which are rising from every pore of my body. Ask my arms which have turned into gentle swings.

Fingers of accusation. Let them be raised. I will chop them off and pick them up and stuff my ears with them. I will go dumb. I will go deaf. I will go blind, but this tiny thing which is a part of me will know me and I will know it by running my fingers over it.

I beg of you. Don't take it away.

Don't overturn my overflowing cups of milk. Don't set fire to the eiderdown I wove with my blood. Don't sever the swings which are my arms. Don't deprive my ears of the music which are its cries.

Don't take it away from me.

Lahore, 21 January

The police have found a new-born baby by the roadside. Its naked body had been wrapped in wet linen with the obvious intention that it should die of cold and exposure. However, the baby was alive and has been taken to hospital. It has pretty blue eyes.

Kingdom's End

The phone rang. Manmohan picked it up. 'Hello, 44457.'

'Sorry, wrong number,' said a woman's voice.

Manmohan put the receiver down and returned to his book. He had read it about twenty times, not because it was anything extraordinary, but because it was the only book in this room. The last pages were missing.

For one week now, Manmohan had been the sole occupant of this office room. It belonged to a friend of his who had gone out of town to raise a business loan. Since Manmohan was one of this big city's thousands of homeless people who slept nights on its footpaths, his friend had invited him to stay here in his absence to keep a watch on things.

He hardly ever went out. He was permanently out of work because he hated all employment. Had he really tried, he could easily have got himself hired as a director with some film company, which is what he once was when he had decided to drop out. However, he had no desire to be enslaved again. He was a nice, quiet and harmless man. He had almost no personal expenses. All he required was a cup of tea in the morning with two slices of toast, a little bit of curry and bread in the afternoon and a packet of cigarettes. That was all. Luckily, he had enough friends who were quite happy to provide for these simple needs.

Manmohan had no family or close relations. He could go

without food for days on end if the going got hard. His friends didn't know much about him except that he had run away from home as a boy and had lived on the broad footpaths of Bombay for many years. There was only one thing missing in his life — women. He used to say, 'If a woman were to fall in love with me, my life would change.' Friends would retort, 'But even then you wouldn't work.'

'It would be nothing but work from then on,' he would answer.

'Why not have an affair then?'

'What good is an affair when the initiative comes from the man?'

It was afternoon now, almost time for lunch. Suddenly, the phone rang.

He picked it up. 'Hello, 44457.'

'44457?' a woman's voice asked.

'That's right,' Manmohan answered.

'Who are you?' the voice asked.

'I am Manmohan.'

There was no response. 'Who do you wish to speak to?' he asked.

'You,' the voice said.

'Me?'

'Unless you object.'

'No ... not at all.'

'Did you say your name was Madan Mohan?'

'No. Manmohan.'

'Manmohan?'

There was silence. 'I thought you wanted to talk to me,' he said.

'Yes.'

'Then go ahead.'

'I don't know what to say. Why don't you say something?'

'Very well,' Manmohan said. 'I have already told you my name. Temporarily, this office is my headquarters. I used to sleep on the city's footpaths, but for the last one week I have been sleeping on a big office table.'

'What did you do to keep the mosquitoes away at night? Use a net on your footpath?'

Manmohan laughed. 'Before I answer this, let me make it clear that I don't tell lies. I have slept on foothpaths for years. Since this office came under my occupation, I have been living it up.'

'How are you living it up?'

'Well, there's this book I have. The last pages are missing, but I've read it twenty times. One day, when I can lay my hands on the missing pages, I will finally know what end the two lovers met.'

'You sound like a very interesting man,' the voice said.

'You are only being kind.'

'What do you do?'

'Do?'

'I mean, what is your occupation?'

'Occupation? None at all. What occupation can a man have when he doesn't work? but to answer your question, I loaf around during the day and sleep at night.'

'Do you like your life?'

'Wait,' Manmohan said. 'That is one question I have never asked myself. And now that you have put it to me, I'm going to put it to myself for the first time. Do I like the way I live my life?'

'And what is the answer?'

'Well, there's no answer, but I suppose if I've lived my life the way I've lived it for so long, then it's reasonable to assume that I like it.'

There was laughter. 'You laugh so beautifully,' Manmohan said.

'Thank you.' The voice was shy. The call was disconnected. For a long time, he kept holding the receiver, smiling to himself.

The next day at about eight in the morning, the phone

rang again. He was fast asleep, but the noise woke him up. He yawned and picked it up.

'Hello, this is 44457.'

'Good morning, Manmohan sahib.'

'Good morning ... oh it's you. Good morning.'

'Were you asleep?'

'I was. You know I have become spoilt since I moved here. When I return to the footpath, I'm going to run into difficulties.'

'Why?'

'Because if you sleep on the footpath, you have to get up before five in the morning.'

There was laughter.

'You rang off abruptly yesterday,' he said.

'Well, why did you say I laugh beautifully?'

'What a question! If something is beautiful, it should be praised, shouldn't it?'

'Not at all.'

'You are not to impose conditions. I have never accepted conditions. If you laugh, I'm going to say that you laugh beautifully.'

'In that case I'll hang up.'

'Please yourself.'

'Don't you really care if I get upset?'

'Well, to begin with, I don't wish to upset myself, which means that if you laugh and I don't say that you laugh beautifully, I would be doing an injustice to my good taste.'

There was a brief silence. Then the voice came back: 'I'm sorry, I was having a word with our maid. So you were saying that you were partial to your good taste. What else is your good taste partial to?'

'What do you mean?'

'I mean ... what hobby or work ... or, shall I ask, what can you do?'

Manmohan laughed. 'Nothing much except that I am fond of photography — just a bit.'

'That's a very good hobby.'

'I have never thought of it in terms of its being good or bad.'

'You must have a very nice camera.'

'I have no camera. Off and on, I borrow one from a friend. Anyway, if I'm ever able to earn some money, there is a certain camera I'm going to buy.'

'What camera?'

'Exacta. It's a reflex camera. I like it very much.'

There was silence. 'I was thinking of something.'

'What?'

'You have neither asked me my name nor my phone number.'

'I haven't felt the need.'

'Why not?'

'What does it matter what your name is? You have my number. That's enough. When you want me to phone you, I'm sure you will give me your name and number.'

'No, I won't.'

'Please yourself. I'm not going to ask.'

'You're a strange man.'

'That's true, I am.'

There was another silence.

'Were you thinking again?' he asked.

'I was, but I just can't think of anything to think about.'

'Then why don't you hang up? Another time.'

There was a touch of annoyance in the voice. 'You're a very rude man. I am hanging up.'

Manmohan smiled and put the phone down. He washed his face, put on his clothes and was about to leave, when the phone rang. He picked it up. '44457.'

'Mr Manmohan?' asked the voice.

'What can I do for you?'

'Well, I wanted to tell you that I'm not annoyed any more.'

'That's very nice.'

'You know while I was having breakfast, it occurred to me that I shouldn't be annoyed with you. Have you had breakfast?'

'No, I was just about to go out when you phoned.'

'Oh, then I won't keep you.'

'I'm in no particular hurry today, because I have no money. I don't think there'll be any breakfast this morning.'

'Why do you say such things? Do you enjoy hurting yourself?'

'No, I'm quite used to the way I am and the way I live.'

'Should I send you some money?'

'If you want to. That will be one more name on the list of my financiers.'

'Then I won't.'

'Do what you like.'

'I am going to hang up.'

'Hang up then.'

Manmohan put down the phone and walked out of the office. He came back very late in the evening. He had been wondering about his caller all day. She sounded young and educated and she laughed beautifully. At 11 o'clock the phone rang.

'Hello.'

'Mr Manmohan.'

'That's him.'

'I've been phoning all day. Could you please explain where you were?'

'Although I don't have a job, I still have things to do.'

'What things?'

'Loafing about.'

'When did you come back?'

'An hour ago.'

'What were you doing when I called?'

'I was lying on the table and trying to imagine what you looked like, but I have nothing to go on except your voice.'

'Did you succeed?'

'No.'

'Well, don't try. I'm very ugly.'

'If you are ugly, then kindly hang up. I hate ugliness.'

'Well, if that's the case, I'm beautiful. I don't want you to nurture hatred.'

They didn't speak for some time. Then Manmohan asked, 'Were you thinking?'

'No, but I was going to ask you ...'

'Think before you ask.'

'Do you want me to sing for you?'

'Yes.'

'All right, wait.'

He heard her clear her throat, then in a very soft, low voice she sang him a song.

'That was lovely.'

'Thank you.' She rang off.

All night long he dreamt about her voice. He rose earlier than usual and waited for her call, but the phone never rang. He began to pace around the room restlessly. Then he lay down on the table and picked up the book he had read twenty times. He read it once again. The whole day passed. At about seven in the evening, the phone rang. Hurriedly, he picked it up.

'Who's that?'

'It's me.'

'Where were you all day?' he asked sharply.

'Why?' the voice trembled.

'I've been waiting. I haven't had anything to eat, although I had money.'

'I'll phone when I want to. You ...'

Manmohan cut her short. 'Look, either put an end to this business or let me know when you will call. I can't stand waiting.'

'I apologize for today. From tomorrow I promise to phone both morning and evening.'

'That's wonderful.'

'I didn't know you were ...'

'Well, the thing is that I simply can't bear to wait and when I can't bear something, I begin to punish myself.'

'How do you do that?'

'You didn't phone this morning. I should have gone out, but I didn't. I sat here all day fretting.'

'I didn't phone you deliberately.'

'Why?'

'To find out if you would miss my call.'

'You're very naughty. Now hang up. I must go out and eat.'

'How long will you be?'

'Half an hour.'

He returned after half an hour. She phoned. They talked for a long time. He asked her to sing him the same song. She laughed and sang it.

She would now ring regularly, morning and evening. Sometimes they would talk for hours. But, so far, Manmohan had neither asked her her name nor her phone number. In the beginning he had tried to imagine what she looked like, but that had now become unnecessary. Her voice was everything — her face, her soul, her body. One day she asked him, 'Mohan, why don't you ask me my name?'

'Because your voice is your name.'

Another day she said, 'Mohan, have you ever been in love?'

'No.'

'Why?'

He grew sad. 'To answer this question, I'll have to clear away the entire debris of my life and I would be very unhappy if I found nothing there.'

'Then don't.'

A month passed. One day Mohan had a letter from his friend. He said he had raised the money and would be returning to Bombay in a week. When she phoned that evening, he said to her, 'This is my kingdom's end.'

'Why?'

'Because my friend is coming back.'

'You must have friends who have phones?'

'Yes, I have friends who have phones, but I can't give you the numbers.'

'Why?'

'I don't want anyone else to hear your voice.'

'Why?'

'Let's say I'm jealous.'

'What should we do?'

'Tell me.'

'On the day your kingdom ends, I'll give you my number.'

The sadness he had felt was suddenly gone. He again tried to picture her, but there was no image, just her voice. It was only a matter of days now, he said to himself, when he would see her. He could not imagine the immensity of that moment.

When she called next day, he said to her, 'I'm curious to see you.'

'Why?'

'You said you would give me your phone number on the day my kingdom ends.'

'Yes.'

'Does that also mean you'll tell me where you live? I want to see you.'

'You can see me whenever you like. Even today.'

'Not today. No, I want to see you when I am wearing nice clothes. I have asked a friend of mine to get me some.'

'You're like a child. When we meet, I'll give you a present.'

'There can be no greater present in the world than meeting you.'

'I have bought you an Exacta camera.'

'Oh!'

'But there's a condition. You'll have to take my picture.'

'That I'll decide when we meet.'

'I shan't be phoning you for the next two days.'

'Why?'

'I'm going to be away with my family. It's only two days.'

Manmohan did not leave the office that day. The next morning he felt feverish. At first he thought it was boredom because she hadn't phoned. By the afternoon, his fever was high. His body felt on fire. His eyes were burning. He lay down on the table. He was very thirsty. He kept drinking water all day. There was a heaviness in his chest. By next morning, he felt completely exhausted. He had trouble breathing. His chest hurt.

His fever was so high that he went into a delirium. He was talking to her on the phone, listening to her voice. By the evening, his condition had deteriorated. There were voices in his head and strange sounds as if thousands of phones were ringing at the same time. He couldn't breathe.

When the phone rang, he did not hear it. It kept ringing for a long time. The suddenly there was a moment of clarity. He could hear it. He rose, stumbling uncertainly on his feet. He almost fell, but steadying himself against the wall, he picked it up with trembling hands. He ran his tongue over his lips. They were dry like wood.

'Hello.'

'Hello, Mohan,' she said.

'It is Mohan,' his voice fluttered.

'I can't hear you.'

He tried to say something, but his voice dried up in his throat.

She said, 'We came back earlier than I thought. I've been trying to call you for hours. Where were you?'

Manmohan's head began to spin.

'What is wrong?' she asked.

With great difficulty he said, 'My kingdom has come to an end today.'

Blood spilled out of his mouth, making a thin red line down his chin, then along his neck.

She said, 'Take my number down. 50314 ... 50314. Call me in the morning. I have to go now.'

She hung up. Manmohan collapsed over the phone, blood bubbling out of his mouth.

Afterword: Uncle Manto's Death

This account of Manto's last moments was written soon after his death by his nephew Hamid Jalal, who was also married to Zakia, younger sister of Manto's wife, Safia.

Were uncle Manto to one day rise from the Miani Sahib graveyard in Lahore where he is buried and walk into the house, I am quite sure what I will do. Ignoring the miracle of his second coming, I will say to him: 'Of all the irresponsible things you did in your life, the most irresponsible by far was your death.'

Pakistan was playing India in the second test at Bahawalpur at the Dring Stadium. I was in the commentators' box, assisting the Indian commentator, Talyar Khan, when someone said there was a long-distance call for me from Lahore. When I took the call, my first reaction to the news that uncle Manto had died that morning was not one of grief but anger. How could he just up and die leaving his wife and three young daughters all alone! But I kept calm. I asked where he had died. Home, I was told. This was reassuring because I was afraid he might have died at some odd place, in a *tonga*, a restaurant, in a publisher's office, or a film studio, anywhere.

I returned to the commentators' box where one of my friends looked at me inquiringly. On a piece of paper I scribbled just one line: The umpire finally gave Saadat Hasan Manto out this morning.

Uncle Manto had survived several appeals, but today his impatient and reckless innings had at last come to an end. Had he been a cricketer, I can say confidently that he would never have become the kind of alert and careful batsman that Hanif Mohammad was. Incidentally, he was greatly looking forward to seeing him open for Pakistan in the third test at Lahore. This I learnt a day after he died. It was one of his last two wishes. A day before his death, he had told his friends in a restaurant: 'Let Hamid Jalal come back and I will go with him to watch Hanif play.'

His other wish was to write a story about the woman whose dead and naked body had been found by the side of a road in Gujrat some days earlier. According to news reports, the woman, along with her infant daughter, had been abducted by unknown men from the local bus stop and raped by six of them. She had finally managed to run away, holding the baby. There was not a stitch on her body and she had died of cold in the night, along with her child. Uncle Manto had been much moved by this tragedy. That afternoon, some visitors had come from Gujrat and told him the details. I am sure that evening he must have drunk far more than he usually did, which is what probably killed him.

He went out that evening and came back very late. Some time later, he vomited blood. My six-year-old son who was standing next to him asked why he was spitting blood. 'It is not blood,' Manto said, 'I am chewing a betel leaf.' Then he cautioned him not to tell anyone in the house what he had seen. He ate his dinner as usual and went to bed. Nobody could possibly have suspected anything was wrong. My son kept his part of the deal. It is quite possible that uncle Manto did not consider the blood he had vomited of much consequence either. He was, in any case, always reluctant to discuss his health with members of the family because it invariably led to renewed demands that he should stop drinking.

It was well after midnight when he woke up his wife. He told her that he was in intense pain and had lost a lot of blood through vomiting. He said his liver had probably packed up. His wife woke everyone up. She did not know what else to do. It was not the first time uncle Manto had faced a health crisis. There had been many before and every time he had come out alive. Nobody could imagine that he had only a few more hours to live. However, I think the umpire's finger had started rising slowly upwards much earlier in the evening.

From what I have heard about his last moments, I can say that for a long time it did not occur to him that he was dying. A doctor had been called and had given him a shot, but his condition had not improved. His pulse was sinking and there was no relief from the pain. He was also constantly spitting blood. In the morning, the doctor had said that he must be moved to hospital.

Uncle Manto was fully conscious when the doctor had suggested that he be moved. 'Don't take me there. It is too late anyway. Let me lie here in peace,' he had said. This was too much for the women in the house who began to wail, which made him angry. 'I don't want anybody to cry,' he screamed. Then he hid his face under the blankets.

This was the real Manto. He had always lived an open life and now that he was dying he did not want anyone to look. Whether he was angry with himself or with his drinking which was leading him to an early grave, I cannot be sure.

An ambulance had been sent for. Once or twice he had uncovered his face and said, 'I am very cold. I don't think I would be so cold even in the grave. Cover me with more blankets.' A few minutes later, his face had reappeared from under the blankets. There was a strange light in his eyes. 'In one of my jacket pockets, I have three rupees and eight annas. Add a bit to it and get me some whisky.'

Nobody was willing to do that, but he kept insisting. To keep him quiet, a pint of whisky was brought. He looked at the bottle with a strange kind of satisfaction and said, 'Pour me two measures.' As he uttered the words, a spasm gripped his entire body.

Even at the moment of death, he felt no self-pity at all. He must have known that he was dying, but he did not allow himself to get sentimental. He did not send for the children, nor dictate a will, nor express a last wish. Perhaps for men like him, there is no dividing line between life and death. Anyway, his life and his soul had already been transferred to his books, assured of immortality.

On his death-bed, the only thing uncle Manto asked for was a drink. Death and drink had become indistinguishable from each other. He knew that just as there could be no physical victory over death, there could be no physical victory over drink. He was always a rebellious man and, now that he was dying, he had decided to revolt against death too. He hated to be beaten. He wanted to face death now with his face hidden under the blankets so that nobody should see his final defeat.

A lesser man than uncle Manto would have perhaps thought of dramatic gestures to ensure he should be talked about nicely after he was gone. He would have wanted his family to say that while he did not quite live according to the book, at the time of his death he was a changed man. But uncle Manto hated hypocrisy. His only dramatic act in the face of approaching death was to ask for a drink. In this last story, he himself was the central character.

Had I been present, it is possible he might have talked to me and reminded me of the story of the man with the snake. I would have understood and mixed him a drink myself. The story was simple. There was a man, who, despite the remonstrations of his friends, had kept a highly poisonous pet snake. One day the snake had bitten him, transferring all its venom into its master's body. Before the man had died, he had picked up the snake and chewed its head off.

As the ambulance braked in front of the house, uncle Manto asked for whisky again. A spoonful was poured into his mouth, but I don't think he was able to swallow more than a few drops. The rest ran down his chin. At about the same time, he lost consciousness. This was the first time in his entire life that he had lost control over his actions. He was lifted from the bed and placed in the ambulance.

When it arrived at the hospital, the doctors rushed in, but uncle Manto had died on the way without regaining consciousness.

Translated from the Urdu by Khalid Hasan

Glossary

adda   place where *tongas* (*q.v.*) pick up passengers

badmash   criminal or tough guy

bania   Hindu money-lender

bhabi   sister-in-law. Close friends also often address each other's wives as *bhabi*

Bhagwan   Hindu name for God

bhai   brother

burqa   long, enveloping garment worn by Muslim women in public

burra   big, as in *burra sahib*

chaddur   thick shawl

chokra   boy

chokri   girl

dada   Bombayese for a tough guy, a local godfather

dak bungalow   rest houses built for British officials in far-flung parts of the country

darshan   act of granting a formal audience to devotees

dupatta   shawl made of fine muslin

fakir   mendicant, a holy man without fixed abode

ghazal   lyrical Urdu love poem, often sung

gitpit   onomatopoeic term for spoken English

goonda   tough guy, criminal on police files

gora   fair-skinned. Common description for a Briton

halakat   death

Hindostora   half-jocular name for Urdu-speaking people in the Punjab

Id   twice-yearly Muslim festival

ikka   one-horse carriage

jamadar   non-commissioned rank introduced in the Indian army by the British. Still exists in India and Pakistan

jani   Punjabi slang for darling

Junagarh and Hyderabad   former princely states in British India which acceded to Pakistan, though both had majority non-Muslim populations. Annexed by India soon after independence

kanjar   male member of a traditional courtesan family

kirpan   dagger worn by Sikhs as part of religious obligations

kotha   place where singing girls perform

lakh equal to 100,000

Lathi   steel-tipped staff carried by police

malashia   masseur

Maulana   Muslim religious divine

Maulvi   as above

mohalla   residential area or quarter. In the old days, people of the same profession tended to live in the same quarter, hence for example *sunar mohalla*, the goldsmiths' quarter

murdabad   death to …

panwala   betel-leaf seller

Pir   Muslim holy man, often with followers

raaga   musical scale sung or played in the classical mode. In the Indian-Pakistani classical tradition there are *raagas* for every mood and season of the year, to be performed only at specific times of day, night and season. *Raaga Maulkans*, which has a pentatonic scale, is sung at night and is one of the most sombre in the entire repertoire

Ramadan   the month of fasting in the Islamic calendar

sadhu   Hindu holy mendicant

sala (male)   mild swear-word, otherwise wife's brother

sali (female)   as above, but wife's sister

seth   rich man, also term of social respect

shagird   apprentice, student or henchman

shalwar   loose-fitting trousers

Sian   affectionate Punjabi pronounciation of Singh

Sikhni   female Sikh

subedar   highest non-commissioned rank in British Indian army.
Still exists in India and Pakistan

tehmad   loin cloth worn by men in the Punjab

thumri   short musical composition based on a *raaga*. It is light-
hearted and flirtatious, with lyrics bewailing separation from
the beloved

tonga   horse-drawn carriage

yaar   close friend, pal

zindabad   long live ...

Proper names are almost always modified or abbreviated among
family and close friends. Thus Ram Singh will become Ram
Singha, Rashid will become Sheeda, Tirlok, Tirloka and Khalid,
Khalda or Khaldi.

MORE ABOUT PENGUINS

For further information about books available from Penguins in India write to Penguin Books (India) Ltd, B4/246, Safdarjung Enclave, New Delhi 110 029.

In the UK: For a complete list of books available from Penguins in the United Kingdom write to Dept. EP, Penguin Books Ltd, Harmondsworth, Middlesex UB7 0DA.

In the U.S.A.: For a complete list of books available from Penguins in the United States write to Dept. DG, Penguin Books, 299 Murray Hill Parkway, East Rutherford, New Jersey 07073.

In Canada: For a complete list of books available from Penguins in Canada write to Penguin Books Canada Ltd, 2801 John Street, Markham, Ontario L3R 1B4.

In Australia: For a complete list of books available from Penguins in Australia write to the Marketing Department, Penguin Books Australia Ltd, P.O. Box 257, Ringwood, Victoria 3134.

In New Zealand: For a complete list of books available from Penguins in New Zealand write to the Marketing Department, Penguin Books (N.Z.) Ltd, Private Bag, Takapuna, Auckland 9.